Folklore of County Wexford

Folklore of County Wexford

Diarmaid Ó Muirithe
and Deirdre Nuttall

EDITORS

FOUR COURTS PRESS

Set in 11 on 13 point Ehrhardt for
FOUR COURTS PRESS
Fumbally Lane, Dublin 8, Ireland
e-mail: info@four-courts-press.ie
and in North America for
FOUR COURTS PRESS
c/o ISBS, 5804 N.E. Hassalo Street, Portland, OR 97213.

A catalogue record for this title
is available from the British Library.

ISBN 1-85182-453-7

Printed in Great Britain
by MPG Books Ltd, Bodmin, Cornwall

For Joyce Alexander and in memory of Steuart Alexander

And for Marie Heaney

Contents

Introduction

This book is what the late Jack Devereux from Kilmore Quay would have called a *glad-bag*, and he had in mind a budget hung in the country house-wife's cupboard: a cornucopia of family trinkets and treasures gathered over the years, often dipped into for the bitter-sweet pleasure of remembering times past. For this is a sampler of folklore from a county which is, to extend the metaphor, itself a glad-bag of a place, in which history has placed Irish, Norman, English, Flemish and Scandinavian to live in harmony, for most of the time, for over a thousand years.

The real authors of this book are many. Firstly there are the full-time collectors of the Irish Folklore Commission, a body established by the Irish Government in 1935 and replaced in 1971 by the Department of Irish Folk-lore, University College, Dublin. 'If I were a poet,' wrote Bö Almqvist, professor *emeritus* in that department, 'I would write out the names of these collectors in verse.' May we mention in particular Jim Delaney from Wexford town, still with us, still collecting, at well over the four score.

Let us also pay tribute to the National Teachers, the unsung mainstay of Irish cultural activity in the arid thirties. It was indeed a stroke of genius on the part of James Hamilton Delargy, the man who lead the work of the Commission, to recruit the teachers in collecting folklore. The astonishing work of the teachers is reflected in the Schools' Collection, housed in the archives in the Department of Irish Folklore, University College, Dublin: it comprises 1,100 volumes. The teachers sought the help of the children under their care; the children, in their turn, sought the help of their parents and grandparents, of neighbours and family friends; and it is heartening to hear that, up to this day, a stream of visitors comes to the Department to re-acquaint themselves with songs, stories and other traditions left by their parents or grandparents to posterity.

Tomás Ó Ciardha, better known in south Wexford as Tom Carey, a voca-tional teacher, worked on his own; his contribution was immense. His day's work was only beginning when he closed the door of his classroom, it would

seem. Mary Dunphy from the Irishtown, New Ross, was another who collected outside her school. We must mention, too, the Butler family, well represented here.

Not all the lore within the covers of this book comes from the volumes
stored in UCD. Some of Wexford's famous Christmas carols are included, as
well as a mumming play from the last century; for these we thank the Devereux
family in Kilmore Quay. But the vast majority comes from Delargy's price-
less archive.

The material drawn from the archives of the Department of Irish Folklore, University College, Dublin, National University of Ireland, is published
by kind permission of the Head of the Department of Irish folklore which
holds the copyright of the original material. We owe a debt of gratitude to
Professor Séamas Ó Catháin and to Críostóir Mac Cárthaigh for their help.

We hope that this little sampler of the lore of our native Wexford will
bring a degree of pleasure to all who will take it up and read it.

Diarmaid Ó Muirithe, Co. Wicklow
Deirdre Nuttall, Ciudad de Las Casas, Mexico

Summer 1999

TECHNICAL NOTE

The footnotes cite the source documents. IFC denotes Irish Folklore
Commission, Main Manuscript Collection. IFCS denotes Irish Folklore
Commission, Schools Collection. Where these abbreviations are used, the
number appeearing before the colon denotes the volume; the number after
the colon, the manuscript page number(s).

Historical

A song about King James [1]

I was great at one time with the butler, Mr Davidson, up at Castleboro, and he told me that the cufflinks King James gave to Mr Carew were still in the possession of the family. He told me he had seen them himself, but at that time they were at the Carews' bankers. I made a poem about it and here it is.

I

I had a dream the other night, a very strange one too,
And the strangest thing about it was the most of it was true.
In my dreams I had companions, though I quite forget their names,
There's but one I can remember, an old gent called King James.

II

He was the king of England then, and I believe of Scotland, too,
He also was a papist and of course he had to go;
They brought William here from Orange to give him tally-ho,
William was his son-in-law; that made matters worse;
All those mighty rows are bad but a family one's a curse.

III

At the Boyne in Meath a fight was staged and a crowd of people came,
I went, too, or thought I did, of course 'twas all a drame.
Most likely, James was dreaming, too; he got cold feet that day,
And skipped away and so did I to Dublin city gay.

1 Narrated by the author, Thomas O'Gorman, aged 87, farmer and labourer, of Castleboro, to James Delaney, full-time collector, in 1954. The stanzas are irregular. IFC 1344:117–20.

IV

Tyrconnel wasn't to be seen, I heard he was in bed,
He had too much wine the night before and couldn't raise his head.
But her ladyship received us and kindly asked us in,
Though she looked a trifle worried, when she saw it was the King.

V

She feasted us right royally and everything looked bright
Until she asked his majesty for news about the fight.
I can't describe my feelings, when I heard the old monarch say,
"The Irish are no good to fight, they promptly ran away."
My lady never seemed to mind but smiled up in his face,
Saying, "My compliments, your Majesty, on having won the race."

VI

We soon took our departure and the next thing that I knew
We were down in Castleboro with one Mister Carew.
He owned an ancient castle, by the winding Boro's strame,
Near the bridge of Och na gCapall, with that fine old Irish name.

VII

I ne'er forget the kindness of the family one and all,
They insisted we should rest that night in Castleboro Hall.
After we'd fortified ourselves and finished up our drinks,
James stood and handed young Carew a pair of golden links.

VIII

Years afterwards the truth was known, just by the merest chance,
That King James was with me there that night, while on his way to France.
Although James had gone forever, the gold cuff-links still remained
In that old castle by the Boro where King James was entertained.

A story about King James [2]

This is what local tradition says about King James after he passed through Dublin still steering south. James steered on through Wicklow and Carlow, into Wexford. He was making his way to Duncannon Fort where he was sure of shelter and a chance of a ship back to France.

He halted his horse and the foot of Sliabh Coillte (a hill near New Ross, Co. Wexford) at a little house right above the village of Aclare (New Ross). The mountain was then covered with trees. The little farmhouse was well hidden among the trees, the real thing for a king on the run.

When he knocked on the door, a homely little woman answered him. He told her his horse was tied and that he himself needed some refreshments. The little woman took him inside and gave him new milk, brown bread, butter and honey. It was good stuff enough for a retreating and abdicating king. When he was well rested, he praised the beauty and scenery of the place. He then told her that he came from a great battlefield.

She asked him what the rest of his family did, and if they were safe. Then James explained that he was the king and was leading the Irish army at the Boyne and how they ran away. But, the little woman said, "Irishmen don't run away in any kind of a fight, and an Irish army wouldn't run away at all." Then James said, "Well, I won't say they ran away, I will just say retreated."

Then she wanted to know what was the difference between a runaway army and a retreating army. James told her that when an army is in retreat, it should keep in close communication and dispute every inch of the ground with the enemy, take up such positions that would command the superiority of fire and hinder the enemy's advance in every possible way. "Why, my dear woman," said James, "a good retreat is a lovely thing." "Oh faith," said the woman, " 'tis yourself knows all about it, and if you didn't you wouldn't be here so soon from the Boyne."

James said no more but got ready to depart. He handed the woman a gold coin. She closed her hand on it and pressed on him to stay longer.

He drew her attention to the coin and asked her did she see anything remarkable about it. She examined it closely, and suddenly exclaimed: "In troth, Sir, 'tis like yourself." "Yes," said James, "that is my head you see on that gold coin. You can keep it in memory of our meeting." The woman told him she would do so and prayed that he might always keep his head on his shoulders and keep away from battlefields.

2 Told by Nancy Reagan, a pupil of Gusserane School, New Ross (Mrs Corish, teacher), in 1938. Nancy's informant was Martin Walsh, Rathimney, Gusserane. IFCS 872:72–6.

That gold coin of the king remained in the family for years in Aclare and according to an account in the *New Ross Standard* it is in Aclare somewhere still.

King James headed south once more, this time to the castle in Rathimney, where he stayed one night only. The people in the castle of Rathimney at the time were in some way connected with the commanding officers of Duncannon Fort who were fighting on the side of James.

On the morning he left Rathimney Castle for Duncannon Fort. He attended Mass at the Poll Church a short distance from this Castle. This church is now in ruins.

Cromwell in Wexford[3]

In bygone days when the Cromwellians visited the town of Wexford, a sad and terrible disaster occurred in the Bull-Ring when Cromwell and his men massacred hundreds of people as well as Fr Raymond who, while the terrible butchery was going on, spoke words of consolation and encouragement to the people clustered around him. After that horrible slaughter, his blood is said to have run like water to the river Slaney. The massacre at the Bull-Ring being completed, the troops thirsting for blood and plunder pushed on to the Friary, and there slaughtered many priests and people. After their destruction, the floor of the church was purple with the blood of the martyrs.

The penal times[4]

There is a mass path in Kilscantlon, Co. Wexford. Fr Brian Madden said first mass in Kilscantlon and second mass in Carnagh in the penal times. The soldiers followed the priest, and when he heard them coming he hid underground. One day the soldiers came when he was saying mass; the priest threw a look at them; they had guns ready to shoot him. The priest made some kind of a sign and the soldiers dropped dead on the ground. It was the will of God that killed the soldiers. They were Protestant people living there, and beside where they were living the priest said mass. These Protestant people told the soldiers to kill this priest. The soldiers that dropped dead are buried in

---

3 Told by C. Hynes, School Street, Wexford, a pupil of Presentation Convent (Sister Bernard, teacher), in 1935. IFCS 880:116.   4 An incident related by William Burke of Carnagh, New Ross, to Nancy Corcoran, Garryduff, Campile, a pupil of Gusserane School, New Ross (Mrs Corish, teacher), in 1938. IFCS 872:101–2.

Kilscantlon. There is a house built there now and a man named David O'Connor is living where the priest said mass.

The 1798 Rebellion

A PRIEST OF 1798 [5]

There was two priests hung at Old Ross. They hung men there at Whitney's Bridge. 'Twas a major, or something very high up in the army but he was a very good man entirely. There was another man too, very high in the army, Hanrick was his name, and he was also a fairly good fellow. But old Hess and the Whitneys and the Hornicks, they were walking devils. The priest was hiding in Frizzel's house anyway, and he was safe enough. This day, anyhow, Frizzel was in Ross, or somewhere, and while he was out, ould Hess and a party of his soldiers came along and they took the priest. They knew he was hiding in the house, so they watched until Frizzel was out to come along and take him. They brought out the priest and they tied him under a horse's belly with ropes, and they rode off into Wexford. They used to hang them there on the bridge. The priest of course got a terrible time of it going – being tied under a horse's belly, and the horse galloping – it must have been awful. Some time after, when they were gone, Frizzel came back from town or wherever he was, and he knew by the frightened look on his wife's face that there was something wrong. He asked her what was the matter; and she told him, how that Hess and his men came along and took the priest away. He never said another word, only ran out and mounted his horse again and went on the way to Wexford as hard as ever he could gallop; and he overtook them just as they were going into Wexford. He was only in the nick of time, for they would hang him the minute they landed, and he knew that, of course. As soon as he got up to them, he called on them to halt, and they did. Then he ordered them to let the man down; and what call had they to take him. Hess said that, "Wasn't he a priest?" "It don't matter," says Frizzel, "he's my prisoner, so let him down." Begor, they let him down; and off they went without another word. The priest was all cramped up when they let him loose, and he wasn't able to walk hardly. So Frizzel put him up on the horse, on the saddle, and he took a hoult of the bridle himself and he led the horse on by the head. They went on that way for a couple of miles or so, and the priest says to him: "It is too bad to have you be walking and I up here." "I'm afraid," says Frizzel, "that you would not be able to walk very much after the usage you got coming

5 Told by Edward Fitzgerald, Kilscanlon, Ballinaboola, New Ross, to Tomás Ó Ciardha (Tom Carey), a teacher and folklore collector, of Cushinstown, New Ross, in 1938. IFC 577:154–9.

here. But if you think you are able, walk for a little while, it might loosen out your limbs a bit, and I'll get up." So the priest got down and he tried to walk a bit but he wasn't able. So Frizzel got down again and he was going to walk again. "Let you get up," says the priest "and I'll get up behind you." But Frizzel said that the mare was travelling all the morning and that he galloped her as hard as she could go coming after Hess, and that she would never be able to carry their two. That it might kill her. And at the time the mare was all one white lather of sweat. "Get up," says the priest, "and you will find that she will not be one bit the worse after it." Begor, the two got up on the mare, and they came along. And still as they came along, the mare was getting cooler; and as they were getting near Dononore she was as fresh as when she was taken out of the stable in the morning; and when they were coming in their own avenue she began to caper. Begor, Frizzel began to think that there was something in it, and he says to the priest: "You must have done something to the mare when we were coming along," says he, " 'tis fresher she was getting as we came along; and now I am hard set to hould her at all." "Well," says the priest, "whatever was done or not done, Dononore will never be without a good horse." No more it aint. There is always the best of horses in it ever since. 'Twas never yet without a good horse. "Well, now" says Frizzel to him, "you will have to do something now to the person that informed on you." "Oh, no," says the priest, "we must forgive him." "Well," says Frizzel, " 'Twas a Catholic up in Rochestown that informed on you;" and he told them the name and all; "and you will have to leave some mark on them; if not, you'll be no friend of mine anymore." "Well," says the priest, "all I say is this, that there will always be a fool or an idiot in them to the end of time." And isn't that true? There was one in the family ever since.

THE CAPTURE OF BAGENAL HARVEY[6]

There was a lot of high bushes and cover on the Saltee island unlike now. The soldiers searched all the island and were coming away, seemingly, without finding any of the men they were looking for. As they were coming away from the island, a woman came out on the beach and waved a white apron. Another version is that she came out to throw out potatoes. My mother always maintained that she waved her apron to the soldiers to betray Harvey and his comrades. They were hiding in a cave that was screened by bushes and that's why the soldier never saw them in their first search.

They were taken to Wexford and tried. Bagenal Harvey was beheaded and his head placed on a spike over the jail gate. The body was given to the people and it was buried in Mayglass in the Harvey vault.

6 IFC 1344:450–1. Same collector and informant.

Near the jail gate were a lot of trees and a man from Bargy spent three days and three nights in one of them. He lay hidden there, as there was a guard on the jail gate. He had a long crooked wire and was trying to get Harvey's head off the spikes. He got off the head at last and it was buried with the body in the old Wexford jail [later the County Council offices].

KELLY, THE BOY FROM KILLANNE [7]

Kelly, of Killanne, was not born in Rackard's house as people say. My grandfather, O'Leary – my name was O'Leary, too – was seventeen years of age when the Rebellion broke out and he told me the place where Kelly's house used to be. The house is gone many years. It was behind where Rileys live now. Riley's house faces the road, but Kelly's was behind where that house is now of Rileys. It was a big long thatched house, with the gable end towards the road. Doyles lived where Rackards live now.

Kelly's sister was going to marry a Doyle and one of Doyle's sisters was going to marry Kelly. He was wounded at Ross but got back to Killoughrim wood. He was arrested in Killoughrim wood, I always heard. The girl, Doyle, followed him to Wexford, where he was executed.

Kelly's land and house were confiscated. Part of the land belonging to Kelly was where the Doctor's residence was in Killanne, and where the dispensary is now.

THE BEGINNING OF THE REBELLION

My grandfather and his father were on the mountain above Kiltealy bringing home turf. They could see the road clearly and the Redcoats making for Boolavogue. "Unyoke and come home quickly," says his father to him, "the row is up." The whole road was covered with Redcoats and he knew then that the Rebellion had started.

Where Orpens is now, a Mr West lived, a Protestant minister. He was rale good to the Catholics. He got a pass for my grandfather's father to move about. He tried to get protection for the whole of Grange, but didn't succeed. He did get protection for a good part of Grange, so that the people were not molested, but he couldn't get protection for Carrigeen.

After '98 a man called Lampere lived there, I think.

---

[7] The following four accounts were collected by James Delaney in 1954 from Mrs Elizabeth Byrne of Milltown, Grange, aged 87. Much of Mrs Byrne's lore was imparted by her grandfather. IFC 1344:163–7.

MRS GRACE AND THE REDCOATS

Mrs Grace was living opposite to where Wat Furlong, of Corrigeen, is living now. There's no house there now. Things were settling down this time. She was out spreading clothes she was after washing. It was a rale warm day and she [...] noticed one of the Burkes running from the direction of Furlong's and the soldiers after them. She saw him running down through the land.

The soldiers came into the yard.

"Warm day," they said.

"It is," says she, "and I think you should come in and I'll give you a drink to refresh you." She did it out of cleverality to give Burke a chance to escape.

The soldiers all got noggins and drank a big tub of crame on her.

When they were leaving, one of them turned.

"For the toss of a pin, I'd shoot you, me auld dame," says he.

"For what?" she says.

"I know what you did," says he, "you brought us in here to let that croppy get away."

A YEOMAN

During the Rebellion the people used to be afraid to go out for fear of the Yeos. My father told me a story about his grandfather. He was afraid to go out. But this day he had to go out as they were short of flour. He said he'd go out to the mill. He wasn't gone far when he fell into an ambush of military who were hidden at each side of the road.

"Ah, me auld rogue," said they, "you were out plundering' and robbin' all night. Kneel down there and we'll give you a few minutes to say your prayers."

My father's grandfather knelt down to say his prayers, when who come along but a Protestant man named Warren. Warren was a Yeoman himself.

"What are you doin' there, Jack?" he says.

He told Warren that they were goin' to shoot him.

"Get up out of that," says Warren, "I'd like to see anyone who'd point a gun at you."

My father's grandfather got up and went off about his business.

Some time after the Rebellion, Warren would have been killed in the town of Enniscorthy only for Jack Leary. Warren had an awful tongue when he got drunk and used to give out about the Catholics.

They were kicking him about the street in Enniscorthy and would have killed him only Jack Leary said, "Leave that man alone," and he told them how Warren had saved his life when the soldiers were going to shoot him during the Rebellion.

GOFF OF HORETOWN [8]

In the time of '98 there was a fellow in Horetown by the name of Goff. He was an Englishman, of course, a big landlord, priest hunter and all the rest of it. At that time the road ran from Horetown up the ould lane by this house. The road below going on to Camross wasn't there at all then. It went up right by this house and on to Kilgarvan. Hardly any of the roads that are there now were there in those times. They were all only ould lanes. There was hardly any cars then either; 'twas on foot or on horseback they used travel. Well, this Goff that lived in Horetown. 'Twas the way he got the two townslands of Asaggart and Shanoule as a gratuity from Cromwell. Well, after the big battle of Horetown in '98 the Irish won and the English had to clear. The Croppies run 'em out of it. This ould fellow Goff was running away after the battle and a party of Croppies after him; he made his way along up this way. My great grandfather was working in the field out there at the back of the house, cutting faggots. He had a whole lot of them out and he had them in cocks along the ditch. Goff came on up to him and he nearly died. "Oh save me, save me!" says he. "They're after me." "What can I do for you?" says he; "if they find me sheltering you, I'll be in as much danger as yourself." He begged him to do something to save him anyway. "Well," says he, "the only thing I can do for you is to put you in under one of these cocks." He lifted up a cock and the lad crawled in under it and he put a few more of the faggots up against him and left it so. He went and cut away and took no more notice of him. 'Twasn't very long 'til the crowd came along tearing, looking for him. They asked me great-grandfather if he had seen anyone passing. He looked up and he pretended he got an awful fight. "There was no one that I seen anyway," says he, "but they could pass and I mightn't see 'em." "Come on, men," says the captain. They passed on, and he went in, had his dinner and came out again. Goff called him from under the heap of faggots. He went over to him, "Will you go into Ross," says Goff "and there's a captain of a vessel there" – he told him his name and all – "and tell him I want to get away with him." "All right," says he, "I'll go." He went to Ross, anyway, and he happened on this captain, and he told him the whole lot. "All right" says the captain, "bring him along." "But how's he going to get in here?" says me grandfather, "I'm not going to chance bringing him." The captain gave him the name of a man in the town and told him to bring in a load of hay to him and that Goff could be hiding under it, and that this man would get him away all right. Next day he got Goff under the load of hay and jogged along the way of Ross. 'Twas

8 Collected by Tomás Ó Ciardha from Mrs John Carroll, Assagart, in 1937. IFC 437:116–19.

getting dark when he got into this yard in Ross. He threw off the hay and got out of Goff. He got away in this vessel with the captain, and he stayed away for a few years until everything was quiet again. He came back again then and he gave his tenants the devil of a time. He really scourged them over rent. The ould man had right to set fire to the cock of faggots when the devil was in under it. But he was no good – yerra, people had no guts in them times.

AN INCIDENT OF '98 [9]

I

There are soldiers in the market-place,
The judge is in the town,
And justice stern-faced, hand-made law,
Now wears her darkest frown.
'Tis the year of tears and troubles,
'Tis the year of blood and fate,
Of blackened hearts and roofless houses,
        The year of '98.

II

For the prisoners to the courthouse
The soldiers clear the way,
The fate of two young lives
Shall be determined to-day.
Through surging lines of clansmen
The youthful rebels pass,
But not an arm is raised to save –
Stands mute each gallowglass.

III

The people's hearts are broken,
Their hopes are dead and gone,
They hardly dare to breath a sound,
Each face is scant and wan.

9 A recitation, collected by Joseph O'Donoghue, of Ballytramont, Castlebridge, a pupil at the Christian Brothers' School, Wexford, in 1938 (Brother Healy, teacher), from Mrs Mary O'Donoghue of Ballytramont. IFCS 881: 21–7.

For heavy as an avalanche,
Swift as the lightning's flash,
Upon this patriot's plot had fallen
The English vengeance lash.

IV

The land they thought with arms to free
Was but the faster bound,
And hearts that freedom's hopes had raised
Are dashed again to ground.
The judge is seated,
Round the court, like statues, soldiers stand.
The two, whose doom this day shall fix,
Are fettered hand in hand.

V

Two noble youths with clear grey eyes,
And glance that never quails,
Their lips are set and bloodless
But their courage never fails.
And only when that Judas-friend,
Less calmly far than they,
Stands in the box and faces them,
Do they at length give way.

VI

Oh! then the memory of the past
Springs up their souls to rend;
They curse the hour when trusting hearts
Called that black traitor friend.
'Tis over now; the foreman's lips
Have spoken the fatal words,
And there from out the silent crowd
A woman's voice is heard.

VII

"Oh, judge, asthore, oh, judge my lord,
Ye'll give me leave to speak,
I'm all they have, God help them, now,
Their mother old and weak.
Himself is dead, those long long weary years,
The love of them two boys is all the poor old widow cheers.
One's not my own; his mother died when he was very young,
But sure I love them both, my lord,
Ye'll save them both, aroon.

VIII

"And may the heavens be your bed,
May all the saints look down and bless you.
And you'll have the prayers of all that are in the crowd."
Then rose a murmur strong and deep.
And all that anxious crowd,
For mercy on the widow's sons, prayed earnestly aloud.

IX

The judge was moved with pity,
But duty tied him down.
He tried in vain to steel his heart,
He tried in vain to frown.
"These men are all this day you have,
They toil that you may live,
The mercy that I can I'll show,
His life to one I'll give.

X

"Take then your choice –
Your husband's child whose mother is no more,
Or he, who, to the sire of both,
You in your bosom bore."
A cruel choice, a bitter task –
She bowed her aged head,

Some bitter tears coursed down her cheek,
Then she looked up and said,

XI

"I thank you judge, but Oh! my lord 'tis hard;
How can I choose between the boy I bore, and him I reared?
Judge asthore, choose yourself,
Take which you please to save,
If I sent one to death, I'd not sleep quiet in my grave."
"Good woman, I can do no more,
One dies; it's right, and just.
Which life is spared, depends on you,
So take your choice, you must."

XII

One moment more and then she spoke,
"Oh! Mike, my darling boy,
You know 'tis not I love you less,
I'd die for you with joy,
But Patsy's mother is dead, asthore,
And he has none to take his part.
So him I choose, oh! Mike, this day
'Tis broken is my heart.

XIII

"But Patsy's mother is dead,
And it's you will see her soon,
And tell her that I saved her boy,
God bless you, Mike, aroon."
A cheer arose from out the crowd,
The judge's eyes were dim,
"Take both thy sons, thou noble heart,
Thou shalt not weep for them."

XIV

Then to the prisoners, "Go," he said.
"If Irish hearts be true,

Learn that with justice England's rule
May mingle mercy too."

MEN OF WEXFORD [10]

I

Men of Wexford, halt not, pause not,
While you still have work to do,
Wipe away that burning plague spot
That too long has hung on you.
'Twas your shores were first invaded,
By a Saxon band;
Wexford slept not then, nor dreaded
To attack them on the strand.

II

'Twas our sires first bled for freedom,
'Twas their blood was last to flow;
And should our own country need them,
        We have hearts to face our foe.
Though they poured their blood like water
Free on many a hard-fought plain.
All this carnage, gore, and slaughter
But cemented Erin's chain.

III

In the times of every danger,
Wexford took a noble part,
Can the bonds of slavery change her,
Will she show a craven's heart?
No, by every link that binds us
To the bright but bloody past,
Erin still shall ever find us,
"Slow but sure" to win at last.

---

10 A patriotic song collected by an unnamed pupil of Gusserane School, parish of Tintern, in 1938 (Mrs Corish, teacher). IFCS 872:41–2.

IV

Let the past direct and guide us,
Let the present ever show
That no change can e'er divide us
Practised by the wily foe.
Then once more let Wexford rally,
And keep up the bloodless fight,
Let each mountain, rock and valley,
Ring with – Persevere! Unite!

BARGYMEN AT THE BATTLE OF ROSS, 1798 [11]

Captain John Boxwell [pronounced locally Box'ell J.D.] was killed at the battle of Ross in 1798. He had been an artillery officer in the British Army before the Rebellion. Whether he joined the Insurgents before the battle of Ross or not, I can't say. He took a contingent from Bargy to Ross. The Bargy men were all famous shots as they lived by the gun, shooting fowl on the Lough, which was then not reclaimed. They say that Boxwell was put in charge of the artillery at Ross. Nick Kelly died at Ross. He was one of the men who went with Boxwell. His grave is now in Grange cemetery in Kilmore. Another man who went with Boxwell was White of Ballyburn. White did great work with his gun. The English had snipers at the back of the chimneys to pick off the Insurgents but White tumbled them out of it like sparrows.

Kelly was wounded about the leg. He was making home with White after the battle and somewhere this side of Ross, they saw a crowd of Redcoats coming. They got into the land and hid in a knock [hillock]. Kelly left bloodstains on the road and about the gate, where they entered the field. The soldiers saw the blood on the road and about the gate and they went in and began to prod about the knock with their bayonets. They happened on Kelly but missed White. They killed Kelly. Kelly was a married man of about thirty-five years of age and, according to the old people, he had eleven children. White brought home word to Kelly's wife of her husband's death.

His (Kelly's) wife and eldest daughter went with a mule and common car from Kilmore to Ross. The car had solid log wheels. They brought the body home and buried him in Grange cemetery. They kept the old log-wheeled car

11 Related by Jack Devereux, fisherman, of Kilmore Quay, to James G. Delaney in 1956. IFC 1399:200d–200f.

for years as a kind of memento of that time. An old man named Reville told me that he often had seen the car.

Two others who went with Boxwell to Ross were Richard Barry, from Neams-town, and Mat Coughlan from Moortown, Tomhaggard.

Death of Boxwell   Boxwell was wounded at Ross and was coming home, but was caught by the Redcoats on his way and despatched. Boxwell had a house in George's Street, Wexford [official name of this street, Oliver Plunket St., though it is never called anything but George's Street: J.D.]. When he had gone to Ross, his wife and family moved into town to the George's Street house. One day she was looking out through the window into the street and she suddenly screamed and fainted dead in the room. Some of the servants rushed to her and soon brought her around. Then she told the servant that a British officer had passed by the window riding on her husband's white horse.

Many years afterwards a grandson of Captain Boxwell's was coming from school in England, home through Waterford and Ross. While they were resting the horses at Ross, the young lad went out the Wexford road for a walk. He got talking to an old man who told him that he knew where Captain John Boxwell, his grandfather, was buried and that he could bring him to the place. The young lad was to go back but never did. The body was buried in a grove of trees.

This last paragraph about Boxwell's body was told to John Devereux by the son of the young lad to whom the incident happened. For the rest of the account about Boxwell, he heard it from an old man, John Howlin of Grange, who died three years ago, aged 84.

A story about Daniel O'Connell [12]

Many fireside stories are told about the liberator Daniel O'Connell which did not appear in the book of his life. Tradition tells us of a good story about a boy seventeen years old who was sent to the fair for the first time to sell young pigs. His father and mother followed him later on, to see what kind of a salesmaster Jack would make. As Jack stood beside the creel of pigs, he was pondering over what a great young man he was when a tobacconist came up and said, "How much for the pigs?" "Twenty four shillings," replied Jack, meaning twenty four each, but did not say it. "Bought again," said the tobacconist, "Bring them in to my yard." Jack delivered the pigs – twelve in number. The

12 Collected by Nancy Ryan of Garryduff, Campile, a pupil of St Leonard's School, parish of Tintern (Mary B. Dunphy, teacher), from Richard Ryan of Garryduff, in 1938. IFCS 871:436–8.

buyer paid him one pound four shillings. "Fourteen pounds eight shillings is my money," says Jack. "Come on with the rest of it." "I asked you how much for the pigs," said the buyer. "You said twenty-four shillings, take yourself out of this or I'll get you arrested." "Oh tare-an'-ages," says Jack, "what will I do?" "Go home and rear another litter of pigs and I'll buy from you," said the tobacconist. Jack came out on the street, the first he met was his mother. "Oh, mother," says he, "what will I do? I only got two shillings apiece for the pigs." "Bad scran to your impudence," said the mother; "is that the sort of an *amadán* of the devil I reared?" A crowd soon collected around the pair and the incident was discussed. "Go to O'Connell," was the cry. Jack went and stated his case. O'Connell gave it thought for some time and asked Jack would he allow a bit of his ear to be cut off. Jack said, "Yes," the whole ear if he wanted it to defeat his opponent. "Now," said O'Connell, "go up to the tobacconist, make a bargain with him; get him to sign it with his own hand, his charge of what tobacco would reach from the top of your right ear to the sole of your foot. I have a friend living in the Cape of Good Hope where I will send this bit of an ear, and by the time he will have what tobacco will reach to the Cape of Good Hope he'll very likely pay you double for your pigs." Jack went back to the tobacconist and asked him his charge for what tobacco would reach from the top of his head to the sole of his foot. He measured Jack and told him seven shillings and six pence. He gave him his signature of the bargain. "Now begor," says Jack, "you'll be an ould man again you'll have it made, for the top of my ear is a long ways on the road to the Cape of Good Hope by now." The tobacconist looked perplexed. "I will go to O'Connell," says he, "and he'll do you." "Begor do," says Jack, "two O'Connells if you like." The tobacconist went to O'Connell and told his story. "It is true," said O'Connell. "His ear is on the road. What about giving Jack four times the price of his pigs and my fee?" He willingly gave down the money.

The hedge school in Annagh [13]

About fifty years ago there was a hedge school in Annagh. It was carried on in an old outhouse of Mr Donohoe's. It was situated beside the road, about three miles from Monaseed school. The name of the last teacher was Richard Carey. He was a lame man. He taught reading, writing, and arithmetic. There was only one long desk in the school and each class sat in this desk while writing, while the others were sitting on forms. There were about twenty

13 Related in 1937 by James Smyth, a pupil at Monaseed School (Nicholas Dempsey, teacher). The boy's informant was Patrick Behan of Hollyfort, Gorey. IFCS 889: 56–7.

pupils present every day. Each one of them had a framed slate and a slate pencil. They had no headline copies, but the teacher used to write a headline on the top of each page. He was a beautiful writer. There was no fire in the school, but there was a hole in the corner of the school and the master often lit a fire in it. Then there would be a smoke and they would run out till it would clear. The ruins of it are to be seen still.

Two evictions

AT COOLTHAWN [14]

About fifty years ago, a man lived in Coolthawn, which is about a mile from Monaseed school. His son and daughter-in-law lived with him also.

He was very poor and he was unable to pay the rent. Then twelve policemen under an inspector came to evict them. When they came to the house, the door was bolted, the windows were barred and the man refused to go out. The police then bored a hole with a crowbar in the end wall. Then the man threw boiling water out through the hole and also an iron bar. The police once took the bar and the people made them give it back. The priest got very angry with the police and he advised the inspector to withdraw his men lest there would be bloodshed. So he withdrew his men and the man was never put out of his house, because the Land War ended soon afterwards.

AT COOLROE [15]

In the year 1888 the evictions of Coolroe took place. A family was being evicted because they did not pay the rent to the landlord in power at that time. The evictions took place on 6 September. At half-nine a band left the village of Ballycullane followed by police and people from all parts of the Co. Wexford, and paraded after a party of soldiers who were going to evict the people from their home. When they arrived at the house, they found it all barricaded with a great heap of clay. Twelve men were inside; they had half the roof off, several gallons of boiling tar and water, iron bars to smash ladders, and food for several days. They fought for one day; it was getting dark, when Canon Doyle came through the people and told them to surrender. They did, and eleven of them were taken as prisoners.

14 Collected by K. McDonald, a pupil of Monaseed School, Gorey (Nicholas Dempsey, teacher), from Johnny Redmond of Craan, Gorey, in 1938. IFCS 889: 67–8.   15 An account collected by Vincent Egan of Boley, Ballycullane, a pupil at Gusserane School, parish of Tintern (Peter Corish, teacher), from David Egan, aged 63, in 1938. IFCS 871: 171–21.

Rivalries

Sectarian suspicions

THE PROTESTANT CHILDREN WHO REFUSED TO BLESS THEMSELVES [16]

There's no doubt about it but the Protestants were a very black crowd too when they got the chance.

I often hear the mother telling how she used be keeping company with a Protestant fellow down near Nash. They were very great, "talking" to each other for a brave length. Begob, they had a row, anyway, and they fell out. And whatever words passed between then he says to her, "The greatest day I was ever with you I couldn't stick you." That's a fact.

There was a man living down in Horetown in a place called the Deerpark. He was a Protestant. Well, he had two children a little boy and a little girl. They used come up every evening to Mrs N's for the milk: the mother used send them up. And nearly every evening they'd come, Mrs N would give them a wedge of bread and butter and a cup of milk that was all the go then, don't you see. Well, she often and often attacked them to make them bless themselves. Well, she said that the hand would break off them before the arm would go to the forehead. They wouldn't do it, no matter what she'd do. 'Twas engendered into them, you see.

A PROTESTANT AND A HOLY WELL [17]

In the townland of Kinnagh, St Martin's well is situated at present. But in years gone by it was situated opposite its present place.

An old legend is as follows. One day a Protestant brought his horse to the well to drink. The horse refused to drink, but the Protestant pushed his head

---

16 An anecdote collected by Tom Carey from Maurice Carthy, a farmer aged 79, of Camross, in 1938. IFC 520: 145–6.　17 A story collected by Mary Walsh of Rinnagh, Ballycullane, a pupil of Ballycullane School (John Doyle, teacher), in 1938. Mary heard the story from her mother. IFCS 870: 323.

down. The horse's head dropped off, and the well sprung up in its present place.

A lot of people leave badges and pictures there, as a thanksgiving. One family keeps a small lamp burning by the side of the well.

Old people say that blindness was cured, by going nine times in succession to the well, and putting the water on the afflicted place. Up to the present day, small blemishes such as warts are cured in the same way.

HOLY COMMUNION [18]

There was a Protestant family living in Cushinstown. They had a little Catholic girl working with them. She was very religious and went to mass and Communion every morning. A child of the Protestant family aged ten, when she saw the Catholic girl going to Communion every morning, asked her what did she receive when she went to Communion. The girl said, "The Body and Blood of our Lord." The Protestant girl asked the other girl would she bring it home to her the next time until she saw it. She said she would. When the Catholic girl went to Communion next day, she slipped the Sacred Host into her hankerchief and brought it home. When she got back, the first thing Dora asked her was, "Did you bring me the Sacred Host?" The girl then took out her handkerchief and what she found there was a drop of blood.

THE DIFFERENCE BETWEEN A CATHOLIC GIRL AND A PROTESTANT GIRL [19]

The priest asked Mrs H., a Protestant, would she let one of the servants come up to the chapel for a few minutes to stand for a child. There was Catholic servants and Protestant servants working in H.'s at the time. Well, the priest came and asked her would she let one of the Catholic servants come up. Mrs H. asked him into the house, and she brought him into the drawingroom, and she was very nice to him. After a while anyway she says to him, "Why not bring one of the Protestant servants up with you? What's the difference?" says she.

"There is," says he, "and a great difference."

"Begob," says she, "I can't see where the difference would be."

"Ah well, there is," says he, "and a great difference."

And there was a girl in the hall, one of the servants, and she washing out

18 A story collected by Kitty Power, Dunmain, New Ross, Gusserane School, parish of Tintern (Mrs Corish, teacher), in 1937, from Mrs Jack Murray of Terrerath. IFCS 872: 152–3.   19 Collected by Tom Carey from Nick Cleary of Horetown in 1938. IFC 520: 249–51.

the hall; she had a tub of water and a piece of cloth and she down on her knees working.

Mrs H. was mad to get him to explain to her what difference it would make anyway, and she said he'd have to explain it before she'd let the girl go. "Ah very well," says the priest. So, he called for a Catholic girl and a Protestant girl, and two candles. He lighted the two candles and he gave one to the Catholic girl and the other to the Protestant.

He told the Protestant girl to dip the lighting candle in a tub of water, and take it up again. She did; she dipped it down and brought it up again, and when she brought it up the candle was out.

Then he told the Catholic girl to dip her candle. She did, and then the priest told her to take it up again. She did, and when she brought up the candle 'twas lighting away. "Now Mrs H." says the priest, that's the difference now, between a Protestant girl and a Catholic girl."

Begob she never said another word; but she let the girl go with him. But wasn't it very strange how the candle kept lighting for the Catholic girl. I suppose she had the light of faith and the other one hadn't. But that's a fact truth; that happened for a fact. I often hear me father telling that.

A FUNNY STORY: THE PROTESTANT PUPS [20]

There was once a half-tinker who went around swopping and selling asses and different kinds of animals. Once he had a litter of pups and he was trying to sell them, when one day he knocked at the rector's door and asked him to buy some of the pups, that they were good Protestant pups.

It so happened that the parish priest was a friend of the rector's and on this particular evening the priest was at the rector's house for tea.

The rector brought the pups into the room where the priest was, and, after discussing the matter with the priest, he gave them back to the man and said he would not have them.

Not long after, the man called to the priest's house and asked him if he would buy some pups from him and added that they were good Catholic pups.

Then said the priest, "Do you remember not long ago you called to the rector's house and told him that they were good Protestant pups and now you tell me they are Catholics?"

"Yes, Father", said the man, "but their eyes weren't open then."

20 Related by David McDermott, a pupil of the Model School, Enniscorthy, Seán Ó hEideáin, teacher in 1937. IFCS 873: 174–5.

A RUDE STORY ABOUT A MINISTER[21]

An auld minister was in Killanne one time, and he said he'd preach a little sermon that'd make one half of the congregation laugh and the other half cry. He had the congregation around him. It happened that he had an auld bad seat in his trousers, anyhow. The part of the congregation behind him was generally always laughing; and the part in front with the pitiful tales he told them about the tortures of hell would have tears dropping out of their eyes.

When he had come to declaring about the rewards of the just, they'd be all enjoying the beauties of heaven and the never-ending happiness. So when he had finished praising the joys of heaven he'd tell about the tortures of the damned in hell and he said, "You'll go down, down, down!" and as he'd say that he'd be stooping down down down himself. "O! can't you see the depth of it, can't you see the width of it!" and the crowd behind roared laughing at his bare arse and the people in front weeping over the pains of hell. They didn't know what the others were laughing at.

TRAVELLING PEOPLE[22]

Travelling folk still call at my home as it is a very old custom in Ireland. However, they are very scarce now since the County Home was built and the old-age pensions and widows' pensions came into operation here. Still, the tinsmith, cheery and light-hearted, without a home for shelter, travels along from place to place begging alms for his maintenance, and training his children in the same direction so that they in turn will maintain themselves as cheap as their ancestors. They swop donkeys; they also make tinware to sell. The majority of the tinsmiths buy drink for the money received. In many cases their tinware is not as much sought-for now since the enamel became so cheap and much in use, but the swop still continues.

They mostly travel in groups; the better-off parties have caravans to sleep in brought around by an old donkey or jennet. The poorer class look for shelter in the farmer's barn or any place at all that would keep them dry for the night.

These people are sometimes very interesting. Of a long winter's night the neighbours congregate to the house where these lodgings are given and listen to the thrilling stories and funny yarns these folks do tell.

When morning comes, they generally ask for tea, sugar, milk and a little egg with the budgets across the shoulders of the men and the women with

21 Collected by James G. Delaney, Parnell St, Wexford, from Walter Furlong, aged 83, a farmer of Carrigeen, Grange, parish of Rathnure, in 1954. IFC 1344: 255–6.   22 An account collected at home by Nancy Ryan, a pupil of Gusserane School, in 1938 (Mrs Corish, teacher). IFCS 872: 79–81

the bag, off they go, until night comes again, and so they spend their weary life. Most housewives dread their coming as it is almost impossible to get them away without giving them too much and they are never shy.

The most common names of the tinsmiths resorting this district are: Dorans, Cassidys, and O'Connors. They assemble to fairs, races and football fields. When they get a good supply of drink in these places, they sing and shout and are sometimes very rough.

Highwaymen

CAPTAIN GRANT [23]

There is many a story and tale told of robbers in olden times, of their daring deeds in holding up stage coaches and robbing the wealthy and giving it to the poor. There is not many an Irish boy or girl but has not heard of Captain Grant and some of his exploits. I happen to live very near the place where Grant had his cave, although there is no sign of a cave there now, but the place was pointed out to me by my grandfather. It is situated on the banks of the river and quite close to Killoughram Wood. It was here Grant was taken a prisoner by the English soldiers. The story is told that Grant, returning home to his cave after the night's plundering, went into a farmer's haggard and brought some straw away with him for to make his bed and to have a good sleep. I think I heard the name of the farmer that owned the straw. It was a man named Rigley. But, Grant was not long gone into the cave when there came a servant girl for a can of water to the well which was close to the cave. When she saw the mark of straw down along to the cave, she peeped in and there was Grant sleeping soundly. This wicked girl thought of a plan to get Grant taken. Going to the well, she filled a can of water and stole into the cave. Grant having laid his powder and pistols by his side in case of danger, this girl had little trouble in spilling the can of water all over them. She then ran home and sent word to the soldiers where Grant was hiding. It was not long until the soldiers came and surrounded the cave. When Grant heard the soldiers outside the cave, he got up on one elbow, rubbed the sleep out of his eyes, and he gripped his pistol. The soldiers were very much afraid of Grant and they started firing outside. Grant crept to the mouth of the cave in order to have a shot at the first soldier that would come in sight. But, alas, Grant found out he was betrayed and he had to come out and surrender. The soldiers closed in on Grant, but he was a powerful man and he felled the first

23 Collected in 1938 by Laurence Foley of Monglass, Caime, a pupil of Caime School (Liam Regan, teacher), from his grandfather, aged 80. IFCS 893: 6–10.

that came near him but he was overcome by numbers and had to surrender. The soldiers then compelled a farmer to yoke his horse and cart and convey him to Enniscorthy. The farmer who brought him in was a near neighbour of my grandfather's forefathers. From Enniscorthy, Grant was conveyed to Wexford but the soldiers were not sure if it was Grant they had, and a warder had to come from Maryborough to identify him. He was very near escaping out of Wexford as he did out of Maryborough on a previous occasion. It happened that a comrade of his was in Wexford jail at the time that Grant came in. He was after cutting the bars of the windows in his cell and getting out and was working away at the bars on Grant's window and had two of them filed away when he was discovered; so ended all hopes of Grant escaping. My grandfather was not able to tell me the date of Grant's capture and he is near eighty but he believes it was some time about the year 1810.

CAHIR'S DEN [24]

There is a place between the White Mountain and Blackstairs known as Cahir's Den. People visit this place every year on the Sunday following 25 July. This day is called the "Mountain Sunday". This Den is down underneath the surface of the earth, and there is said to be a flight of stairs leading down to it, which only certain people can see. Cahir was a highway robber who lived here long ago and who brought every person he could catch, and killed and robbed them. On one occasion he caught a girl from Ballindoney and brought her to his den. Some people pursued him, but it was all in vain. The girl was never heard of since. He died sometime shortly after this.

FREANY THE HIGHWAYMAN [25]

There was a great highwayman used to be around this part of the country long ago; Freany was his name. He used to spend all his time around here and up around the Co. Kilkenny. The police and the soldiers used always be after him, and there was a big price on his head; but he was always too quick for them. Sometimes he used to turn the shoes the wrong way on the horse's feet, the way the police would go the wrong direction after him. He was a good man, too, supposed to be. He used take from the rich and give it to the poor.

He was supposed to be hiding up in Lacken hill for a long time. Of course, all that hill was planted that time, and 'twas all a great big wood. Well, the old people say that he buried money there on the hill. He went up on the hill and

24 Collected in 1938 by Lizzie Kavanagh, a pupil at Templeudigan School, Ballywilliam, New Ross, from Martin Murphy of Templeudigan. IFCS 901:92–3.   25 Collected by Tom Carey from Michael Carthy, a farmer, of Cushinstown, New Ross, in 1938. IFC 520: 355–7.

he stood at a certain point of it where he could see the castle in front of him, and he buried the money there. He came along some time after and he looked for the money and he couldn't find it. He stood on different parts of the hill and every place he'd stand on it he could see the castle right in front of him. You could see the ould castle from any point of the hill straight fornent you. He tried it several times but he could never again locate the exact spot where he hid the money; and the money is in it yet; 'twas never found. Several fellows went to dig for the money, and several of them dreamt about it, and went to dig for it; but I don't think anyone ever got it, so it is in it still. Freany then he gave up the robbing, and he handed himself up and asked for pardon. Begor, they pardoned him all right, and they gave him a job. He used to be collecting the tolls on the Bridge of Ross after. He was at that job for a good many years after. Me father was able to tell some great yarns about things he did when he was a highwayman; and about all the fellows he robbed, and all the escapes he had from the police and soldiers.

Hurling and football

WHY THERE ARE NO GOOD WHITE MOUNTAIN HURLERS [26]

I asked a man from around here one day, "Why is it that there are no hurlers from around here in the White Mountain? How is it that all the great hurlers come from Castlebridge, Killurin and Killanne and other places down there?"

"What else could you expect," he says. "Nothing will do the fellows around here but go over into Carlow for their wives, and the children they breed are good for nothing. That's the reason there are no hurlers up here."

HURLING AND FOOTBALL MATCHES ON SLIABH COILLTE [27]

Long ago hurling matches were played on the top of Slieve Coillte mountain, the nearest mountain to where I live where the match was played. All townlands and parish matches were finished there. The top of the mountain is level, and at each end of the playground they used to have a big long thin sally with both ends stuck down in the ground. It took the shape of a loop, and, when the ball passed through it, it was counted a score. At each side of the loop there was a man to see if the ball went through, and, when it did, he raised a green flag. All lookers-on would know it was a score. There were also a referee out among

26 An explanation given to James Delaney by Walter Furlong of Grange, aged 83, in 1954. IFC 1344: 77.   27 Collected in 1938 by Bridget Doyle of Nash, Cassagh, a pupil of Gusserane School (Mrs Corish, teacher). Her informant was Martin Doyle of the same address. IFCS 872: 164–8.

the players. Hurleys were made of ash in different shapes and sizes to suit the players. The local carpenters made them. The number of men in each team was seventeen. A match often lasted two and a half hours. The players wore nothing only a shirt and trousers and they wore nothing on their feet. The hurling balls were all made by shoemakers.

Long ago football and hurling were played in a different way to what they are played today. Instead of playing from goal to goal as they do nowadays, they played from ditch to ditch. Thirty years ago one of the roughest matches of the day was played in Foulksmills between a team from Taghmon and another from Campile. The match which lasted for two and a half hours was supposed to be the roughest ever played in the district. They fought and hurt each other until there was only two men left on the field, Campile taking the victory by four "overs" to three. The following is a song composed in remembrance of the match:

Last Sunday morning as the birds in
the trees they did sing,
I handled my old brogues together
and made my way down to Foulksmills.
For today was the day of the contest
Between the Campile boys and Taghmon.
We smoked and we joked on together
For two or three miles of the road.
We came to a racked looking mansion
Which was called Gort tí an óil.
'Twas there we got whisky and brandy ...

Faction fights [28]

In years gone by there used to be a fair at Nash. Where the fair was held was called the Fair Green.

When the fair was over, the faction fight used to begin. A man would take off his coat and drag it along the ground and say, "Any man there to walk on my coat?" Then another man would step on the coat, and then the fight would start.

As there used only be two fairs at Nash, the people in Nash and in the

---

28 Recorded in 1938 by Eily Kehoe of The Maudlins, New Ross, a pupil at the Mercy Convent (Sister M.P. Ní Mhaoldomhnaigh, teacher). Her informant was her mother. IFCS 897: 149–50.

surrounding districts used to prepare for the faction fights months before the fair (for the faction fights) by having blackthorn sticks and ash plants greased and smoking in the chimney for months to have them sound.

The young girls of the districts and places near used to fill their stockings with stones to help their menfolk in the fight.

On St John's Eve there used to be a bonefire on the Fair Green. All the young girls and boys used to have a dance.

On one St John's Eve a girl who was one of the dancers afterwards on the Green went into the neighbouring churchyard, stole the wooden crosses off the graves and with them started the bonfire. While the girl was dancing, a sheegee [Irish, *Sí gaoithe*, a fairy whirlwind] came and swept the girl away and it said that screams of her going through the air were awful and it is said that she was never seen afterwards. And that finished up dances and fairs at the Fair Green of Nash.

	Faction Leaders
New Ross	Gunnips, Bearneys
Nash	Roches, Connicks
Terrerath	Kents
Loughnageer	Whelans

Stories

"Giants"

THE NASH GIANT[29]

There was a giant that lived in a place called Nash, Cassagh, New Ross, many years ago. He was eight feet four inches high. Any time he wanted to get a new pair of boots he always killed a cow and skinned her to have enough leather to make them. It took three tailors three weeks to make a suit of clothes for him. He used to perform great feats in Nash. He was as strong as six men. When pulling tug-o-war he was very supple although being a very big man. He would stand three big barrels side by side; then he would take a 56 lb weight in each hand and leap from one barrel into the other until he landed out clear. He often took up four fair-sized men and carried them all round the fair-green for exhibition. There was a huge stone in the fair field and he was able to pitch it forty yards away and three ordinary men were not able to lift it. He was often known to carry a stone roller on his shoulder a distance of two miles just the same as another man would carry a pike handle. They came from different counties to see him on a fair day in Nash.

Finally he went to America and gave great exhibitions of his strength there. On one occasion he had a challenge with a Russian sailor to carry a heavy weight of lead, twelve hundred weight of shot, from the vessel to the quay. So Gunnifer (this giant's name) carried it one hundred yards and the Russian sailor was defeated. He won a lot of money in America and he became a rich man after.

29 Collected in 1838 by Mary Doyle, of Nash, Cassagh, from Martin Doyle of the same place. Mary was a pupil at Gusserane School (Mrs Corish, teacher). IFCS 872: 172–4.

A WEXFORD GIANT AND AN ULSTER GIANT[30]

Long ago there lived a giant in Co. Wexford; he was famed throughout Ireland for his brave deeds. Another giant lived in Ulster; he had heard of the Wexfordman's great deeds and came to Wexford to challenge him. The Wexfordman was terrified at this, but his wife came to his aid: she told him to get into the cradle and she would do the rest. Then she sang and rocked the cradle. After some time the Ulsterman arrived and asked to see the giant. The woman said he was out, but if he liked he could see the baby. When the Ulster man saw the baby, he put his finger in his mouth to find if he had any teeth.

The supposed baby bit off his finger. The Ulsterman's excuse for going was that he had to be home at a certain time and could not wait to see the father. Seeing the son so big, he wondered what the father was like, and fearing he would be overpowered he went home to Ulster sorrowfully.

ANOTHER WEXFORD GIANT[31]

Long ago there lived a great giant in the Co. Wexford. He used eat people and animals. The people were terrified of him and at last decided to kill him. So, one day as he was walking along the bank of the river Glasha near Kilmishall, a man cut off his head by means of a long slash-hook. When the head was severed from the body it rolled into the river, and floated away with the tide. They buried the body headless. Some time after this the head was found miles away on a bank (when the tide was out), crying, "Raw head and bloody bones who'll I eat now." It terrified the inhabitants, until somebody had the courage to bury the head, in a kind of channel from the river to the bank. But it is said the head can still be heard making noise and splashing in the water.

Cúchulainn visited Wexford in the distant past. One day he was trying his skill. He went up to the top of Bree Hill. He got a great big rack and threw it in the direction of Borodale. It landed in the river Boro, at Borodale. It is said that there is a great jewel hidden there and a dragon supposed to guard it, so that no one can get near it.

JACK THE GIANT KILLER[32]

There was an old woman and maybe there is still; she had one son whose name was Jack. He had lived with her for twenty-seven years, so one day he

---

30 Told by Peggy Codd, a pupil of Sister Angela's at Presentation Convent, Enniscorthy, in 1938. IFCS 894: 52–4.   31 Also told by Peggy Codd, who heard them from her mother, Annie Codd, who heard them from Paddy Kenny of Enniscorthy. IFCS 894: 50–1.   32 Written down by John Walsh, a pupil at Marshallstown School (Seosmh Ó Macháin, teacher), in 1939, from his grandfather, Laurence Walsh, who lived in Tomadilly. IFCS 893: 84–7

made up his mind to go seek his fortune and he plastered up an old potato basket and set sail down the river; so on he sailed until he came to a fine gentleman's palace. So up he went; he met the owner of the palace and asked for a job. The gentleman asked him what he could do. He said he could turn out cows, mind them and bring them in. The gentleman agreed to give him work. He gave him his supper and a good bed. Jack slept well that night but he began to think of his poor mother at home. He got up early next morning and turned the cows out to the field. There was not much grass in the field, so Jack looked around and over the bounds wall he saw a fine field of grass; the grass was two or three feet high in it. Jack pulled out a few stones out of the wall and let the cows into the field. When Jack turned them home in the evening, they were spilling their milk along the road. The gentleman was very pleased, but when he heard that Jack had the cows in the giant's field he told Jack that the giant would eat him if he caught him there. Jack got up next morning and went and put the cows in the giant's field again. They were not long there until the giant came to the gentleman's place to get the rascal who put the cows in his field. He stood for a minute and then he said, "Fee faw fum, I smell the blood of an Irishman; be him dead or be him alive, I'll have his guts for my garter and his blood for my morning's meal." Jack stepped up to the giant and the giant said to him, "Which would you like me, to drive you up in the air a few miles or put you down some feet in the dirt with my big thumb?" "Not so quick," said Jack. "Let's have a trip and a box over first."

The first time that Jack hit the giant he knocked him down. Jack had a little hatchet in his pocket and he cut off one of the giant's heads.

The giant got up but Jack knocked him down again and cut off another of the heads. He got up a third time and Jack knocked him down again and cut off the third head. This was how he got the name of Jack the giant killer. Jack put the three heads in the gap where he used to turn out the cows for stepping stones because it was dirty. Jack set off for the giant's palace. When the housekeeper saw Jack, she started to scream, telling Jack that the giant would kill him. But Jack told her that he had killed the giant and that he was now Master of the Palace. He went around looking at all his fine property but he began to think of his poor mother at home. He set sail once again in the back basket to bring his mother to live with him in the palace. So there they lived happy together and when I was there last they made me the tea and I drank a cup and a half; so if they don't live happy that we may!

A Carrigbyrne Faust [33]

There was a blacksmith living in the Co. Wexford one time and he was very poor. One day a gentleman came riding on a horse to the forge door. He asked the blacksmith to shoe his horse, an' the blacksmith did it, an' the blacksmith asked him for his pay, and the gentleman gave him a hundred pounds for doing it. "But," he said, "you'll have to come with me in ten years for I'm the divil." The blacksmith said he would. But before the ten years were up an angel came to the blacksmith an' she said to him: "You've got very rich lately. There must have been somebody here who gave you money." The blacksmith said that the divil was there. The angel said that he shouldn't have took anything from the divil. The blacksmith said that he didn't know twas the divil until he had the horse shod. The angel gave him a snuff box and she said that whoever went into that box couldn't leave it until he'd tell him. When she was going away, she said that anyone who went up on his apple tree couldn't leave it until he'd tell him. When the ten years were up, the divil came along. The blacksmith told him to sit on his armchair. The divil did so and the blacksmith dilly dallied as long as he could and the divil couldn't get out of the chair, and he asked the smith to let him go, and he wouldn't come back for another ten years. The smith let him go. The ten years weren't long going again and the ould fella an fifty young divils came along. The ould boy wouldn't go in, so the young divils went in. The blacksmith kept the young fellas adin for a long time an' at last the ould fella went in. The smith said to him, "You've great powers and I bet you you couldn't go in this box." The divil went in and the fifty young fellas followed him. The smith wouldn't let him out and the divil asked him to let him out, and that he wouldn't come back for another ten years. The smith agreed. The ten years weren't long going and the divil came along and the smith forgot all about the apple tree and he locked the door and was going off with the divil. When they were passing by the apple tree, the divil went up for an apple and of course he couldn't get down. He was there for two months, and at last the smith let him down. The divil never came back again and the smith lived happy ever after.

* *adin* = within

---

33 Told by Josie Kehoe of Carrigbyrne School, parish of Newbawn, in 1938 (Mary Curtis, teacher). Josie's informant was Henry Condon of Carrickbyrne. IFCS 882: 506–8.

The three maidens who set out to seek their fortunes[34]

Once upon a time there lived a woman who had three daughters. Their father died when they were young. Two of their names were Margaret and Lizzie and the youngest daughter's name was Jane. Their poor mother found it very hard to provide for them. She used to work with the farmers making hay in the fields, milking cows and picking potatoes.

Now the eldest girl reached the age of eighteen years, and she consulted with her mother as to her future. The girl wished to go and seek a living for herself. At first the mother thought she was too young to face the world, but then as she was so eager to go the mother thought it better to let her off.

"Kill me a chicken and bake me a cake and I will go to seek my fortune in the morning," said the girl.

The next morning she got out of bed early and bade goodbye to her mother and two sisters and made her way as best she could along the road. About midday she was tired travelling and she sat down by the side of the road and helped herself to some chicken and cake. As she sat considering where to she would steer her barque next, she espied a horse standing by the side of the road, a distance off. She came up to him.

He could not eat as the iron bit had cut his mouth since some person had tied him to a tree. She said to the horse, "Let me on your back and take me a piece of the road as I am tired travelling," and the poor horse said, "Oh, loose me from this tree and I will carry you as far as I am able." She replied to the horse, "I will not let you loose. I have something else to trouble me now as I am off to seek my fortune."

So she travelled some miles farther. She sat down again and helped herself to some chicken and cake. She next saw a donkey grazing at the side of the road. When she came up to it, she said to it, "Let me on your back and carry me some distance as I am tired walking." The donkey looked at her and said, "If you take the nail out of my hoof, I will carry you as far as I am able." She answered, "Indeed I will not help you, as I cannot get anyone to help myself."

So she moved on a couple of miles further on, and she again sat down and helped herself to some chicken and cake. Now she continued on her journey and next she met a poor sheep and it lying down on the side of the road with a line of bees stuck on its back, tearing off the wool.

She said to the sheep, "Carry me a piece of the road, I am very tired." The

34 Collected in 1937 by James Furlong of 6 Abbey Street, Wexford, a pupil at the Christian Brothers School, Wexford (Br D.C. Ó hEilighe, teacher) from Mrs Mary Furlong, aged 72, who lived at the same address. IFCS 880: 444–54.

sheep said, "Will you take these bees off my back as I am nearly dead." She answered, "No, I will not."

She next met a wolf lying behind a cock of hay and he said to her "Oh! will you help me? My poor leg is broken." She said to him, "How did that happen," and he replied, "I was caught in a trap," and she answered, "I cannot help you." She sat down again and partook of the last of the chicken and cake.

She travelled on some miles further until she came to an avenue leading to a giant's castle. She decided she would go up to the big castle and see what it was like and to find out who was living there. When she reached the middle gates of the avenue, she heard a loud barking of dogs. Still she persisted. She came to a big gate on which hung a bell. She lifted her hand and rang the bell twice. A black servant came out to her and said, "What brought you here? Don't you know, this is the giant's castle, and if he finds you here he will devour you at once. However, I will put you in the dog's kennel and I will let you out at day-break."

Now the poor girl slept in the kennel afraid to stir. Just as the clock struck twelve, the giant ran down stairs out of bed and called up all the servants and alarmed the house. He shouted, "Fee! Foo! Fum! I smell the blood of an Irishman. Let him be dead or alive, I will have his blood for my morning dram, I'll have his bones for stepping-stones, and I'll have his guts for garters!"

So he searched the place all around and found her in the dog-box. He ate her up in two minutes.

Weeks and months went by and the poor mother was always worrying over the daughter, but could get no account of her whatever. Now the second eldest daughter came to the conclusion that she would also go to seek her fortune, and see could she find out what became of her sister. She said, "Dear mother, bake me a cake and kill me a chicken and I will go to seek my fortune."

So she went off the next morning early. She walked on for some miles, until she got hungry and tired, and she helped herself to some cake and chicken. She looked around and she saw a horse standing by the roadside. She called out to him, and said, "Give me a lift on your back as I am tired walking."

The poor horse looked, and said to her, "Will you loose this rope which holds me here so tightly and I will take you any-place?" She said to the horse, "Indeed, I will do no such thing, I am only out to help myself."

So she journeyed on a piece further and she next met with a donkey. She said, "Come, donkey, carry me a piece of the road, as I am tired walking." He answered, "Oh! take the big nail out of my hoof and I will carry you any-place." She replied, "No," and she said that she would not wait for him.

The poor donkey shook his head, and said, "Oh God help us! you are the second girl that passed this way and refused to do a good turn." "Well," she said, "I am out to seek my fortune. I am afraid it will turn out a hopeless one."

Now she travelled a couple of miles further and she sat down and helped herself to some cake and chicken.

While she was eating, it occurred to her that the other girl the donkey spoke of was her sister. "If so, I am on the right road," she said.

She still kept travelling on for about a mile of the road until she met with a sheep lying down. It said to her, "Oh, will you do something for me? My back is full of bees. They are tearing me to pieces." She said, "What sauce! I have nothing else to do only wait on you!" The sheep said, "You are the second girl that passed this way, who would not do a kind turn for anyone."

Next she met with a poor wolf and he lying behind a cock of hay suffering from a bad leg, and he said to her, "Will you bandage my leg? I am suffering in great pain." She said, to him, "I will do no such thing. I am seeking my own fortune. I am sorry I came this way, as I am annoyed with the lot of you." The wolf said, "Go ahead, you will be no better."

She moved on a bit further and sat down and helped herself to the last of the cake and chicken. She travelled about a mile on the road until at last she came to an avenue leading to a big castle.

As it was nearing nightfall she said, "I will make my way up here. Perhaps I will get some account of my lost sister. Anyway they might shelter me for the night."

Just as she had reached the middle of the avenue, she heard the barking of dogs. She was much frightened until she saw the footman approaching her. "What on earth brought you here tonight? You know this is the giant's castle, and if he finds you here, he will eat you up."

She said to him, "Oh! could you put me up anywhere for the night and I will leave at daybreak." He locked her in an old house at the side of the yard, and told her to make no noise.

Now the clock struck twelve. The giant's bell rang and he called up the servants. He said, "Fee! Foo! Fum! I smell the blood of an Irishman. Let him be dead or alive, I will have his blood for my morning dram, I'll have his bones for stepping stones, and I'll have his guts for garters."

So he told his servants to make a search inside and outside the castle. At length they came to the old house where the girl was hiding and the giant immediately devoured her, and that was the end of the second sister.

Now time rolled on and the poor mother was worried about her two daughters. The third daughter was now sixteen and she said, "Mother, bake me a cake, and kill me a chicken, as I too am going to seek my fortune, and I will find out what became of my two sisters, if possible.

Next morning, she bade her mother goodbye, and started off early. She travelled some miles and she sat down by the side of the road and helped herself to some cake and chicken. So, when she had finished she went on further and she saw a poor horse by the side of the road, and he tied to a tree. He said to her, "Oh! will you loose me from this tree, I am in great pain. There were two girls who passed this way before, but I am afraid they are in bad luck."

She said to him, "Certainly I will loose you from the tree." So the horse travelled on beside her as she went along. Next she met a donkey standing on three legs, suffering from a nail in his hoof. He said "Oh! will you take this nail out of my hoof as I am suffering great pain?" She at once drew the nail from the hoof and the donkey was delighted and marched along with her.

She sat down again and helped herself to some cake and chicken. Next she met a poor sheep and it wild with pain from a hive of bees that got stuck on its back. It said, "Oh! please do something for me as the bees are tearing me to pieces." She at once shook off the bees and the sheep was relieved.

Next she met a wolf lying behind a haycock, with its leg torn. She at once bandaged up the leg and had the wolf right again. Next she came in sight of a big avenue leading to the giant's castle. She said, "I think I will try my luck up here."

Now the horse and the ass, the sheep and the wolf, all went with her to guard her, to the giant's castle. It was nightfall by this time. She went up to the gate and rang the bell. The servant man came out and said, "Oh, what on earth brought you here, because if the giant smells you, he will devour you at once. Such was the fate of two girls who came here about a month ago." "However," he said, "I will hide you in the house in the garden," so she and the four animals stole in and lay down beside each other.

Now the clock struck twelve and the giant awoke. He called on his servants and said, "Fee! Foo! Fum! I smell the blood of an Irishman. Let him be dead or alive, I'll have his blood for my morning dram. I'll have his bones for stepping stones, and I'll have his guts for garters."

He tore out to where the poor girl was, and thought to make her his prey. The sheep, the ass, and the horse got stuck in him. The wolf caught him by the throat and tore him to pieces.

"So you see," said the donkey, "a kind turn is not lost."

She was brought in by the servants who handed over the castle and all its gold to her. She sent for her mother and told her all. And herself and the donkey, the sheep, the horse and the wolf, all lived happily together ever after.

They put down the kettle and made the tay and if they weren't happy, that you and I may.

The dog, the pig, and the narrative [35]

A woman who lived in this district got a bit high up in the world, and thought she would like to send her daughter, Matilda, to a boarding school in England to learn to be "grand". When holiday-time came, Matilda came home and spent most of her time reading. One day her mother asked her to tell her the tale she was reading. "Oh! Mother," she replied disgusted, "don't say 'tale', say 'narrative', it's a much grander word." Shortly after that, her mother on looking out, saw a dog running after a pig with the pig's tail in its mouth. Very excitedly her mother cried aloud, "Oh! Matilda, the dog has the pig by the narrative."

A tall tale and a folktale [36]

POTEEN AND A HORSE

There was a man once lived in Kilmore Quay over seventy years ago by the name of John. When he was eighteen years of age he got married and lived very well for a number of years until he found himself the owner of seven children. The poor man then got it hard enough trying to rear them. One morning he turned up late for work and the boss being in a bad temper told him to go home and never show his nose in the place again. Poor John went home and spent a whole week trying to get work but failed. He went out one morning after he having a frightful row with the woman and sat down on the top of a hill, and began to wonder what would be the best thing for him to turn his hand to. He spent a long time thinking and trying to suck comfort out of an old pipe that was as innocent of tobacco as the day it came from the factory.

He suddenly jumped up. "Begob," says he, "I have it, I'll go home and start making poteen; they say it is a great plan of making money. I'll make a little of it first in the parlour and then when I'll have some money made I'll build a house underground and carry on an extensive trade. That's what I'll

35 A funny story told in 1938 by Ena Murphy of Broadway, Lady's Island, a pupil at Lady's Island School (G. Ó Murthuile, teacher). IFCS 878:121.   36 Recorded by Seán Butler: the first from Edward Gough, Kilmore Quay, no date, IFC 106:18–40; the second from Willie Doyle (25) of Glynn, no date, IFC 130–50.

do," says he as he started for home, "but I'll have to be very careful for if the police got wind of it there would be an end put to my little trade in no time."

He told his story to the wife. She said she didn't care what trade or business he started so long as he made plenty of money to support herself and her family. It was not long until John started with the new industry, but he found it very hard to make it up to the mark for a long time. After a time, however, he improved on it and it was not long until he started building the underground house. He used to get sale for the poteen in a lot of counties outside Wexford. He wouldn't sell any of it in Wexford as he was always afraid of the police hearing about it.

It was not long until John was a very rich man, and was not only able to support his family well, but was also able to lay some by for the rainy day. The neighbours couldn't understand at all how he was so well off, because no one knew he was making the poteen. All went very well with John for a long time, until he began to drink, and one day in a public-house he began boasting about the great wife he had and the fine family. Then someone in the public-house asked him how it was that he became so rich lately. John, being full of drink, told him all about the "famous industry" he had started on condition that he would keep it a secret. The man said he would of course.

The next day John and his family were working away in the underground house when a boy came rushing in saying that four policemen were coming to the house in a car. John got an awful fright, but he told his wife and family to bring all the poteen that was in the dwelling house and put it in the underground house. They were not long doing this, and, when all was ready, John had nothing to do but wait for the police. It was not long until the car drove into the yard. They got out of the car and tied the horse to the stable door. They then told John why they came there. They told him that they had heard he was making poteen, and had come to find out whether that was true or not. John told them it was all a lie, that he wouldn't know poteen from water, and told them they had permission to search the place and welcome. The police went inside and searched the house from top to bottom, but could find nothing. John had a secret door in the parlour floor to the underground passage, but it was so well put in that the police never noticed it.

But while the police were inside searching the house the fun was going on outside. It happened that there was an old tub at the stable door half full of poteen that John forgot about when they were hiding it. The policemen's horse was tied to the stable door, and he put his mouth down in the tub to get a drink, but he wasn't long drinking when he stopped as the taste was rather strange to him. But however strange the taste was, it pleased him and he started again and never stopped until he had the tub empty. Well, half a tub of poteen is some drink even for a horse.

When the police had the house searched and could find nothing, they came out and yoked the horse and went in the direction of Wexford. When they were about two miles from John's house they noticed something strange about the horse. They couldn't get him to trot at all, but walk at a slow pace and his head drooping. Then he started swaying backwards and forwards and at last came to a standstill. They then started beating him with a big stick and the horse made an effort to move, but the moment he did he fell on the road and stretched himself out and started groaning.

The police got a fright then, when they saw the horse dying, and didn't know what to do. One of them said he would run back to John Doyle's house, and get John to take the horse off the road for a few shillings and bury him, as they didn't know anybody else in the neighbourhood. The others consented and he went back to John's house. He found John standing at the stable looking into the empty tub. The policeman told him the story from beginning to end. John wasn't a bit surprised, for when he found the tub empty he knew it was the horse that drank it. "Begob," says he to himself, "I'd better get that horse away from them as soon as I can, for if them buckoes get the smell of poteen off him I'll be sent to jail for long enough." He went back with the policeman to the place where the horse was stretched on the road. After some bargaining with them John decided to bury the horse for ten shillings. The policemen then went home. When they were gone John said he might as well make ten shillings more, and took a big knife and put an edge on it. Then he began to skin the horse. Everything went on well until he was nearly finished. He was finishing one of the hind legs, when he cut the inside skin. John noticed nothing until the horse made a kick at him, and then he did get the fright. The horse starting kicking and tumbling on the road. At last he got up and when he did the skin fell off him. Poor John kept looking on at all this with his mouth and eyes open, and who would wonder at him, and he looking at the poor horse walking around and no skin on him. He didn't know what to do with the horse now. He was considering would it be best to shoot him when he saw the horse beginning to graze. This decided him. He put the skin on the horse again, but, when he had it on, he had no cords or ropes to tie it on, and of course it wouldn't stop on by itself. He went and got a few long briars and split them and put a couple of them around the horse's belly and tied him around the head with another. Then he brought home the horse and let him out in the field. He went out the next day to take the briars off the horse, and tie on the skin with cords and make a neater job of it. But when he tried to pull the briars off the horse, he found they had taken root and when he began to pull one off, the horse began to kick. He had to leave him as he was.

After a couple of weeks the fun began. The briars began to grow, and it was not long until they began to bud. After a while he was seen going around in full bloom. The leaves then began to fall away and the berries began to form. They grew until they were as big as apples, and it is stated that one of them alone would make a pound of jam. The horse lived for ten years in this position; in the spring he would bloom out, and in the end of summer would bear fruit.

MOCKLEY THE FOOL

There was a man one time lived in Wexford ages ago. He was married. They had one son. His name was Mockley, but he was commonly called Mockley the fool. He was all the divil for eating; he'd ate and ate an' never could be filled. Now his people were very poor, and they found it very hard to live, and keep a bit in Mockley's mouth.

Times got so bad at last that they had only one cow between them and starvation, so they had to bring her to the fair. Mockley and his mother went to the fair and they were a long time there but couldn't sell the little cow. At about two o'clock in the afternoon Mockley was gettin' awful hungry and he told his mother so. She was tormented. "Begor," says she, "you may stay hungry today be the look of things." Mockley was so mad with the hunger an' everything else that he walked away from his mother an' the cow. He went down the street. At that time on the streets at the fairs there used be stands selling boiled pigs' heads and boiled pigs' feet an' chunks of bread. As Mockley was going by one of the stands, the smell of the boiled meat was too much for him, so he stopped. He picked up one o' the posts off the stand and made a drive at the man in charge. He got such a fright he ran away. Mockley gripped a pig's head in one hand an' a big chunk of bread in the other an' went off down the street eating at his leisure.

His mother never sold the cow that day. When she got home, Mockley was there before her but there was no sign o' the pig's head or the chunk o' bread. His father an' mother talked for a long time that night over the fire an' they came to the conclusion that it was time for Mockley to go an' seek his fortune, as they found it impossible to keep him. When morning came, they told Mockley what they had decided upon.

Mockley was very sad when he heard the news but he knew well enough that his parents couldn't keep him so he was willing to go. Mockley had a little pitcher from the time he was a small boy, and he was very fond of it, so he took his little pitcher with him; he then bid good-bye to his father an' mother an' went to seek his fortune.

He travelled on and on with his little pitcher under his arm until he came to a stream. He sat down by the stream an' rested for a while. He was beginning to get very hungry and didn't know what to do. Suddenly he saw a little trout swimming to and fro in the stream. He put his hand in the stream and caught it. "Begor," says he, "I'll have something to eat now anyhow." "Oh don't eat me, don't eat me," says the little trout, "and anything you can wish for you can have it." "Oh, I don't believe you at all," says Mockley. "If I break my little pitcher, will I get another if I wish for it?" "You will, you will," says the little trout. Mockley then broke his little pitcher and wished for another. The moment he did he got it. He then released the little trout an' set out for home. It was night by the time he got home an' he was mad with the hunger. His father an' mother wondered greatly at him coming home so suddenly an' they were also mad with him for they hadn't a bit to ate in the house only what would do themselves. "You came back very quickly," says his mother to him. "Did you get homesick?" "No," says Mockley. "I have my fortune made." They thought he was fooling them. "Well," says Mockley "if yous don't believe me, listen to this. I wish by my little trout for a good supper on that table." No sooner had he said the words, than there was a great supper on the table, all the grand eatables you could mention. So the three o' them sat in and had a very hearty meal. Mockley soon got to be a very rich man, and his people were also well off. He remained with his own people for about six months and he doing nothing except going around the roads and he dressed up like a gentleman. At the end of that time he took a notion to travel around the world for a couple of years.

So he started off one mornin' and travelled on and on and had a great time. Everything he wished for by the birth of his little trout he got it.

It happened one day that he was passing by the king's palace an' he saw the princess sitting in a window. She was very beautiful and Mockley the fool fell in love with her, but he knew he'd have no chance of her. So he said, "I wish by the birth of my little trout that the princess will have a child for me by this time nine months." Very well an' good. Mockley took a house about two miles an' a half from the king's palace, and stayed in it for a year. When the nine months were up there was a hell of a row at the king's palace, for the princess had a son.

The king was furious and he did everything in his power to find out who was the father, but he never succeeded.

There was an old witch one day passing by the palace and the king came out and asked her advice on the matter. "I'll tell you what you'll do," says the witch; "give a great ball or dance an' invite everybody for miles around to it. Then in the middle o' the night's fun bring out the child, place it in the middle o' the floor, put an apple in its hand an' tell it to give the apple to its father." Very good. The king gave a great dance and invited everybody for miles around the palace. A great crowd came an' Mockley himself came an' he dressed in great style. At about twelve o'clock the king brought out the child and placed it in the middle of the floor and gave it an apple and told it to give it to its father. The child walked around the room until it saw Mockley and walks over to him. "Here, Daddy," says he and, giving him the apple, Mockley got an awful fright when he heard what the child said. He looked around him but couldn't escape. The king then sent for the princess and asked her did she ever see this man before. She said she didn't. The king told her she was a liar, that she knew well enough this man was the father of her child. He ordered a boat to be built an' when that was done he put it out on the water an' ordered Mockley an' the princess an' her child to be put into it, an' let them go where they like.

When they were on the water for a couple of hours, says Mockley to himself, "I wish by the birth of me little trout that there'll be a grand mansion with a whole lot of attendants an a bodyguard of soldiers outside by the side of this lake."

When they came to the beach they saw the grand mansion. "This is my mansion," says Mockley to the princess, "what do you think of it?" When the princess saw the grand mansion, she was surprised. She never saw it before, but she was delighted when she saw the inside, for she was never in such a mansion before, an' it was ten times a better an' a grander mansion than her father's palace. So Mockley an' the princess got married an' they lived happily for a long time.

After some time the princess said she would like to see her father again, so they invited him an' all the nobles, to a grand feast at Mockley's mansion. That night they were drinking wine out of gold cups, and when the attendants were washing them up they found out that one of them was missing, so they told Mockley. Mockley said to himself, "I wish by the birth o' me little trout that I'll find that cup in the king's pocket." Mockley then told all the guests that the cup was stolen an' that he was sorry he would have to search everybody there. So he started to search an' he searched away until he came to the king. "Sure you're not goin' to search me," says the king. "Why not," says Mockley; "everybody must be searched." So he searched him and found the cup in his pocket and held it up for everyone to see. The king was in an awful state then as he didn't know how the cup got into his pocket, and he was also ashamed to look anybody in the face.

"I don't know how that cup got into my pocket," says he, "it is very strange." "Not a bit more strange than how the child got into the princess," says Mockley the fool.

The story of the frog in the well[37]

There was a man one time and he had only the one son. The son grew up, and, at about the age of twenty, he was as fine a young man as was in the country. He started "talking" to a young lady that lived a few miles away, and they fell in love with each other and they decided to get married. The girl's father was a very rich man, a real big fellow, and he didn't want the daughter to marry this fellow at all. He didn't like him, it seems. Well, this ould fellow he had a witch in the place and he got her to work some kind of enchantment on the boy to get him out of the way. The witch didn't know what 'twas all about, or why he was doing it; but she had to do it. So one day she was down by a well that was near the house, and this boy happened to come along. The ould witch hit him with a wand, or whatever she had, and there and then she changed him into a frog. He was there in the well, hopping about for a long time, and nobody put any *suim* [interest] in him no more than another frog. Begob, one day the girl of the house – that's the young lady he was courting – she came to the well herself for a can of water. She dipped the can down in the well for to get the water, and what came up inside the can but the frog. He came up to the top of it and he spoke to her:

> Oh! take me home, me own fair lady,
> Oh! take me home, my own true love,
> Don't forget the world's in water
> For you are my own true love.

Begor, the girl ran home with the can of water and the frog inside in it. She ran in to her father and she told him about it. "Oh, papa," says she, "the quarest thing you ever seen happened. I brought up this little frog in the can out of the well; and he spoke to me and asked me to bring him home with me." "Oh! musha," says the father, "maybe the poor little fellow was cowld. Take him out and put him on the chair there by the fire." The girl got the tongs out of the fire and she caught the frog with it and she put him on the chair. She was afraid to catch him with her hands.

After some time the girl and her father sat down to their dinner; and they were only just sitting down to it when the frog spoke up again and says:

> Oh! I am hungry, my own fair lady,
> Oh I am hungry, my own true love,

37 Narrated by Patrick Doyle of Old Ross, a stonemason, to Tom Carey in 1938. IFC 577: 254–8.

Don't forget the world's in water
For you are my own true love.

"Do you hear that?" says the girl to him. "Musha," says the father, "I
suppose the poor fellow is hungry. Bring him over here to the table and let
him ate a bit." So she got some stuff for the frog and she gave it to him. The
frog sat down, and then he says, "A knife and fork, me fair lady: a knife and
fork, me own true love" etc. "He wants a knife and fork now," says the girl.
"How could a frog work a knife and fork?" "Sure give it to him anyhow, and
let us see how he will work them." So she got the knife and fork and she gave
it to him. Sure the frog worked them the finest ever you seen. "Begob," says
the father "he's a brave fine frog. He's able to work away at them as good as
anyone." That was all right until about eleven o'clock that night when 'twas
about time to go to bed. The frog spoke up again:

Oh! come to bed, me own fair lady,
Oh! come to bed, me own true love,
Don't forget the world's in water,
For I am your own true love.

"Oh," says the girl, "how am I to take a frog to bed with me?" She didn't
like the idea of taking a frog into bed with her. "Oh, musha" says the father
"sure, he won't take up very much room. He's not so big; and can't you take
him with you." After great persuasion anyhow he wrapped the frog up in a
shawl or something and she brought him up to her bedroom and she put him
into her bed. He was fine and snug in it. There was a bit of him on the pillow,
and a bit of him in the bed. There wasn't much of him anywhere. As soon as
the frog was nice and snug in the bed, he says, "Come in to bed, me own fair
lady; come in to bed, me own true love; Don't forget the world's in water, For
you are my own true love." The girl didn't want to go. But the father per-
suaded her. He told her a frog was the cleanest animal out, and what harm
would he do her. So she went anyhow. As soon as she was in the bed, the lad
spoke up again: "Put out the light, me own fair lady; put out the light, me
own true love; don't forget the world's in water, for you are my own true
love." She put out the light anyhow, although she thought damn hard of doing it. After some time, anyhow, she went off to sleep, and she never woke
anymore until morning. When she awoke in the morning, she let one roar out
of her; and she ran down to her pa. "Oh, papa," says she "the finest foxy man
you ever seen is above in me bed." It seems enchantment was broken that
night, and he got back to his own shape again. But, to make a long story short,

they got married very soon after. They had childer in basketfuls and they threw 'em out in riddlefuls. All they gave me was a glass backside and I slid here to Old Ross and I'm here yet. So there's the story now for you about the Frog in the Well.

Mumming plays

A fragment of a mumming play [38]

Mummers were very common in Wexford twenty or thirty year ago. They used to dress up in paper caps and green ribbons and do a kind of a dance. There were twelve men on a set and they carried sticks in their hands and kept time to the music by hitting the sticks together. Every man used to say a rhyme at the start. This is how the Captain's rhyme went:

Attention pay, kind friends, just listen for a while
Until you hear the heroic deeds of those boys from Erin's Isle.
Twelve patriots we represent and nobly fought to right old Erin's wrong.
Soldiers, saints, valiant king and warriors brave and strong.
The first he is St Columcill who once provoked the state,
Left Erin's shore, ne'er saw it more, for why he will relate.
Brian Boru he is the next and crushed the haughty Danes,
He is here to tell how long and well in old Erin he did reign.
Art MacMurrough is the next, old Leinster's sept he swayed;
The great King Richard and his knights he ne'er obeyed.
Owen Roe O Neill, no prince more grand in the lordly race of Neill,
Benburb he won it with the spear and wore a Spanish mane.
Sarsfield too you'll hear him tell of Limerick's battered walls,
Where women fought, caring not for fire and cannon ball.
The brave Wolfe Tone, at whose very name the coward would shake with fear,
Lord Edward too of "Crom aboo", you'll also meet him here.
Likewise John Kelly from Killanne to tell of Ros Mhic Treoin,
Brave Michael Dwyer whose pike flashed fire at the rising of the moon.

38 Collected by Mícheál Mac Aodh of Carrig-on-Bannow from Martin Cullen, a labourer from the district, in 1936. IFC 417: 14–20.

Robert Emmet young and fair has something got to say
Of what he did, and how he strove to smack the tyrant's sway.
Fr John he is the last: his name we all revere,
A heroic priest who doubtless led the dauntless Shelmaliers.
In Leinster's vales and Leinster's plains great deeds of them abound,
While Ulster hills and Connaught glens have heard the slogan sound.
Of music too we have galore by artists proved with skill.
The first of all on him I call: Step forward Columcill.

Kelly from Killanne's rhyme

You have heard with pride the heroic deeds of which those gallants tell,
Columba's fame has blessed this Isle, yet far from it did dwell.
Sarsfield speaks of Limerick's walls, O'Neill of Benburb's vales,
If you will, now I will relate no less a heroic tale
Of how was fought the fight at Ross that sealed old Erin's fate
In the year of thrilling memories, dark yet glorious Ninety Eight.
From Wexford town the boys marched out; we camped on Three Rock hill.
From thence we sped and won Taghmon and likewise Foulks's Mill;
Still on we kept our onward march and all along the way
Brave stalwart men did join the ranks from Barony Forth to Bannow Bay,
And braver hearts to those men's breasts never yet did burn,
Than those that camped on the fourth of June on the Rock of Carrigbyrne.
A clarion sound in the morning dawn, it o'er our slumbers broke.
The green flag proudly floated high above the forest oak.
And down each slope and down each height
And in every hand was seen a ten-foot pike.
Or the deadly sight of a pitchfork pointed keen.
There from all sides came trooping, through the summer night,
Old men whose heads were hoary and youths in wild delight.
Scarce had the first rays of the dawn outshone the cloudless sky,
Six hundred hands had clutched their pikes to carry Ross or die.
Brave Father Roche he blessed their ranks and with a loud "hurray!"
Like lions we sped down the hill. Oh Heavens! what a day!

Ros Mhic Treoin from battle walls that chain-shot on us fell,
Our ranks were mowed like corn, and bullets on us fell.
Still on we sped, I led the ranks of Bargy's daring men,
While Clooney led the boys of Tintern ...
On past the spot where young Furlong fell, there his young body lay.

A thousand throats sent forth a cry: Revenge shall we have this day.
Faster now and faster still up to the gates we go,
We have reached at last ...
Ah, now the pikes are up against the foe.
Ah, who could stand those pikemen, brave children of the soil,
Soon down the street came an ocean flood of Saxon blood like oil,
And in the thickest of that fight a female form was seen,
Molly Doyle, the heroine who fought beneath the green.
Our men fatigued from loss of blood and scorched with the burning sun,
Were falling back, when thro' the ranks a nimble gorsoon ran,
The green flag waving in his hand, saying, "Follow me who dare."
Once more the redcoats we did rout in terror and despair.
Across the bridge, like frightened deer, twas there we lost the chance,
For Harvey on that flying foe would not let me advance.
My tale is told, my task is done, though more I could relate,
But Father John, that faithful priest, I cannot ask to wait.

The Forth and Bargy Mummers' Play [39]

Here I am, the captain brave, I lead no rebel throng,
But a chosen band of heroes grand, to Kilmore we do belong.
For mirth and sport we do resort, and for diversion play,
And with our skill great nations fill with terror and dismay.
So, gentles all, good order keep, and strict attention pay,
And listen to those heroes grand, and what they've got to say.
The first he is the grand Prince George, may fortune on him smile,
Close followed by St Patrick, the patron of our isle.
Napoleon Bonaparte comes next, of great fame and renown,
Close followed by Lord Wellington, who swears he will pull him down.
The Czar of Russia he is next, a monarch of great fame,
He is followed by the Grand Signor, most terrible to name,
Likewise a learned Doctor, to who great fame is due,
Close followed by the Polish King, his glory to pursue.
Next comes a mighty champion, Lord Nelson is his name,
And as for Julius Caesar, you know his ancient fame.
Dan O'Connell he's the last, and the greatest of them all,

---

39 The manuscript of this nineteenth-century mummers' play was in the possession of Jack Devereux of Kilmore Quay, fisherman, and former leader of the Kilmore carol singers. The manuscript, according to him, is of Rosslare provenance.

He fought against his foreign foes, and did not mind the storm,
Till a Christian state he set compleat, en suite and fully formed.
I'm certain sure you can endure Dan's freedom to repeal,
For Irishmen elected him, that never wanted bail.
So now my verse is ended, and I have no more to say.
And for our jovial merry men, we have them at a call.
We have a band of music grand, which always bore the sway,
So appear our great Prince George, till we hear what you have to say —

Enter Prince George
Here I am the great Prince George, old England's royal king,
My royal name, I do proclaim, was famous on the wing.
When wars of blood over Europe spread, my ground I firmly stood,
Surrounded by those briny waves, my walls were made of wood.
The entire ocean I command, the seas triumphant ride,
My royal fleet no match could meet, not in this world wide.
From Columbus's shore, I brung great store, from India treasure drew,
From east to west, it is confessed, of me all stand in awe.
Those good and just and gracious laws in the empire I have made
That all honest men may now rejoice, and the wicked are dismayed.
Scotland and Wales never fail, being faithful to their king,
And our Irish heroes stout and true, will sure a victory bring.
So, gentles all, I must conclude, though I have more to say,
So appear above, St Patrick, and meet me on the way.
It is my life I do not dread, nor any colour fear,
So enter in, St Patrick, and boldly meet me here.

St Patrick speaks
The Pagan laws I did destroy, one true God to adore,
And the Christian church did firmly plant, to stand for evermore.
This nation I did consecrate, great rulers did ordain,
Till your tyrant band did invade our land, and our sacred laws profane,
This nation you did plunder o'er, for to maintain your crown,
Our churches you have robbed them, and our abbeys you pulled down.
With laws most strict you did inflict, who dared complain you hung,
Oppression sore for long we bore, yet to our claims we clung
Till that tyrant Cromwell next came o'er and nothing with us leaves;
Full fifty thousand of my sons, he sold for British slaves.
Although my sons have bravely fought, for to maintain their right,
Yet all the honour they received, were foremost in the fight.

Our British sovereign he is dead, and cannot hear our cry,
Our good and just and gracious king, our wants he will supply.
So cease, Prince George, I pray thee cease, give persecution o'er,
Or perhaps one day, like ancient Greece some friends might us restore.

Wellington speaks
Patrick, dear, pray hold your tongue, be peaceful in your mind.
Here is your only friend, who for you will prove kind.

St Patrick speaks
To hold my tongue, proud Wellington, I utterly detest,
For Dan O'Connell is the man that knows your temper best.

Dan O'Connell speaks
Proud Wellington, from flattery come, make known those simple things,
To use your practice on brave men, you'd shame a race of kings.
At Waterloo, you know it's true, where the Irish bravely fought,
That won the field, that raised you up, to the glories you have sought.
So, Irishmen, strike for your blood, say boldly what is there given,
Your bolts and bands, your chains and wrongs, as a crying sent to Heaven.

Prince George speaks
For the wrongs I have done to St Patrick's sons I will humbly make amends.

St Patrick speaks
If that be so, Prince George, both you and I are friends.

The Captain speaks
Now since St Patrick and Prince George are one, no danger need we fear
And if fickle friends dare with us contend, they will quickly disappear.
Cromwell he a tyrant was, and now that knave is dead,
He died full sore against his will, because he lost his head.
So you valiant sons that truly bled, promotion on your smile,
Like Wellington at Waterloo, and Nelson on the Nile.

St Patrick speaks
Yes, Prince George, my valiant sons shall the British flag maintain
And shall firmly stand, at your command, in safety you may reign.
We will have days, when parties cease, and friendship will unite
And, Wellington, you need not fear that threatening Muscovite.

Around each shore our guns shall roar, like rattling thunder peal,
And our foes shall dread the British lead, and the sons of Granuaile.
We'll have harmony, contents and peace, we'll all sit down at ease,
All foreign foes, that us oppose, we'll blow them off the seas.
The history of my life's been short, I've got no more to say,
So enter in, Napoleon, and meet me on the way.
As my life, I value it not, nor any colour fear,
So enter, Napoleon Bonaparte, and boldly meet me here.

Enter Napoleon Bonaparte
Here am I, Napoleon Bonaparte, a conqueror of renown,
It's with my skill, and might deeds, great nations I cut down.
France and Spain I did obtain, Russia and Prussia too,
I crossed the Alps and Pyrenees, great nations to subdue.
The Portuguese I did them squeeze, the Poles and Saxons all,
The Danes and Swedes I did submit, and obedient to my call.
Ancient Italy I vanquished, and the states of Germany;
The Egyptian troops and Mamelukes before me I made flee.
I fought my way, by land and sea, to no mortal did I yield,
The powers of Europe, when combined, I beat them in one field.
I fought them three days two to one, like hero stout and true,
Till Marshall Ney did me betray, on the field of Waterloo.
So, gentles all, I must conclude, you know it all right well,
For to relate all my exploits, it would take one year to tell.
So enter in, Lord Wellington, and meet me on the way.

Enter Lord Wellington
Here I am, a noble Lord, great Mars's warlike son,
The martial signs they shone on me, they call me Wellington.
My titles great augment my fate, though being an Irishman,
Exalted high in dignity, and you a Corsican.
Hold, you ambitious tyrant, until I shall draw near,
And relate to you a word or two, that will not take a year,
On Britain's isle, where fortune smiles, you dare not to advance;
I fought my way by land and sea, and conquered you in France,
What desolation you have spread, o'er our country wide and large,
With persecution and cruelty, I lay it to your charge.
I really think such vaunting pride does not become you here,
Your lawless band, out of this land, I quickly will them clear.
But ill-got gains don't prosper long, and so it happened you,

For vengeance did you overtake, on the plains of Waterloo.
I bet you in Spain, as everyone sees,
I conquered you in the Pyrenees,
I, Wellington, tell what is true,
I fought and won and slew them, on the plains of Waterloo.

Napoleon speaks
At Arcoli, and Austerlitz, my value it was tried,
At Marengo I let them know, the Austrians I defied.
Proud Wellington, all nations know, one hour you would not stand,
With your British crew, at Waterloo, to fight me single-hand;
But, for British gold, my cause was sold, to a man upon that day,
Who, for recompense, his throat cut since, his name was Castlereagh.
But my misfortune to relate, the Prussian horse did flow,
With direful rage on my retreat, commanded by Suelow.

Wellington speaks
Now, Irishmen, all danger's o'er, Napoleon is gone to rest,
So meet the Russia's Emperor, and do not with us jest.

Enter Czar
Here I am, the Russian Czar, in costly robes I'm drest,
A terror to the Grand Signor, a glory to the rest.
The Christian standard I displayed, the Turks I did dispel,
And also, with my mighty fleet, blocked up the Dardanelles,
My royal arms such conquests made, three Pashas I laid low,
Which caused Mahomet's rapid flight from his great seraglio.
Those infidels I did subdue, and ancient Greece restore,
And now the cross most brilliant shines, and the crescent is no more.
Proud Wellington, you speak too much, on Bony's cruelty,
Sure, I do find you, and, the Turk, 'gainst Christianity.
Your greatest efforts I defy, the Turks I will upset,
If I am provoked my sword to draw, you will learn to regret.
When my Polish subjects did rebel, how dare you interfere,
May England mourn, and ne'er return, so home this message bear.
Gentles all, I must conclude, though I've got more to say,
So enter in the Grand Signor, and meet me on the way.

Enter Grand Signor
Here I am, the Grand Signor, known by the badge I wear,

No king or prince that rules this earth shall dare with me compare.
Full fifty nations I give law, they me a tribute pay,
Woe to the Frank or Nazarene that will not me obey.
The Muscovite of late has dared, my empire to annoy,
If he profane my holy lands, the gods will him destroy.
You boast of the Dardanelles you blocked, my naval force defied,
You reflect upon my British friends, who your defects supplied.
If that Nazarene, I find out, by Mahomet's cap, I swear
His body into two I'll cut, or with wild horses tear,
To find him out for long I've sought, but in case he may be here,
Right out of hand, I do demand, he quickly shall appear,

The Czar speaks
The Czar of Russia, he is here, his courage for to try,
He's willing for to meet you here, where shot and shell do fly.
Hold, hold, you tyrant Turk, and pest of human race,
You monster vile, you this earth defile, all nature you disgrace,
Your god Mahomet I detest, it is by his cap you swear,
You boast of British friends you've got, but not one fig I care.
No power on earth that fills with awe shall stop my grand pursuit,
Till Mahomet's race I'll extirpate, from Europe, branch and root.

The Grand Signor speaks
Ah, silly Russian, dost thou think my name to extirpate
Or to destroy my kingdom grand, that was decreed by fate;
My capital you thought to take, but since you were beside,
My lofty walls for to surround, would take a full day's ride.
Where in my court you did fifty crowns behold, of Asia's stores of silvery ore,
And a shining mass of gold, so now your life defend;
'Tis with my steel your blood I'll spill, or Mahomet is at an end.

The Czar speaks
You detested wretch, I am your match, your god did you deceive,
Full fifty thousand infidels I sent there to their grave,
Your boasting pride I will put down, and tarnish your half moon,
You infidel, go down to hell, and there receive your doom.

They fight. The Grand Signor falls. The Captain speaks
Ah, Russian brave, I do demand, can you to me explain,
What Prince is that lies bleeding there, by whose hand was he slain?

The Czar speaks
Ah yes, my friend, there bleeding lies the mighty Grand Signor,
With my Russian steel I made him feel, as thousands did before.
Let his wandering ghost to Eblis go, and there Mahomet tell,
The Grand Signor, he is no more, 'tis by my hand he fell.
But if a doctor you can find, his skill pray let me try,
Although I slew him in my wrath, I wish he may not die.

The Captain speaks
A Doctor grand I do demand, if one can here be found,
For to restore the Grand Signor, he shall have fifty pound.

Enter a Doctor
Here I am, a Doctor, though my fees are not so low,
To cure even a mean object, for that I would not go.
Let me receive one thousand pounds, and then I will go to bail,
That Mahomet's wounds I will dress and cure, and make him sound and hale.

The Captain speaks
Be quick, Sir Leech, and I shall see you paid, if life remains,
Be quick, our hero's blood does flow, two hours he has been slain.

The Doctor speaks
Yes, he has received a deep and deadly wound, yet I think his vital parts are
    sound,
I've often seen a case in worse condition, cured by the aid of a good physician.

The Captain speaks
Any fear of your being an impostor?

The Doctor speaks
Who, me an impostor?

The Captain speaks
Yes, you an impostor.
Many impostors like you I have seen, pray tell me where you have been.

The Doctor speaks
I have been to Montpellier, there I spent a full half year,

London Temple, it seemed high, it's on my way I passed it by.
I went from that to Patcher's Ram, saw doctors there not worth a damn,
And if you grant me your belief, I climbed the Peak of Tenerife.
My travels are great, none can contend, it's twice I saw the world's end.

The Captain speaks
Your travels, Doctor, are great, you are good, I am sure,
But you did not say what you can cure.

The Doctor speaks
I can cure what I think fit; by cunning death I can outwit
The pox, the palsy and the gout, and if the devil's within I'll run him out.
My granny's brains I did pull out, and washed when at a running spout,
They were not sound, I left them there, and stuffed the wounds with granog's
    [Irish *gráinneog*, hedgehog] hair,
I then bestowed her two cat's eyes, and ever since she's twice as wise;
Her chattering tongue her teeth wore out, I put a gatepost in her mouth.

The Captain speaks
Your experience is great I can't deny, but what sort of medicine do you supply?

The Doctor speaks
To tell you that it's Latin I should speak, such information you could not take,
Such instructions I could not give, for it's by such means we doctors live.
But my skill I'll exert, with all my care, some costly medicine for to prepare,
This well applied I do maintain, he never after shall complain.

The Captain speaks
Rise up, rise up, the Grand Signor, and the truth to me tell,
What mighty wonders have you seen when on the field you fell.

The Grand Signor is restored to life, and speaks thus
My wandering ghost aloft did float, when on the field I fell,
Dreadful were the sights I saw, most dismal for to tell.
While hovering o'er the Stygian lake, descending to the shore,
I met my old friend Charon, and he safely sailed me o'er.
Saying Mahomet, dear, I am your friend, the truth to you I tell –
The place where you are doomed to go, the Christians call it Hell.

With fiery flames, and red hot chains, and melting cauldron's glow
When I did descend to see my friend, I found 'twas frost and snow,
Where my bones might freeze to adamant, and that for evermore,
Were it not that some strange magic art did life to me restore.
The history of my life being short, and spoke without delay,
So enter in Lord Nelson, and meet me on the way.
As my life, I value not, nor any foeman fear,
So enter in, Lord Nelson, and boldly meet me here.

Enter Lord Nelson
Here I am, Lord Nelson, that ne'er knew what was fear.
At the age of sixteen in Greenland I killed a savage bear.
Lieutenant to the *Victory*, my courage is assured,
A letter of marque, and I showed sharp action with my sword.
Here I am, Lord Nelson, rear admiral of the Blue,
No man that breathes this vital air proved to his king more true.
Should I relate each warlike feat, it would take up my time.
It is a history I should write, and not this simple rhyme.
Through fire and blood, I firmly stood, to serve my king upright,
For neither flames nor tyrant's chains did ever me afright.
A glorious conquest once I won, which made Great Britain smile;
The fleet of France, I made them dance, in Egypt on the Nile.
With cruel rage I them engaged, and fought most manfully,
Their fleet so great I did defeat, no man escaped but three.
My leg and arm were there shot off, likewise I lost my eye,
Yet France and Spain they sore complain, with me they cannot vie.
I close pursued, by night and day, and sought at length in vain,
I wished to meet that combined fleet, and pride of France and Spain,
At Trafalgar I them did overtake, where crimson ran the flood;
A dreadful conquest there I made, and sealed it with my blood.
So, gentles all, I must conclude, I've got no more to say,
So enter in, the Polish King, and meet me on the way.

Enter Polish King
Here I am, the Polish King, that stood in time of need,
My sword I drew against the Turks, all Europe I have freed.
You Western heroes make great boast of conquests you have won,
You boast of Kings, and royal things, for shame what have you done?
Like wrangling dogs, which each devour, and do no Christian work,
One day you might your force unite, to rout the haughty Turk.

One day in blood, alone I stood, on me did all depend,
Till Mahomet's standard it must fall, or Vienna have an end.
From morning till the sun went down, the slaughter did remain,
Full thirty thousand of our sons lay scattered on the plain.
'Twas with a slow and steady pace we advanced along the plain;
We halted every fifty yards, to prime and load again.
With Imperial guns and thundering drums, we raised the hue and cry,
You'd really think Vienna's fate would surely rend the sky.
So Christian Europe, now rejoin, give thanks to God and me,
For in that war if I had to fall, all heathen you would be.
Now gratitude is dead and gone, the world may plainly see,
Amongst them all, I'd no friends at all, in my extremity.
As for my life I value not, nor any colour fear,
So enter in, Julius Caesar, and boldly meet me here.

Enter Julius Caesar
Here I am, great Julius Caesar, of whom all nations stand in awe,
I'm the greatest hero of my age, the world ever saw.
The Roman Empire did me obey, its laws I did dictate,
They placed a crown upon my head, for being so truly great.
The hundred battles I have won, one thousand I have slain,
I never yet engaged in fight, but I have victory gained.
The Muscovite, I would him smite, those savage hands cut down,
Yet France and Spain may sore complain, with legions of renown.
To Britain's shore, I next called o'er, it's now an altered place,
When first that nation I did subdue, 'twas of a savage race.
'Twas Satan's work, to raise the Turk, known by his savage yell,
He'd do no such thing, when I was king, if he came straight from Hell.
You Western heroes make great boast, you're not worthy of a crown,
When you up let old Satan get, you dare not pull him down.
Kind Providence did me befriend, I must submit to fate,
Those cruel brutes, they did combine, to me assassinate.
Now, gentles all, I must conclude, I've got no more to say,
So enter in, O'Connell, and meet me on the way,

Enter Daniel O'Connell
Here I am, the great O'Connell, from a knightly race I came.
My royal habitation lies in ancient Derrynane.
I am the man they call brave Dan, who stood your friend on all occasions
And the first MP that ever sat of the Catholic persuasion.

For my country's wrongs I deeply felt, they filled me with vexation
And our cruel foes for to oppose, I formed an Association.
'Tis certain sure, the Church most pure, should persecution bear,
But the penal yoke was lately broke, by electing me in Clare.
To Parliament straightaway I went, in hopes to free our nation.
Wellington and Peel, I made them yield, and grant emancipation.
That still-born pact, the Stanley Act, supports the haughty Church's ambition,
Those various tithes I have laid aside, by a total abolition.
The Catholic rent I underwent, to break and wreck in twain,
Those tyrant's chains, from off those plains, they bound up with disdain,
For thirty-three years, it plain appears, our rights to us denied,
They may regret they have borne away their Union as their pride.
And from that time in chains so were bound, for justice we appealed,
We swore that day that come what may to this we would not yield.
By St Patrick's sons you have laurels won, and been raised to dignity,
Our brothers' cries you did despise, and our country's misery.
So now your cause, and penal laws, I'll expel, by exhortation;
Those notorious tithes I'll lay aside, or in blood I'll steep the nation.
Your tyranny won't frighten me, nor your hellish emigrations,
Your infernal ends, they stood your friends; if I live I'll free the nation.
Now, gentles all, I must conclude; I have no more to say,
So enter in, the Captain, for to conclude the play.

The Captain speaks
Ladies and gentlemen that there before me stand,
You have heard of our performance, while in a foreign land,
I being the brave commander, with courage bold I stood,
And often to my waist in streams of precious blood.
(There's not a hero that can boast of such a gallant train.
Not Alexander, Hannibal, nor Caesar of great fame.)
Through burning sands, and desert lands, and o'er the Alps we crossed,
And our hands and ears were often badly bitten by the frost.
After a gallant victory, and such a fearless toil.
It's here we stand, with sword in hand, on Wexford's lovely soil.
The praises of our mummers' band throughout this isle abound
So I hope you will good order keep, while warlike music sounds.

The end of the play.

The mumming [an elaborate sword-dance] starts.

The supernatural

The banshee, also known as the Bow

THE BOW [40]

The Bow is said to be the demon of the air. The old people in Ireland always believed in the Bow. It is said that she is a small woman and that when she was a girl she had a long head of hair which she was always combing.

She was very proud of her hair and it is said that when she died she was too bad to go to Heaven and too good to go to Hell and God sent her on this earth to cry after certain people when they die. She makes her path through the fields and on the hills. She goes around at night crying and keening and her cry is like the cry of a young child.

When a person out of the family she follows dies, she comes around on that night and cries under the window sill and everyone is afraid of her. When she is crying she is always combing her hair with a bone or a steel comb.

It is said that when you meet the Bow you should not say anything or do anything to her. If you are passing on her path and happen to step on it, she will be at your back when you look around, and you must get off to let her pass. It is said that she is very wicked if you touch her. People who hear or see her get a very big fright.

A TEACHER SEES THE BANSHEE [41]

Between fifteen and twenty years ago a lady by the name of Miss Dunphy, NT, Irishtown, New Ross, heard the banshee.

One night Miss Dunphy went to bed and after a long sleep she was awakened by a noise. Her bedroom window faced down the Irishtown. When she woke up she was dazed by sleep. She heard screams. At first she thought

---

40 A story collected by Peggy Byrne of Bree School, parish of Clonmore, in 1938 (Seán O Braoin, teacher). IFCS 902: 245. 41 Told in 1937 by B. O'Brien, a pupil of the Mercy Convent, New Ross (Sister Ní Mhaoldomhnaigh, teacher). IFCS 897: 151–2.

it was the howling of dogs, but as the screaming came nearer it filled the whole vault of the heavens. Then all of a sudden it struck her that it was the banshee.

The lady got out of bed and went to the maid's room. She woke the maid and told her she had heard the banshee. Then the maid said "Come over to the window until we see what she is like."

But Miss Dunphy did not go over. The maid looked out the window and she said: "That's she, all right."

"What is she like?" Miss Dunphy asked. The description she gave her was:

At first she looked like a huge tangled ball of wool but as she came nearer she assumed a woman form. After a time she sat on the corner of the Bosheen and started keening and combing her hair. After a while she disappeared.

That same night the Banshee was heard in Ryleen and in the Maudlins and on that very night a man named McCaully died in the Maudlins.

It is said that the banshee follows families whose names begin with "O" or "Mac".

THE BANSHEE'S COMB [42]

Once upon a time when the banshee was supposed to be about there were two men passing by one night and they took her comb. They ran home as quickly as they could and the banshee after them.

She stayed outside all night crying for her comb. So in the morning they went to the priest and asked him what would they do.

He told them to let down the window a little bit and to hand out the comb with a tongs. So they did, and she took the top off the tongs.

They had seven fine fat pigs for the fair, so when they got up in the morning the seven fine pigs were dead. So the next morning all the feathers were off the hens, so they had to make jackets for the hens. So that is the end of that story.

A BANSHEE FORETELLS A DEATH [43]

One night in the month of October, about seventeen years ago, a woman named Mrs Carton went out to meet her daughter, who was in town. All of a sudden the banshee started to wail inside a ditch. She went on a little further, and she

---

42 The story is attributed in IFCS 870: 137, Templetown School (Charles Hearne, teacher), 1938, to Patrick Colclough.   43 An anecdote related by Ellen Crean of Adamstown School (D. Curtis, teacher), in 1937. Ellen heard the story from her mother. IFCS 900: 61.

met a messenger saying that a woman named Mrs Livingstone had just died. This was the woman who owned the field in which the banshee wailed.

A dead priest says mass [44]

Once upon a time, a very long time ago, there was a woman and she went to the church to say her prayers. She fell asleep. When she awoke she saw a priest coming out of the vestry. He said, "Is there anyone to answer mass?" The woman said nothing. He was dressed in his vestments.

The next day the woman told the priest her secret. The priest told her not to tell anyone else. He told her also to stay there the next night. He stayed with her. About twelve o'clock that night the dead man came out of the vestry and said, "Is there anyone to answer mass?" The live priest said, "Yes," so the dead priest said mass and the other priest answered it.

When mass was finished, the dead priest told the other man that while he was alive he was told to say a mass but he never said it and he could not rest easy until he said it so that he came back to say it.

Buried treasure

A HOARD AT KILLESK CASTLE [45]

Killesk Castle is now the ruins of a castle built by the Normans. It is believed to contain some hidden treasure which consists of gold sovereigns. It is said that a big black bull is minding it. Long ago when the old people were hiding this money they sacrificed an animal or a person who was to come and guard the money, and a bull was killed to mind this treasure. Two men ventured to look for this money as they heard of it being there. They brought shovels and spades with them to dig for it but it was all in vain. This castle is situated in the townsland of Killesk on Mr Colfer's farm.

A HOARD IN THE BORO RIVER [46]

On the Boro, the tributary of the Slaney, there is a deep hole. This hole is

44 Story collected from Patrick Colclough, of Templetown, Fethard-on-Sea, in 1939, by an unnamed pupil of Charles Hearne's Templetown School. IFCS 870: 140–1.   45 Told in 1938 by Martin Forristal of Knockea, Campile, aged 78, to Nellie O'Connor, a pupil at Killesk School, Horeswood parish (Margaret Sutton, teacher) IFCS 873: 23.   46 Collected by Peter Murphy, a pupil of the Christian Brothers' School, Enniscorthy (Brother Mac Oireachtaigh, teacher), from Philip Murphy, a postman, in 1937. IFCS 893: 250.

known in the locality as "the Soldier's Hole". This was the camping place for the soldiers in 1798. There was a small bridge spanning the water.

One night a man was run from his home because he was a "rebel". This man had gold in a trunk in his possession. When he was routed, he grabbed the gold and made for the bridge.

He was in the centre of the bridge when he was shot by the soldiers. He fell into the water, gold and all. It is said that when the man hit the bottom he changed into a serpent. A diver attempted to recover the gold but the serpent would not let him go near it.

THE TREASURE HIDDEN AT THE BABE'S GLEN [47]

A treasure is hidden in the centre of a wood about six miles north of Enniscorthy. This place is called Kil Aughrim. The spot where the treasure is hidden is called the "Babe's Glen". It was hidden there by a wealthy young man named Howlan before the rebellion of 1798.

One night he put all his possessions which consisted of bars of silver and gold into a coach and brought them to the "Babe's Glen", and buried them there. He then cut the coachman's head off and buried him with the treasure. Howlan buried his wealth because his life was in danger and he was a Yeoman also and was afraid the rebels would burn his house.

One night three men thought they would try and unearth the treasure. A farmer named Roche gave them picks and shovels to dig. (He himself was there also.) It happened that one of them struck the chest. Suddenly a strange thing happened.

They heard a noise louder than thunder. They looked around in amazement. Thundering up the little path was a carriage drawn by a pair of headless horses and a headless coachman driving it. The men ran for their lives.

The headless man followed Roche to his house. Roche ran upstairs and locked himself in his bedroom. The headless man shook the door so much that the end wall of Roche's house fell next day.

The devil in Loftus Hall [48]

Loftus Hall is a great big house, down hear the Hook (Tower of Hook). The fellow that lived in it he was the landlord over all that part of the country. He

47 Collected by James Hendrick, a pupil of the Christian Brothers' School, Enniscorthy, from Aidan Hendrick, a labourer, of The Duffry. Same MS source as the previous item. 48 Collected by Tom Carey of Cushinstown from Patrick Doyle, a stonemason from Old Ross, aged 71, in 1939. IFC 600: 375–81.

was supposed to be as bad a man as could be picked. He was supposed to be after swindling all the money he could out of other countries, and then he came over here to swindle all he could here. Well, this fellow used give a great spree two or three times a year; and he used invite the whole country to them. The worst type of people he could gather up he used have them there. He even used have young ladies from the back slums of Dublin, he was such a great fellow. Well, he gave a great spree this time, anyhow. Every time they used have a spree they used have a great hunt that day. They used to meet, in their red coats, all the gentlemen of the country and go off to Johnstown to hunt the deer. They had a great hunt this day; and that evening they all got back to Loftus Hall, and fitted themselves out for the big spree. They were to have supper first, and then they could go dancing, or playing cards, or anything they liked. Begor, they were just going to sit down to the supper when a strange gentleman rode up to the hall door. He had a red coat on him and he was riding a jet-black horse. He pulled up to the hall door and he stopped. All the gentry inside they were asking each other who the stranger was, and no one knew him. "He's a gentleman anyhow," says the boss, "you'd know by the look of him. I think we'll ask him in." "Oh, do!" they all said. "Ask him in anyhow." So the boss went out and he welcomed him, and told him to come on in. So the lad put up his horse in the yard, and walked in. And, sure, who was he but the "Real Boy" himself. They are sat down to supper; and of course they had the finest of everything to ate and to drink. When the supper was over, the boss told them that they could go to the ballroom and start dancing, or if they liked they could go playing cards in another room. Whatever they liked themselves. They could go out if they wanted to, and do whatever they liked. Begor, this strange man said he wouldn't dance but that he'd go and play cards. Of course he couldn't very well dance I suppose on account of the cloven leg. They fell in for a card game anyhow, and they played away all night, until about nine or ten next morning. Then they ate a feed, and they played away until 2 or 3 o'clock in the evening. And all the time the rest of the crowd were dancing, or courting, or some devilment like that. About two or three o'clock, all the crowd said that they might as well be hitting for home. So all the horses were brought out and yoked, and brought around to the front door. There was a whole line of carriages as far as from this over to John Roberts's gate. There was over a hundred of them in it. Every coachman got up, and all the people got in to the carriages. They told the horses to "go on", but the horses couldn't move. The legs were going up and down like that, the very same as they were trotting, but no carriage was moving. They never moved an inch out of where they were. They got out and they tried all they could to get them to go; but 'twas no use. So begor, the boss said, that the best thing they could do was to come in, and dance away again, until the next day. None of them ever suspected anything, of course. In they all went again. The horses were unyoked and put back in the stables; and all the crowd turned in, and they started to dance and play again until morning. The next morning about nine o'clock they all yoked up again to go home. But 'twas the very same go. The horses' legs would go up and down all right; but they wouldn't move a peg. Begor, they began to get a sort suspicious about it. The boss asked them did they ever see anything like it happen before, and they all said they didn't. 'Twas the most peculiar thing they ever seen, they said. Begor, he told them that the only thing to do was to come in again and hould on until tomorrow and maybe everything would be all right. So they did. And this stranger was there all the time, playing away; and a couple of the women were after getting really mad about him. They thought he was the nicest fellow they ever met. The next morning they yoked up again, but 'twas just as bad as ever. They were in a hell of a state then entirely. They didn't know what to do. They all said that there must be some devilment, or some enchantment going on. They sent for the minister, and there was a couple of ministers there at the party; but they couldn't make out what was wrong. They didn't know what to do then. They knew there was some enchanted person in the place. Begor, there was a couple of Catholics there in the place — servants; and one of them said to the boss that they should send for the priest. And sure the boss, and all that crowd would just as soon shoot the priest as send for him. But, begor, they said they'd chance it anyhow. So they did send for him. There was a priest in Templetown at the time, Father Broaders was his name, so one of the servants went to him and told him the whole story. Begor, when the priest heard the story, he knew well that there was something very serious the matter. So himself and the parish priest came along. Fr Broaders was only the curate, I forget now what the parish priest's name was.

On they came anyhow, to Loftus Hall. And, begor, when the boyo seen the priest coming he flew upstairs into one of the top rooms. The people seen what he did, and begor they partly guessed then that it was he that was doing the devilment. When the priest came in, he knew that the boyo was there; and he enquired for the stranger. They went out to see was his horse there and there was no sign of him anywhere. Up they went upstairs after him — the two priests. Fr Broaders went first, and the P.P. went after him. Fr Broaders opened the door and looked in to this room; and whatever sight they met there, it must have been terrible, for the P.P. made to run back. "Come here," says Fr Broaders to him. "Isn't your faith any stronger nor that?" So begor he came back again and stood his ground. Fr Broaders then attacked the boyo, and asked him who he was. He said that he had a command to take everyone that was in the place; and he said that he was going to hold them there, and keep them in the place; and that he would finally take them all to a "palace" he had prepared for them. The priest then ordered him to leave the place, and begor the lad wouldn't. He ordered him three times to go, but he wouldn't stir for him. "And how long do you intend to stay?" says the priest. "I'm going to stay for seven years, until I have everyone here taken." "Well, you will stay here for seven years," says the priest, "but you will take no one; and you'll never leave this room for all that time." So the priest put him there in the room for seven year. The room was all built up around him – door and windows and all built up. The horses were outside under the carriages and they couldn't get them to move an inch. The priest went out and held up his hand and made the sign of the Cross, and the minute he did they all moved off. So they all went back home to wherever they came from; and they never came near Loftus Hall any more. A whole lot of the people that were there, and seen what happened, they changed their religion, and became Catholics. The ould boss of the place then, he said that he wouldn't live there anymore, and the devil in the same house with them. So he sould it out and went off to live somewhere else. They tried to get him to turn, and become a Catholic, but he wouldn't. He said he didn't mind what happened a damn bit. He said it always took one devil to conquer another. So he stayed as he was. Well, when the seven years was up then, 'twas out through the roof of the house the devil went; and the mark is to be seen there still where he went out. You could see where the rafters were burned and all. And for years after the hole was in the roof, and no matter how they'd repair it, it would be there still after them. I don't know, whether it is that way still or nor. I think it is. 'Tis nuns that are living in the place now.

The devil and the dog [49]

It is said that the divil passed through Wexford on many occasions. Of course he was not always in his own shape, but however he was the divil anyhow. I heard a story one time about a man that had the divil in his house and he didn't know that he was there at all. This man you see had a little dog and he was very fond of him as he was a great animal for performing tasks of all kinds. It was a very delicate kind of a dog and used to get sick very often and the man was very anxious about him every time that he would get sick, for he

[49] Collected by John Butler of Foulksmills, from Thomas Doyle, a farmer aged 69, Newbawn parish, in 1939. IFC 600: 275–7.

was afraid of his life that he was going to die; and he used to send for all classes of cures and tonics for him when he would be sick. One day this man's mother complained of not being too well and, begor, he had to send for the priest and the doctor; and they came and said that nothing at all much was the matter with her – that she would be all right in a couple of days. The doctor went off home and the priest remained behind to talk to the man of the house and all that, and while they were talking the man said to himself that he would show the wonderful dog that he had to the priest. He used always keep this dog out in a little house to himself and the two of them went out to the house to see him. When they got to the house he was not there at all and he said that that was a strange thing, as he had never known the dog to be away from home at all. They searched all around the place and they could not find him any place and the man said that maybe he was inside. They went in and they searched all around the house and they could not get him at all. They tried every place and at last they found him in under the bed and he coiled up as tight as he could be. The man called him out and he would not come; and then the priest got suspicious and he said that he mustn't be right at all or he would come out. So the priest himself went in under the bed and then the dog walked out all right, and he stood in the middle of the floor and his head down. The priest turned on the man, and said he: "You must be a born fool not to know that it was the divil that you have in the house," and the dog looked up at him and said, "You needn't say a word at all now. I was your own dog for five years and you did not know it at all." That was an awful shock for the priest, for he knew that he had a dog, and he went away, and he never could get any account of him any place. The divil has the power to turn himself in to whatever the dickens he likes, and it is a usual thing for him to turn into a dog or a cat or some animal like that.

The fairies

THE CHANGELING [50]

There was once a man living in the parish of Adamstown. He was married and had one child. When this child was about ten months old, the father began to notice that it was very witty and had some very old sayings and nobody was ever able to make him cry. The father began to think that his child was "no right thing" and began greatly to fear that that it had something to do with the "good people".

50 A story collected by John Butler of Glynn parish in 1938. Informant not named. IFC 106: 2–6.

One day while he was ploughing he broke some part of it. He went to a lot of forges for miles around but none of the smiths were able to weld it. One morning he got up and told his wife that he would have to buy a new plough. The child was listening with all his ears in the cradle. "You don't need to buy a new plough, Daddy," says he; "go up to Enniscorthy where there is a good smith and tell him to weld that plough-iron between a blue and a red flame." The man got an awful fright when he heard this talk coming from his son and he scarcely eleven months old.

He yoked the horse and drove into Enniscorthy and told the smith what the child had said. This was one of the most famous smiths in Wexford at the time, and he wondered greatly at what the child had said. "Well," says he, "that is one of the greatest secrets of my trade and not many smiths in Wexford know it but myself; it's my opinion it's a fairy-changeling you have," says he. "When you go home," says the smith to him, "tell him that the fairy rath is ablaze." The man got the plough-iron welded and went home. The child was sitting on the doorstep waiting for him and began clapping his hands with delight when he saw the plough-iron welded. "You got it welded at last, Daddy," says he in the voice of a very old man, "I did, my son," says the father, "but when I was coming by Jim Doyle's field I saw the fairy-rath in one great blaze." "You don't say," says the child, "that the fairy-rath is on fire," and his two eyes opening wide. "I do, begor," says the father. "O, Lord," says the child, "my bellows is surely burned," and away with him through ditches and hedges in the direction of the rath.

THE LEPRECHAUN AT RATHIMNEY [51]

About fifty year ago ghosts and fairies were far commoner than what they are now. There was a young soople fella lived in a place called Rathimny in the parish of Tintern. He was going across a field one day and he seen a lurechan [leprechaun]. He was a fine active young fella so he made a run at the lurechan and caught him and although he turned and twisted this way and that way he succeeded in houlding him. "If you tell me where there's money hid, I'll let you go," says the fella, but the lurechan said nothing only twisted and twisted trying to get off. "'Tis well known that the like of you know lots of secrets about money that's hid," says the fella, but the boyo in his hand tried harder and harder to get away. "If you don't tell me this instant minute," says the man, "I'll sweep off your head," and he put his hand in his pocket and took out his knife. "There's money hid in the middle of this field," says the

51 Collected by Mícheál Mac Aodha of Carrick-on-Bannow from Martin Grady, a labourer, in 1937. IFC 481: 281–2.

lurechan, "and there's a boochalawn [ragwort] growing over it." The young fella looked round the field and there wasn't a weed to be seen but one big boochalawn in the middle. He was delighted with himself and he let go the lurechan and he vanished in a second. He got up next morning as soon as the daylight had come in. He got a spade and a pick and set out for the field but when he got there he couldn't believe his eyes, for every inch of the field was covered with boochalawns.

A STORY [52]

There was a man named Colfer living in Bannow seventy or eighty years ago and he went to America. He got on fairly well and after a while he joined some secret society and got to know another man from the Co. Roscommon. Himself and the man from Roscommon got to be very great and one night they were drinking together in a taproom. "I wonder what's me poor ould mother doing at home now," says Colfer. "Well, I'll tell ye" says the other man, "there's a griddle on the fire an she's just finished making a cake o' bread and she's ready to bake it. Would you like to go home to night and see the people at home," says he. "It wouldn't be very easy to get from here to Bannow tonight," says he, "but if it can be done I'll go." "Very good," says the Roscommon man, "come on down to the quay." The two went down to the quay and the man hauled up a small little boat just big enough for two. "Are we going across in that?" asked Colfer. "Yes," says the other man, "and on the peril of your life, don't speak a word to anyone from the minute you put your foot in this boat until you get back here again." Colfer promised that he wouldn't open his mouth and they got into the boat and started off. In a short space of time they drew into the quay at Bannow and Colfer jumped out and went home. He walked into the kitchen just as his mother was taking up a cake o' bread. They all flocked round him and asked him this question and that question, but he stood at the dresser and never opened his lips. After a few minutes he walked out and down to the boat and set out again for America, and soon got across again. "Well," says the other man when they had landed, "did you speak to anyone?" "I didn't," says Colfer. "It was well you didn't," says he, "for if you had we were finished." Colfer came home to Bannow again when he was an old man and he often tould about the night he come home in the little boat, and he said he seen hundreds of imps and divils flying round the boat when they were on the journey.

52 Collected by Mícheál Mac Aodha from Michael Murphy, a labourer from Danescastle, in 1937. IFC 481: 289–91.

ANOTHER CHANGELING STORY [53]

Long ago there lived a woman who had one child. The fairies took the child and put an ugly one in its place, with a huge head and staring eyes, who did nothing but eat and drink.

The woman was very grieved at having such a creature in the house, instead of her own bright, bonny baby. She sought advice of the neighbour. This person was very wise. She told her to take the ugly baby and place it on the kitchen hearth, then light the fire, and boil some water in two egg-shells. At this the ugly baby would laugh; then the fairies' power would be over.

The mother did as she was told, and when she put the egg-shells in the fire with the water in them, the fairy child exclaimed:

> I'm as old it's plain
> As your age once again
> But never have I heard tell
> Of cooking in an egg-shell.

Then the fairy laughed right merrily and as soon as it laughed there appeared a lot of little people carrying the right child, who laid it on the hearth, and then they went off, taking the fairy child with them.

ANOTHER CHANGELING STORY [54]

There were some people working in a field near Lady's Island. They were tying corn. One of the women left her baby asleep on the headland. The owner of the field said he would look after the baby for her. As he watched the woman's child, a fairy came and took away the child and left her own in its place. The fairy child commenced crying as soon as it was laid down. When the mother heard the child crying, she ran to take it up, but she was kept back by the old farmer. The fairy woman kept walking up and down in the adjoining field. But in the end she could not stand her child's crying. She came back with the woman's child and took her own. The woman never left the child out of her sight again. This happened over a hundred years ago.

---

[53] Related by Mary Barnwell in IFCS 879: 166–7, Mayglass School, 1937 (Seosamh Mac Shomáis, teacher).   [54] Collected by Patrick Kearns from Mary Power of Martinstown, Killinick, aged 75, in 1937. IFCS 881: 405, compiled in Christian Brothers' School, Wexford, by Brother D.C. Ó hEilighe.

WILL O' THE WISP [55]

I had remained in Wexford town one evening, longer than usual, and set out for home about nine o'clock in the evening, the time being early Winter. I had the company of a neighbour on the road, and then had, in order to avoid a long way to my house, to cross through many fields.

I had not gone very far, when I saw a bright light before me, moving slowing. From the moment I saw it I became nervous, because it seemed to be coming nearer to me; and I thought I could see a shadow of a person holding it. Then it moved away again but never passed out of my sight. I went on, knowing that I was going in the direction of home but it was strange that my own roof was not to be seen, and at last the thought struck me that I was being led astray by the light, as I should have reached home in half the time. I stopped and turned my back on the light, but no matter which way I turned the light was before me.

I thought of a plan which I heard my mother and Mrs Dalton talking about. She said, "One day as we were lost in a wood we turned our coats inside out, because it was a way for keeping away the fairies."

I did this too, and on the minute the lantern disappeared and I found myself in Hollymount, about four miles from my home.

THE KILLIANE LEPRECHAUN [56]

The leprechaun is known by various names in this locality as "lutharagaun" the "Merrily Gog" "Jack 'o the Lantern," "Will 'o the Wisp" and the "little green man". He is about two feet in height. He wears a green coat with a red cap which tapers to a top. Out from the top of this cap comes a tassel. He spends most of his time making and repairing shoes under the bucholaun [ragwort]. He also minds gold.

Tom Waters of Rathjarney caught the leprechaun. The leprechaun told him to look behind him to see who was coming. He did so and when he looked back the leprechaun was gone. Tom caught him, thinking that he would deliver up his crock of gold which he had, but he was too clever for him.

It is a common belief around here that he lives under ferns and under bushes at the banks of rivers, in holes in rocks and under the blackthorn bush.

55 A story collected by Joseph Donoghue, Castlebridge, from Mr Jordan, Kismisten, aged 81, in 1937. IFCS 880: 390–1, compiled in Christian Brothers' School, Wexford (Brother D.C. Ó hEilighe, teacher).   56 Collected by Patrick Maguire of Killiane, Drinagh, a pupil at Piercestown School in 1938. IFCS 879: 347 (Máirtín O Cléirigh, teacher).

Strange happenings

THE BIG BLACK DOG [57]

In years gone by a big black dog used to be seen on Terrerath hill. He used to roll down the hill every night, and everyone was terrified of him, as he used to turn into a big ball of fire. At last some men said that they would get together and fight the black dog, as everyone began to think he was an evil spirit. They armed themselves with stones, and had any of the men lost their nerve, they would have failed. They stoned him into a small narrow lane and ever since this lane is called "The Devil's Lane" as the black dog is supposed to be there still. The following are the names of some of the men who stoned the black dog: James Kent, Tom Kent, Watt Murphy, Pat Murphy, Henry Foley, Simon Kent, James Murphy, Larry Doyle, John Kent. They are all dead now.

THE NASH BONEFIRE [58]

The following story is told in connection with a place called Nash about two and a half miles from here. On the fair green of Nash, which is known as Carraiginaminogue, it was usual to hold bonefires at times of rejoicing.

This evening a dance was in full swing. The boys and girls from near and far were enjoying the dance and the bonefire was blazing at its height. During the dance the bonefire died down and one of the girls said she would not be long procuring some firewood. She went off laughing to a near-by graveyard. She gathered some of the old crosses that were lying about, brought them back and flung them on the bonefire. After a short time a scream was heard. The girl was seen to rise up and disappear in the air with the clouds and nothing was ever seen or heard of her again, only her apron was got on brambles or briars near the place. This ended the bonefires on the fair green of Nash.

THE HAUNTED KILN AT BALLYSOP [59]

There was once an old kiln in Ballysop on Mr Doyle's land and it was haunted. It was said that there used to be greyhounds singing in the kiln and that they were heard by several people. There were also lights seen in this kiln.

One night, a priest was going to a sick call and he saw a light in the kiln, and he heard the greyhounds singing. It was beautiful and they were saying,

57 Told by Vincent Campbell, a pupil of Aughclare (Aclare) School, Horsewood parish, who recorded it from Honor Gaffney of Aclare, 'who heard it from the old people'. IFCS 870: 109 (1938).   58 From the same pupil in Aclare School, but in IFCS 873: 112–13.   59 Collected by Josie Caulfield of Ballykerogue from her father. Also from IFCS 873: 133–4, Aclare School.

"Stay and listen, stay and listen," but the priest did not stay. He went on and it is said that the greyhounds were trying to stop the priest so that the person he was going to see would die before he got there.

THE HOUSE BUILT ON A MASS PATH [60]

In Camblin, about two English miles from Ross, in a field of the Causey there was a mass path. The people around used to go to mass by this path to Ballykelly.

After some time the people started going to mass to Ross and the mass path was closed. People built a house in the field where the mass path was, and before they were three months living in it, they had to leave it. Every night as soon as they would go to bed, the bed clothes would be pulled off the beds and no matter how often they put them back, they would be pulled off again. The chairs used to be tumbled around the floor in the morning. If any delph were left overnight on the table, it would be found on the floor, broken in the morning.

Every night, as regular as the clock, this went on. The noise of the chairs and the rattle of the delph would begin as soon as twelve o'clock came. No one could sleep, so in the end they had to leave the house, and after some years it fell from damp and neglect and no one would ever sleep a night in it after that.

My father, Richard Shannon, told me this and he was reared in Camblin about ten yards from the house. When he was a boy, only the old ruins were there, but he used to hear my grandfather and the other old people talking about it. The stones of the house are all covered with grass and weeds now and no one would touch a stone, all the people are so much afraid of what would happen.

Evil spirits

BUTTERMAKING AND THE EVIL ONE [61]

It was believed by the people long ago, that certain people were under the power of the devil, and that they could "take away" other people's butter, that is, that you could churn and churn away for hours, and no butter would come.

60 Collected by Nellie Shannon from her father, Richard. Also from IFCS 873: 170–2, Aclare School.   61 Related by Honor Gaffney of Aclare to M.E. Campbell, teacher at Aclare School, in 1939. IFCS 873: 180–1.

If the butter was "taken", the milk would rise in froth all over the churn but there would be no butter. Sometimes the cream would have an awful smell.

The power was supposed to be got from the Evil One on May morning by skimming a well before the sun rose. There was a rhyme to be recited whilst the skimming was going on. A piece of whitish fat or butter with milk dropping from it was supposed to be left at the door of the house where the butter was to be taken. The people of the house would know then that they would have no butter when churning.

The cure for this was to get the coulter out of a plough and put it in the fire and redden it in the devil's name. Then the person who had "taken" the butter would have to come into the house whether he or she liked it or not, and then of course everyone would know who their awful enemy was.

PETTICOAT LOOSE [62]

A girl, who was known by the name of Petticoat Loose, killed her mother and father, and two children, one without Baptism. She herself died soon afterwards, and on a certain spot, where she killed the people, she used to appear. One night a man was passing by on a horse and she appeared to him and he took her up on the horse, and the minute she mounted, the horse staggered. The man remarked that he never noticed the horse stagger like that before. She replied, "The horse never carried such a weight before, for I carry many tons of sin." The man then let her dismount and journeyed home. In the morning he found the horse dead. He mentioned the matter to a priest, who later visited the place. To him she also appeared. He asked her her business and she said "I am here to kill anyone who passes by." He said to her, "By whom are you sent?" "By the devil," she replied. "What did you do?" he asked. "I killed my mother and father," was her reply. "You could get pardon for that," said the priest. She then told him she killed the children, one without Baptism. The priest then told her that it was the unbaptised child that cursed her and had banished her for ever.

Witches

A CHARM STORY [63]

Once upon a time there was an old woman who travelled around from house

62 Related by Kathleen Ronan, Mountgarret, New Ross, a pupil in the Mercy Convent, in 1938 (Sister Ní Mhaoldomhnaigh, teacher). IFCS 897: 175–6. Kathleen heard the story from Mr T. Whelan of The Irishtown, New Ross.   63 Told in 1938 by Kathleen Ronan, a pupil of the Mercy Convent, New Ross (Sister Ní Mhaoldomhnaigh, teacher). IFCS 897: 247–9.

to house begging her bread. She came to a certain house, one day, and the owner was suffering from a violent toothache.

The old woman promised to cure his pain on condition that he should wear a certain charm, which consisted of some words written on papers. She forbade him ever to open the papers or read the words. The man took the charm, wore it, and, as the old woman had foretold, the pain which had been so violent, ceased.

The man's wife feared that the old woman was a witch and one day when her husband had gone out to work, she found the charm in his coat which he had left behind. She longed to open it to find out what secret it contained. On doing so, what was her horror when she saw the fatal words! Written in clear handwriting where the following words:

Toothache, toothache, fare thee well,
Until we meet in Hell.

Knowing, then, that her husband had been cured by the power of the devil, she immediately burned the charm. When he returned home in the evening she told him how he had been deceived by the wicked witch. They both agreed that it would be easier for him to bear the toothache in this life than to sell his soul to the devil by wearing the wicked charm which the old woman had given him.

A WITCH AS A HARE [64]

There was a woman who lived in Rathkyle, and there was a small farmer living near her who hadn't many cows.

This man could never get any milk from the cows so he said there was somebody milking them at night. He got a couple of fellows to watch the cows this night to see who was milking them, and they had two greyhounds with them. They watched for a long time, but at long last a hare came along and began to suck the cows.

The men set the greyhounds after her and she went along till she came to the woman's window and the hounds caught her goin' in through it, an' they took a piece out of her hip, but she got in through the window after all. This hare was supposed to be the woman, and it is said that she had always a sore hip after that.

---

64 Told by Alice Murphy, a pupil of Adamstown School (D. Curtis, teacher), in 1938. Her informant was John Lacey of Coolnagree, Adamstown. IFCS 900: 42–3.

The black lamb and the dead[65]

It is a custom amongst the people, when throwing away water at night, to cry out in a loud voice, "Take care of the water", or literally from the Irish, "Away with yourself from the water," for they say that the spirits of the dead and buried are then wandering about. It would be dangerous if the water fell on them.

One dark night, a woman suddenly threw out a pail of boiling water, without thinking of the warning words. Instantly a cry was heard as of a person in pain, but no one was seen.

However, the next night a black lamb entered the house, having its back all freshly scalded. It lay down moaning on the hearth and died. Then they all knew that this was the spirit that had been scalded by the woman, and they carried the dead lamb out reverently and buried it deep in the earth.

Yet every night at the same hour it walked again into the house, and lay down, moaned and died, and after this happened many times the priest was sent for and finally by the strength of his exorcism the spirit of the dead was laid to rest. The black lamb appeared no more, neither was the body of the dead lamb found in the grave, when they searched for it, though it had been laid by their hands deep in the earth and covered with clay.

The dead coach[66]

About fifty years ago there lived in the Faythe an old woman by the name of Mag Curran and at the same time the "dead" coach used to be heard going around at midnight. The people of that time were very superstitious, but old Mag used to laugh at their fears. She boasted one night that she would stay up and see the "dead" coach herself. Her neighbours told her not to do it, that something awful would happen to her.

One night when everybody had gone to bed old Mag got out behind the door to wait for the "dead" coach. It was not long before she heard a rumbling noise coming down the Faythe. At first she felt afraid but her curiosity got the better of her and she put her eye to the key-hole to watch.

She saw that the horses and driver were headless, and just as they were

65 A story supplied in 1938 by Thomas O'Neill of 16 William Street, Wexford, a pupil of the Christian Brothers' School (Brother Ó hEilighe, teacher). His informant was Matthew O'Neill of the same address. IFCS 880: 404–5.   66 A story written down in 1938 by John Shudell of 8 Upper John Street, Wexford, from John Roche, aged 84, who lived on the same street. Master Shudell was a pupil of Wexford Christian Brothers' School (Brother Ó hEilighe, teacher). IFCS 881: 69–71.

passing, while she was still watching, the driver raised his whip and lashed out at the door. The whip going through the key-hole struck her in the eye and blinded her.

The next morning the neighbours found her lying screaming in the hall behind the door, and her eye had to be taken out though she lived a good many years after.

The "taking eye" [67]

There was a house down in Carne where a lot of cows were kept, and a lot of butter was made. The occupants were very prosperous with their cows and they supplied a lot of poor people with milk, as they were very good even though rich. They used to keep their cream in crocks all around the dairy on a big flag floor.

The time had come to churn the cream, so they put the horse to the churn, as they used to churn with a horse that time; by driving the horse around in a ring in the yard. They churned for half a day and could get no butter; so, weary and annoyed, they said that they would leave it until the next day.

The next morning they started to churn again with no result. They gave up that day. They tried again the third day and there was no result. Thinking that there might be something wrong with the milk, they emptied it into tubs and put in fresh cream, and started off to churn again. They held on churning that way for a week but all in vain.

On the evening of the last day a neighbour came in and said, "What are ye doing with the milk?" as everything was full of milk by now. They told him that they had been churning for a week and had no butter. "That is very queer," he said, "why don't ye go to the 'fairy-man' on the mountain?"

One of them got on a horse and brought Ned the fairy-man back with him. When Ned came in, he told them to throw every sup of milk out in the shore, a thing they thought hard to do. But he told them that everything in the dairy should be emptied and the crocks and tubs washed out.

He went around the house and laid his hands on the crocks and tubs. He came out to the door of the dairy and called the farmer and he said, "You are giving milk to a woman who is taking all your profit." He told the farmer that she lived down the lane near the farmer's house. The farmer instantly knew who the woman was, because he used to give her milk for charity. Ned the

67 A story collected by Patrick Sinnott of Drinagh, Wexford, a pupil of Wexford Christian Brothers' School in 1938 (Brother Ó hEilighe, teacher). His informant was Mrs Morris of Drinagh, aged 62. IFCS 881: 76–80.

fairy-man said that she had the "taking eye", and never to give her milk without getting in exchange even a penny or a half-penny.

On Monday they started the churning again and the dairy was scarcely able to hold all the butter. The people said no matter who they gave milk to after that they would charge a penny or a halfpenny for it.

Going astray at night [68]

You'd often hear tell of people going astray in the night. Well, that's a fact. I know several men that went astray in this locality. I went astray meself one night. There was a man living in this lane, he's dead now, and he went out in the field one night, he wanted to have a look at some sheep that were going to lamb. And when he went into the field he thought there were several people in the field with him – and he could see no one. But he felt people walking around everywhere. There was a path going through the field on down to his own place, and when he wanted to find this path to go home the dickens ever he could find a bit of it. He spent the whole night going around, and in the end he didn't know where he was. So he allowed the only thing to do was to sit down and wait till the daylight would come in. And where was he when he came to in the morning, do you think? He was sitting on Cloney's Bridge in Old Ross, about three or four miles away. That's a fact truth. I know the man well, and I heard him telling it twenty times. And he could never make out how it happened. But that was where he was in the morning. I went astray meself one night too, much the same way. I was away seeing an uncle of mine that lived about three or four miles from this place. I left the place to come home about nine o clock, and I got home here about half past nine or thereabouts. When I came home I had to go out in the field to see some horses that I had out there. 'Twas a grand night, well, 'twas fairly dark, there was no moon nor anything, but 'twas a grand night for rambling all the same. Well, when I was going across this field anyway, I thought there was thousands of people in the field with me. I could hear the rumbling of voices all around me, and I could feel people walking every way and the dickens a bit of me could see any one. I went all around the field to find the gate and I couldn't. I went around it a hundred times I suppose and couldn't find it – and I wouldn't go over the ditch. Sometimes I could see the gate, as I thought I'd go on straight to it and all of a sudden a great big mountain would get up in front of me, and I'd find meself at the ditch. In the finish I sat down and took off me

68 Collected in 1938 by Tom Carey from Nicholas Fitzgerald, a farm worker aged 74, from near Foulksmills. IFC 544: 133–6.

boots and socks; and in one minute I could see the gate right at me and I had no trouble at all finding the way. Only for that I suppose I'd be in the field all night. They say that if you took off your boots or your coat that you would find the way after a while but not to go over a ditch. They say that if you went astray like that in a field, that you should never go out over a ditch, only out a gate, or a gap. They say that if you go over a ditch that you'll get plenty to carry you – plenty help to carry you. Sure that's what happened this man I was telling you about, Lar was his name. When he went astray in this field he went over the fence. He thought he only went over the one fence; and sure in the morning he found himself and he sitting on the Bridge of Old Ross.

The pooka [69]

The pooka used to travel around that part of the county as well as the fairies. This thing was somewhat in the shape of a horse, and he used to travel through the country at an awful speed, and he used to make very little noise at all. Some people had stories about him and said that on one occasion he happened on a poor man that was travelling home and he was very old and was hardly able to walk. The pooka came along to him and asked him had he very far to go, and he said that he had; and begor, he got a great fright when he heard this yoke talking and he said that he was all right, that he was well able to walk home. The pooka asked him to get up on his back and the old man was afraid to refuse, and he got up and away the horse goes as hard as ever he could, and the lad was clinging to him for dear life, and the pooka was going faster than any horse ever travelled; and he said that the man need never bother his head trying to keep on, as he was not going to let him fall off. The man then loosened his grip and the pooka was able to twist his body this way and that and the man could not fall off no matter if he tried. The pooka kept up his gallop and he was not long doing the journey. Then he stopped all of a sudden and let off the man and he fell down on the ground. Then he went off again as fast as he had come. It was all done in such a short space of time that the man did not know whether it was on his head or his heels he was standing.

---

69 Collected by Seán de Buitléar from Thomas Butler, a farmer, aged 66, of Glynn. IFC 608: 15–17.

The nun and the devil[70]

A girl named Lily Myler told me this story of an old nun who was so holy that the devil tempted her. God had told her to fast for some number of days to see would she obey him. One day she was praying in her room when something scrawbed her and she told the nuns, but they said it was the cat. So they locked the room but it was the devil all the time. Then he appeared to her again, dressed in lovely garments, and said to her, "If you do not eat, you will die soon. God is not wanting you to be greater than himself and he is wanting you to die." "But," she said, "I will keep my promise to God", but he tempted her so much that she gave in and as soon as she tasted the food she dropped dead and the devil laughed over her, for he had her for himself.

70 An exemplum collected in 1938 by Madge Browne, a pupil of The Faythe Convent School, Wexford, from her friend Lily Meyler. Both Madge and Lily were from Maudlinstown. IFCS 882: 153–4.

Love and marriage

Marriage customs

GUSSERANE [71]

Marriages occur most frequently before Lent and Advent. May is supposed to be an unlucky month for getting married. There is a rhyme about the days for getting married on:

> Monday for health,
> Tuesday for wealth,
> Wednesday the best day of all,
> Thursday for losses,
> Friday for crosses,
> And Saturday no day at all.

Matches are made in this district. Money is given as a fortune. On a wedding day the couple go to the church and get married. Then they go home to the house of the bride and have the wedding breakfast. When breakfast is over the wedding guests start a dance and remain over till night. That night all the neighbours gather in and have a big "spree". "Fools" visit the house that night. Some people dress up in rags and put an "eye fiddle" [Eye fiddle. Irish *aghaidh fidil*, fiddle face, from the grotesque fiddle-shape of the mask] or mask on them and go in around the house and if they didn't get sweet-cake or whiskey they would go out and do some devilment. But if they got it they would go out and throw off the rags and go in and dance. Some people used to receive them well, but others used to bring Peelers and have them arrested, so the custom died out. When the couple came home after the honeymoon, another dance is held; it is called a "hauling home".

71 Written by Thomas Foley of Rathimney, Gusserane, New Ross, a pupil of Gusserane School, parish of Tintern (Peter Corish, teacher), in 1938. IFCS 871: 285–6.

KILMUCKRIDGE [72]

May was considered an unlucky month for marriage and is still. Saturday was the unlucky day. The bride always got from her mother a white counterpane (crochet or knitted). Mrs O'Byrne's mother remembers but one marriage taking place in a house but that christenings were quite common in houses – the "case of necessity" not being the cause. This was an occasion for a "celebration".

On the wedding day morning the bridegroom, in a carriage (when he could afford one), repaired to the house of the bride elect where there was a feast. Then to church, thence to the bridegroom's house where there was feasting and merry-making till morning.

But immediately after the wedding there was the race for the bride's garters or "bucks" among the guests. This was a race on horseback cross country from the church to the bridegroom's house.

I myself was told details of such a race: how Tom Cullen, Ballyvaloon, beat Paddy Dempsey, Ballyvoodock, although not so well mounted. My informant saw the race and showed me where Cullen went the short cut to win well.

The marriage of widows or widowers was not popular. When darkness fell, the "boys" "blew" them. The "blowing" was done through bottles without a bottom.

FORTH [73]

Long ago there were peculiar marriage customs in the barony of Forth. At a wedding feast, the table was placed in the centre of the floor, the priest sat at one end of it, and the bride at the other, the guests between; the bridegroom waited on the table.

The wedding party often came to church on the famous Forth ponies. Even the priest, if living some distance from the church, rode one; as we know from an old ballad in the Forth dialect.

> Aar was a wedeen ee Ballymore,
> An aar was a hundereth lauckeen vowre score.
> Aar was Theig an' Joane, an lhaung Jauane,
> An a priesth a parieshe on his lhaung-tyel garaane.

72 Collected by Mrs Margaret O'Byrne, of Kilnacooley, Kilmuckridge, a teacher at St Brigid's School, Blackwater, from her mother, aged 82, written in 1937. IFCS 886: 21–2.   73 Collected by Peggy Quirke of Tenchespit, a pupil at Lady's Island School, Carne (Margaret Burke, teacher) in 1938. Her informant was Miss Annie Madden of Hayestown, Murrintown, who was aged over 70. IFCS 879: 197–8.

We append the full text, with translation and notes as published in *The Dialect of Forth and Bargy, Co. Wexford*, ed. Dolan and Ó Muirithe, Dublin 1996. This archaic dialect, called Yola, was spoken in the twin baronies until the middle of the last century. We have amended the child's version.

Ee weddeen o Ballymore

I

Aar was a weddeen ee Ballymore,
An aar was a hundereth lauckeen vowre score.
Aar was Thieg, an' Joane, an lhaung Jauane,
An a priesth o' parieshe on his lhaung-tyel garraane.
Chorus   Ye be welcome, hearthilee, welcome, mee joees,
            Ye be welcome hearthillee, ivery oan.

II

Aar was Parick o Dearmoth, an dhen score besidh,
Wee aa lhaung vlealès an pikkès, to waaite apan a breede.
An a priesth o paireshe on his garrane baun,[74]
Hea marreet dear Pheilim to his sweet Jauane.
Chorus – Ye be welcome, &c.

III

Aar was lhaung kaayle an nettles, ee-mixt wee prasaugh buee,[75]
Maade a nicest coolecannan that e'er ye did zee.
Aar was a muskawn o buthlther ee-laaide apan hoat shruaanès,[76]
An gooude usquebaugh ee-sarith uth in cooanès.[77]
Chorus –Ye be welcome, &c.

---

74 Garrane Bawn is Irish (*gearrán bán*, a white pony). In correct Barony of Forth, it would be "whit caul" –*Tobias Butler* (fl. 1800, a local informant in the dialect).   **75** Prassaugh buee is given by Mr Poole as "yellow weed" (*praiseach buí*).   **76** Shruaanes, Tobias Butler thinks, torn or divided cakes or pieces of such cakes. " 'Tis aul in shruaanes" – *Mr Poole* (a Wexford antiquarian, fl. late 18th century)[It may be scraps (of bread), and " 'Tis aul in shruaanes" would mean, "It is all in scraps "].   **77** "Wooden cans or vessels; some made square, others round, but without handles" – *Tobias Butler.*

IV

Raree met in plathearès, ee-zet in a rooe,
An neeat wooden trenshoorès var whiter than snow.
Heve a dishen an trenshoorès awye, Shaneen;
Drink a heall to a breede. "Shud with, a voorneen."[78]
Chorus – Ye be welcome, &c.

V

A peepeare struck ap; wough dansth aul in a ring;
Earch myde was a queen, an earch bye was a king;
Zoo wough aul vell a–danceen; earch bye gae a poage
To his sweethearth, an smack lick a dab of a brough.
Chorus –Ye be welcome, &c.

VI

Zoo wough kisth, an wough parthet; earch man took his leave;
An a boor lithel breedegroom waithed wonderfullee grieft.
Zoo wough aul returnth hime, contented an gaay,
To our pleoughès an mulk-pylès till a neeshte holy die.[79]
Chorus – Ye be welcome, &c.

ENGLISH

I

There was a wedding in Ballymore,
And there was a hundred, lacking four score;
There was Thadee, and John, and long Joan,
And the priest of the parish on his long-tail pony.
Chorus   You are welcome, heartily welcome, my joys,
                You are heartily welcome, every one.

---

78 Shud with: Irish, *siúd ort*, here's to you.   **79**   The next Sunday or other intervening ec-
clesiastical festival after the marriage which they call "The Rising out-day", when they again
assemble.

II

There was Patrick Ó Deormod, and ten score beside,
With their long flails and picks, to wait upon the bride,
The priest of the parish on his white pony;
He married dear Phelim to his sweet Joan.
Chorus – You are welcome, &c.

III

There was long kale and nettles, mingled with yellow-weed,
Made the nicest coolecannan that ever you did see.
There was a great heap of butter laid upon hot scraps,
And good whiskey served out in wooden cans.
Chorus –You are welcome, &c.

IV

There was choice meat in platters, set in a row;
And neat wooden trenchers far whiter than snow.
Heave the dishes and the trenchers away, little John;
Drink a health to the bride, "Here's to you, my dear."
Chorus – You are welcome, &c.

V

The piper struck up, we danced all in a ring,
Each maid was a queen, and each boy was a king;
So we all fell a-dancing – each boy gave a kiss
To his sweetheart, and smacked like a dab [slap] of a shoe.
Chorus –You are welcome, &c.

VI

So we kissed and we parted, each man took his leave;
And the poor dirty bridegroom looked wondrously grieved;
So we all returned home, contented and gay,
To our ploughs and our milk-pails till the next holiday.
Chorus – You are welcome, &c.

Love songs

THE FLOWER OF CURRAGHMORE [80]

I

I'm wounded by a charming girl, ye kind gods set me free.
She is a handsome tall young girl but does not pity me.
Her gold-like hair and tresses bright hang o'er her gentle face,
'Tis her fair distracting charms first disturbed my humble peace.

II

When I first beheld this angel bright she struck me with delight:
Her bright angelic features sorely increased my sighs;
Her face was like the roses that bloom both red and white,
She is the fairest of all females, she was my heart's delight.

III

For to send forth her praises my eloquence is weak,
For Cupid's dart has pierced my heart which causes me to speak,
You all heard tell of Venus, young Mars did her adore –
I think her far inferior to the Flower of Curraghmore.

IV

Don't reflect on me with scorn when you'll hear of my sad pain,
Or think 'tis youth and folly that makes young men complain,
If she knew my disorder I'm sure she'd set me free.
Take pity, lovely Katie; prove kind and marry me.

V

But what signify my industries, my labours are all in vain,
For she has placed her fancy on some other youthful swain;
Since I can't gain the favour of the girl that I adore,
Broken-hearted I will wander from the Flower of Curraghmore.

80 Composed by Michael Dalton, Rosegarland, Clongeen. Collected in 1937 by Annie Ryan, of
Garryduff, Campile, a pupil of Gusserane School (Mrs B. Corish, teacher). IFCS 871: 373–4.

WILLIE REILLY [81]

In the County Wexford near Taghmon
My love was reared a farmer's son;
I own I loved him just as my life
And I was resolved to become his wife.

To my misfortune I went to walk,
I sent for Reilly with him to talk,
I was deceived by my waiting maid,
She told my mamma what I had said.

My mamma called me immediately,
Saying "Susan, Susan, how can it be
That you're in love with a farmer's son;
When your dada will hear it he'll distracted run.

You know, dear child, he's no match for you;
Besides, a Roman - you know it's true;
Before you'll bring us into disgrace,
We'll have him banished out of the place."

Mamma dear, do pardon me,
There's none I love but my dear Willie;
If I'm prevented to be his wife,
With a sword or a pistol I'll end my life.

"If that be so," my mamma cried,
"I'll ne'er prevent you to be his bride;
So send for Reilly immediately,
When it's past and over we will agree."

My mamma then to the steward did run,
She ordered him for to charge a gun;
He hid himself in the laurel tree
To take the life of my dear Willie.

81 Collected by Mary B. Dunphy, retired teacher, in the Irishtown, New Ross, in 1938. IFC 618: 99–100.

A case of pistols I then drew
And to young Reilly I them threw;
He defended himself right manfully,
And he shot the steward in the laurel tree.

In to Wexford he went straightway,
And he stepped on ship board without delay;
He steered his course to Columbia's shore,
May the Lord be with him, mo mhíle stór.

My father mortgaged his property,
In hopes to drive me to poverty;
His golden riches I do deny,
I will walk the world with my farmer boy.

Broken hearts

AN EXPERT AND HER CURES [82]

Biddy the Knitter lived in a small unlighted cabin situated on Monbeg Hill, in a lane now belonging to Philip O'Brien. She specialized in curing broken hearts, and the local belief that she got much information in the "raheen" [fairy fort] close to the house tended to augment rather than diminish her status.

Love potions were the chief items in her nefarious business, and some vile odours used issue from the cabin as she was always brewing some concoctions for her love-sick patients. She did a roaring trade and it was not unusual to see four or five victims of the *galar* [disease] plodding their weary way to Biddy's lonely cabin. Her treatment was as follows: Some article representing the person's heart had to be left in Biddy's care. A drink of her famous brew was, of course, a most necessary item, after which the patient returned home to wait for a month. Biddy then began her ritualistic ceremonies, which continued together with her nocturnal visits to the "Raheen" until her customer returned after nine days to report progress.

Usually the wound was healed by the end of the month.

A story of one young man who went to Biddy with his broken heart and as he was leaving the token, Biddy asked him who was the young lady responsi-

82 Collected by Peggie Codd of Presentation Convent, Enniscorthy (Sister Angela, teacher), in 1938. IFCS 894: 38–40.

ble, and he told her. "Oh," said Biddy, "I have that young lady's heart here for repairs too."

On hearing this he immediately dumped his purse on the table and said, "Here's my purse and all that's in it, but give me hers this blessed minute."

THE COUPLE WHO ALWAYS FOUGHT [83]

I heard a story once of a man and a woman that used always have a little bit of an argument about things that would go wrong in the home. They used to fight an awful lot, and the most of it all was on account of them having no children. They used to fight and fight, and it would last for a whole day and then the next day they would not speak to each other. This went on for a long time and it was worse matters were getting, and one day they had a divil of a row and the man got as mad as he could be, and he told the wife to clear out of the place and not come back any more. She looked at him and said that he could not do it at all. He said that he meant doing it and she said that she would go; and then he told her that he did not care if she never came back. She collected up a whole lot of things that she owned and said that she was bringing them with her. He saw her taking a lot of stuff that he would want, and he told her that she would have to leave back some of them, and he gave her leave to bring off only the three things that she liked best in the place. "Do you mean that?" said she to him. "I do," said he. So she put back all the things that she had collected and one of the things that she took was her money. And then she brought a pet dog, and then she caught the husband and put him up on her back. He did not know what was the matter with her at all and he got down off her back and asked her what did she mean at all by doing as she did. "Well," said she, "you gave me leave to take away three things out of this place, the three things that I like best. Well you are one of the things that I like best and I am bringing you with me." When he heard her talking like that, he softened greatly and saw that whatever faults his wife had she was very fond of him at the back of it all.

He then said that he was sorry for what he had done, and she was fond of him all right, and it wasn't hard for her to turn around and say that she was also sorry for all she had said. And from that day onwards they lived as a married couple should, and to crown all a child was born to them and they were all as happy as the day was long.

83 Collected by John Butler of Foulksmills from James White of the same place in 1935. IFC 600: 121–4.

Curses, prayers and cures

St Patrick in Wexford[84]

It comes down to us in history that St Patrick never came to Wexford as it had already been civilized before his time, but the following short folk-tale shows us that this is not true.

St Patrick had certain reasons for coming to Wexford on two or three occasions; once when he was driving out the snakes and reptiles, and another time when he was driving out the devil.

When St Patrick was driving out the snakes and reptiles he drove them on as far as Ferrycarrig, about two miles from Wexford town. There was no bridge at Ferrycarrig that time, and he wanted to cross. He saw a lot of men fishing and he asked them would they mind taking him across, himself and the snakes and reptiles. The men said they would of course and got St Patrick and the snakes and all into the boats. When they were about half-way across, the man that was over the men, or that had them employed, told them to turn back and get on with their work. They told him they wouldn't; that they were going to obey St Patrick. But St Patrick told them to take him back and obey their master. They took him back then.

When St Patrick got on the bank again, he took a plate out of his knapsack and laid it on the water and changed it into a big boat. He then got the snakes and reptiles into it and went safely to the other side. When St Patrick thought of the man that wouldn't allow his men to take him across, he got angry and he put a curse on the water, that no fish would ever be caught in it again. The fishermen began to wonder the next morning when they could catch no fish, for they could see plenty of them in the water, and they would even be in the nets and yet when they would draw them in there would be nothing in them.

But when St Patrick found out that it was affecting the poor fishermen

84 A story collected by John Butler of Lambstown, Glynn, from his father, Thomas, in 1935. IFC 106: 160–4.

that were so kind to him, he got sorry for what he had done, and he took the curse off the water again; but he had taught the hard master a lesson.

I got this story from my father who heard it when he was a small boy, but he doesn't known from whom.

The power of the priest [85]

There is no mistake, but a priest have great power if he wanted to use it. There was a priest in this parish one time. Father Cavanagh was his name. He was a great big man: Big Father Cavanagh he was called. Well, one day, he was coming from Taghmon. 'Twas a car he was driving in, one of these traps 'twas all them you'd see that time. Well, he was coming on down the hill of the Craigeog, and he had a boy driving him. Begob, Doran's house was afire. One of the outhouses, 'twas blazing up in the heavens, and there was a devil of a storm blowing straight against them, and 'twas blowing the flames and sparks and all on towards the dwelling house.

Says the boy, "That's Doran's house on fire, and the dwelling house will be burned the way the wind is blowing." Father Cavanagh never said a word, only took out his book and started to read. Well, the boy said that they weren't half way down the hill when the wind was on their back; and of course the house was safe then.

Stories about the Holy Family [86]

Our Lord worked with St Joseph in the carpenter's shop at Nazareth. One day when his Mother was present, he was putting some work together. In turning it over his shoulder, it appeared to the Blessed Virgin in the form of a Cross. This made the Blessed Virgin sorrowful, as she foresaw her Son carrying his Cross to Mount Calvary.

Another story connected with the life of Our Lord relates to birds called cross-bills. Our Lord and his Blessed Mother were journeying together. The cross-bills were always flitting around Our Lord. His mother asked him the reason why these birds were accompanying them. He replied, "We are birds of a feather." His Blessed Mother did not understand the meaning of these words. Later on she remembered when on Mount Calvary.

85 A story collected by Thomas Carey, Foulksmills, from Nick Cleary, a farm worker from Horetown, in 1938. IFC 520: 251–2.   86 Collected by Annie Reddy of Askamore, a pupil of Askamore School, near Carnew, in 1937 (Margaret McGrath, teacher). Annie's informant was John Moore, of Ballytarsna. IFCS 875: 81.

The story of the blessed bread[87]

The favourite bread years ago was wheaten bread. It was made like this: first the wheatenmeal was put in a bowl, then salt and bread-soda was added, and it was stirred well. Buttermilk was then added, and it was stirred again. Then it was kneaded and shaped round or square.

In later ages they began to mix it with water. The bread mixed with water was called "blessed bread". This is why: There was a poor widow living in the north of the county, near Gorey, with a large family of hungry children. She found it hard to provide for them. On one occasion the parish priest paid her a visit and finding her in tears asked her the reason for her tears. She told him she had no bread for the children and no means of getting it. He told her to get some flour and water and to mix it into dough, which he blessed, and told her to keep a small portion for the next cake and every cake after that. The cakes turned out splendid and the blessed dough has gone around the County Wexford for a great number of years, even to the present day.

Prayers

FOUR CORNERS ON MY BED [88]

There are four corners on my bed.
There are four angels on them spread,
Matthew, James, Luke and John
Bless the bed that I lie on.
Here I lie upon my side.
I pray to God to be my guide.
And if I die before I wake,
I pray to God my soul to take.
Waken now or waken never
To God I give my soul forever.
God bless me.

Four corners on my bed
Four Angels over-spread,

87 Collected by Evans Byrne of The Faythe, Wexford, a pupil of the Christian Brothers' School, Wexford (Brother Healy, teacher), from Mrs Byrne of Colbert Street, Wexford, who was aged 70 in 1938. IFCS 881: 127–8.   88 Collected by Kathleen O'Grady of St John of God Convent School, The Faythe, Wexford (Sister Columcille, teacher), in 1938, from Mary O'Grady of 5 Tuskar View, Wexford. IFCS 882: 129.

One to sing, one to pray, and two
To carry my soul away.

HERE I LAY MYSELF DOWN TO SLEEP [89]

Here I lay myself down to sleep,
To God I give my soul to keep;
But if I die before I wake
To God I pray my soul to take.
This I ask for Jesus' sake.

* * *

I shall die, I know not when, where, or how,
But if I die in mortal sin I am lost for ever.
      O Jesus! Have mercy on me.

* * *

O, Jesus who for love of me,
Didst bear thy Cross to Calvary;
In thy sweet mercy grant to me
To suffer and die with thee.

* * *

Virgin Mary, pray for us and those in their last agony and who are to die tonight. Heart of Jesus once in agony, have pity on the dying.

OTHER PRAYERS [90]

To be said in bed: Seven priests singing. Seven bells ringing. Shut the gates of hell and open the gates of heaven and let my poor soul pass in. I don't know when or how or where I may die, but if I die in mortal sin I am lost for ever – *Tom Franey*

---

89 Prefaced by this note: "The following are holy prayers taught to James Carroll, 6th Standard. He lives in Coolinteggart, Hollyford, Co. Wexford. James Carroll told them to the 6th Standard and they were taught to him by his mother. She learned the prayers from her grandmother."Collected by James Carroll, a pupil at Killaneerin School in 1937 (Nuala Bean Uí Chadhla, teacher), IFCS 888: 146.   90 Collected by Tom Franey, Teresa Jordan and Mary O'Leary of Marshallstown School in 1937 (Seosamh Ó Macháin, teacher). IFCS 893: 74–5.

Here I lay me down to sleep, I give my soul to God to keep. Waken now or waken never, I give my soul to God for ever.

* * *

When the clock strikes, say: Jesus, protect me and keep me from sin – *Teresa Jordan*

* * *

> Infant Jesus meek and mild,
> Pity me a little child,
> Sweet Jesus, I implore thee;
> Heart of Mary I adore Thee;
> Heart of Joseph pure and just,
> In these three Hearts I put my Trust – *Mary O'Leary*

The Rosary[91]

The Rosary holds a very high place and traditionally is regarded as a very powerful prayer. I can recall, off-hand, one story in which a person's safety was attributed to the recitation of the Rosary. My nephew, Richard Greene, who is now master of the *Irish Pine*, belonging to Irish Shipping, told me on one occasion that he owed his life to the Rosary. He was very young at the time (1939), and was coming from South America in a British ship called the *Royston Grange*. She was torpedoed without any warning. Not long – a few minutes before she was struck – Green, who was A.B., moved aft and began to say his Rosary. He was not on duty at the time and it was day. He was not long saying his Rosary in this private place – I forget exactly where he stood to say his beads – when the vessel was struck. The torpedo hit just underneath the spot where he was standing previous to beginning the Rosary. But he moved away from that place to a more private spot to say his Rosary without interruption.

He said he does not know why he was moved to say the Rosary at that particular moment, as it was not a habit with him to say the Rosary very

---

91 Written by James G. Delaney, full-time collector, of Wexford town in 1954. IFC 1610: 252–3.

often. So he attributes his safety to the Rosary. He never even got a scratch. *"The Rosary brought us safe."*

Captain Devereux sailed out of Liverpool all his life, but one time he brought with him as A.B. his brother-in-law, a man much older than himself and a man who had spent the greater part of his life in the Wexford schooners. He had been skipper of various home-trade schooners in Wexford, but like many of the old schooner skippers he could neither read nor write. Captain Devereux said he heard old Carroll telling the other sailors about his experiences in the schooners and what they used to do in bad weather: "We used to say the Rosary," he said: "and we always came safe!"

And that to a crowd of British sailors who never even knew what the Rosary was. Captain Devereux was ashamed at his brother-in-law's simplicity. He thought sound seamanship and a knowledge of navigation far more in keeping with a schooner in bad weather!

A poor scholar[92]

There was a poor scholar one time going around, and one day he went in a shop in Taghmon for half an ounce of tobacco. He asked the owner of the shop for half an ounce of tobacco and he wouldn't give it to him. The tobacco used be in rolls that time and there was a big roll of it up on the table. The lad said nothing, only took out his knife and cut off the tobacco himself, and threw the money on the counter to the shopkeeper, and he turned around and said to him, "There's more tailors nor John Donnell; and more shops nor yours; and the grass will grow green at your door before this day twelvemonth." And so it did. He was broke and gone out of it in twelve months.

Sir Walter Whitty and his cat: a story[93]

Sir Walter was to be married to Lady Devereux of Ballymaghyre. Lady Devereux asked Sir Walter to get some rabbits for the wedding. He would not let anyone only himself hunt, so out he went to the burrows and he hunted all day but never a rabbit could he catch.

Returning home at night quite disappointed, what should he see but a white cat perched on a bank of sand. "Bad luck to you, and all your breed,"

92 An anecdote collected by Tom Carey from Maurice Carthy, aged 79, of Camross, near Taghmon, in 1938. IFCS 520: 139–40.   93 Told in 1938 by William Saddler of St Columba's Villas, Wexford, a pupil at Wexford Christian Brothers' School (Brother D.C. Ó hEilighe, teacher). William's informant was Mrs Furlong of 3 Wolfe Tone Villas. IFCS 800: 376–7.

said the knight, taking up a stone. "It's you and the likes of you that have destroyed all my rabbits," and so saying he flung the stone and killed the cat.

When he reached home, he found as usual the old cat sitting at the fire. "Maude killed Jude," he said in Barony of Forth language, which means "Cat, I killed your kitten", and scarcely had he said the word than she curled up her back, sprang upon the knight, and before anyone could save him she had his throat cut.

When the servants came in, they could not see the cat. From that night to this Sir Walter is seen sitting in the hall of the castle with a cat stuck on his throat.

The Whittys ever since hate cats and never keep one in their houses. Lady Devereux, hearing of her lover's death, drowned herself in the well of the garden, in which she is seen walking about dressed in white.

Cures for diseases in cattle[94]

Blackleg in cattle   A short time ago the bone of a cow's leg was found hanging in the chimney of an old house. It seems this bone had been hanging there for years and was kept by the old people of the house as a preventative for Blackleg in cattle.

Fluke   The common bracken or fern which grows by the roadside contains a juice which when extracted cures "fluke" in sheep or cattle.

A charm for churning[95]

There was a woman here on the White Mountain not very long ago. She was a Protestant and she used to churn fifteen pounds of butter from one cow. She used to put a straw rope around her body like an army officer's belt, across the shoulders and around her waist, and put another straw rope around the cow's body.

94 Collected by Kathleen O'Connor of Slevoy, Foulksmills, a pupil at Traceystown School (Mrs Farrell), teacher, in 1938. IFCS 883: 129.   95 Collected by James G. Delaney from Walter Furlong, aged 84, of Grange, Rathnure, in 1954. IFC 1344:109

Various cures

CURES FOR WARTS, CHIN COUGH (WHOOPING COUGH), RINGWORM [97]

To cure warts it is important to get a gravelstone for every wart you have and put them in a bag. Then throw the bag on the road and whoever picked it up first got the warts.

An effective cure for the chin cough [whooping cough] is to go in and out three times under a briar with both its ends growing in the ground.

A good cure for ringworm is to get three furze bushes and redden the stumps in the fire and then draw the sticks one after another around the ringworm as near as you could bear the heat.

CURES FOR HEADACHE, WHITLOW, A STY, A BOIL, WARTS [98]

This is a cure for a headache. Cut a piece of brown paper to fit the forehead, steep it in vinegar and lay it on the forehead, repeat it until the papers get dry.

This is a cure for a whitlow. Put the finger into the boiling potato water three times, when the potatoes are boiling on the fire.

This is a cure for a stye on the eye. The first who has seen the stye on the eye gets a thorn of a gooseberry bush, and point it at the stye three times without touching it.

This is a cure for a boil. Get soap and sugar and mix it together, and make ointment of it, and put it on the boil.

This is a cure for a wart. Put your spittle on the wart for nine mornings.

A CURE FOR CONSUMPTION [99]

Consumption is an awful thing, God save us, when it gets into a family. It will come on one of them and then the rest of them will take it if the others do not make an effort to get away. If they stayed away altogether, they would have a good chance of missing it.

Consumption can be cured in its early stages by the juice of dandelion and bogmint. All you have to do is to go to the bog and you will see plenty of this stuff growing there and bring it on home together with the dandelion and put them down in a pot and boil them. When they are well boiled, they should be squeezed tight together to get all the juice out of them and then thrown away. The juice can be drunk, a little of it at a time. You could take it three or

97 Collected by John Molloy of Dungulph, Fethard-on-Sea, a pupil of Poulfur School (Pat Neville, teacher), in 1938. IFCS 870: 236.   98 From Una Doyle, Great Graigue, Fethard-on-Sea. Same school. IFCS 870: 237.   99 From John Alyward, aged 84, a labourer from Foulksmills direction. Collected by John Butler of the same place in 1939. IFC 618: 311–12.

four times a day and it would do you no harm at all. I've known fellas to take
it that were rotten in consumption and it brought them out of it. There is
nothing that I know of better than it.

A CURE FOR MEASLES FROM THE SAME SOURCE [1]

In the olden times they used to have a great cure for the measles. They would
go out in the fields and pick up all the sheep dung that they could find and
begor this would be brought home and put into a pot and begor I don't know
who the dickens thought of it, but I know it for a fact that it is a genuine cure.
When it would be in the pot for some time, they would strain the water off it
and this is the water that is given to the people that are affected with the
measles. Sometimes it is very hard to get the children to take it, and you know
that it is children that are generally affected with the measles. They would
have to give it to the children and not tell them what it was at all, for if they
did they would not take it. And do you know what it is, it is not hard to take it
at all. It hasn't a bad taste at all. Some of the doctors that are going now would
not approve of it at all, but it is certainly a great cure.

CURES FOR WARTS, SORE EYES, AND "THE BLAST" [2]

In olden times people used to cure warts by getting a stone and by rubbing
the stone on each one of the warts and then put the stone in fancy paper, and
throw it away. The first person to find the stone and pick it up would have the
warts, and the warts would be gone off your own hand. That cure is happening still.

The way to cure sore eyes would be to put the Sign of the Cross three
times by a person's ring; it would be cured after a few days.

To cure the whooping-cough, in olden times, if two people were married
of the same name, and if you got that bread that the woman would make they
say that it would cure the whooping cough.

To cure a cold it would be to boil a snail in milk and for to drink the milk
and the cold would be cured.

To cure a blast in animals – to get forge water; it would be for the person
to go into the forge, without speaking a word and get the water out of the
forge in a trough (if you spoke it would be no good for the person to speak),
you would bring the water to the animal and sprinkle it over the animal; she
would be cured all right after a few days.

---

1 IFC 618: 305–6.   2 "The blast" is a mysterious disease in animals caused by a supernatural
agency. Collected by an unnamed pupil of Ballycullane School (John Doyle, teacher), in 1938.
IFCS 870: 290.

A CURE FOR CHIN COUGH [3]

A cure for the chin cough is if you happened to find a hairy-molly [hairy caterpillar] and put her in a cloth, and tie it around the person's neck with the ailment, and accordingly as the insect decays away the chin cough will go away too. If you get bread from the children of whose parents are of the same name, it is supposed to cure the chin cough too. The roots of comfrey boiled or scraped, and made into a plaster with the white of an egg is a cure for a sprain. Spunk leaves [leaves of colt's foot] are good for a severe cut. If you boil water and put a corner of a towel into it and put it as hot as you could bear it on the back of your neck, it will cure a headache.

Long ago when people wanted a cure for the whooping cough they put the person in between an ass's legs three times and making the sign of the cross each time. Scutch grass was boiled and the water of it drunk for rheumatism. When people had the toothache, they took Easter water with pepper in it. Children who had the whooping cough were given food left behind by a ferret. This lightened the cough but it did not cure it. Two Cahills married can cure evils by putting three drops of blood on them. When seven sons are in a family one after another, the seventh is supposed to have a charm.

Bees' wax would also cure corns. Rub the wax on the corns and it will cure them. Two pieces of limestone well rubbed together, and wet them, and rub them until [word missing] come on them will cure warts.

CURES FOR RUPTURE, CRAMPS, CORNS [4]

Like most other places in Ireland, Aclare has many old cures, which the people believe in. The following are some of them:

A ruptured child is supposed to be cured if it is passed three times through the bole of an ash tree.

A child with whooping cough is supposed to be cured if it is passed three times under a jackass.

The soft bark of the alder is said to cure warts. There are also several wells here, the water of which is believed to cure warts also.

Another cure for warts is: For every wart take a small stone. Rub it on the wart it represents and then bury it. The wart is supposed to disappear in nine days.

---

3 From Kathleen Forristal of Killesk School (Margaret Sutton, teacher). Kathleen came from Knockea, Campile. Nano Harte of Tinnock, Campile contributed cures for whooping cough and rheumatism; and Nellie O'Connor of Knockea contributed cures for corns and warts (1938). IFCS 873: 47–8. 4 Collected by unnamed pupils of Aclare School (M.E. Campbell, teacher) in 1938. IFCS 873: 137–9.

Elm sap cures burns and scolds. Boiled furze blossoms and the juice strained is a cure for cramps and internal pains. A cobweb tied tightly around a cut has the same effect.

If you lose your way in a field at night, you should turn right around and bless yourself, and you would then know your way home.

Penny-leaves [pennywort] are applied under an old clean cloth to corns. Every second night they should be changed, and the corn will fall out after a week.

Ivy leaves boiled are also good for corns. They are supposed to disappear after a week or so.

A bit of sheep's wool, cut off near the sheep's back so that the oil is in it, is good for ear-ache if put in the ear.

A gooseberry thorn if stuck in a sty on the eye, is supposed to cure the sty, and it will not come any more.

A live frog put in the mouth and left there until it jumps out is supposed to cure toothache.

The heart of a raw onion is good for ear-ache if placed in the ear.

In a hole in one of the rocks of Sliabh Coillte, there are little stones to be found. If one of these stones is placed in the mouth, it is supposed to cure tooth-ache.

The clay off Fr Clancy's grave in Terrerath graveyard is believed to cure toothache also. The clay is put in the mouth. After a while when the pain ceases, the clay is spat out.

Another cure for warts is: Stick a thorn in a snail, and make her froth. Rub the froth on the wart. Put the snail up on a bush, and if she has withered in nine days the wart will disappear also. Lime is supposed to cure warts also.

The lick of a dog's tongue cures a cut.

Another cure for toothache is to put a dead man's tooth in your mouth, and leave it there for a few minutes, and it is said when you would take it out the toothache would be gone.

These old cures were given to the schoolchildren by the old people around.

The holy well at Ballytramin [5]

St Nicodemus' Well   There is a holy well called St Nicodemus' Well at Balla-tramin, Co. Wexford. It is situated in a small wood. There is a protecting wall

5 Collected by George Murphy of Thomas Street, Wexford, a pupil of the Christian Brothers' School (Brother Healy, teacher), in 1937. George's informant was Patrick Davis, also of Thomas Street, aged 70. IFCS 880: 301.

built around the well. Its patron saint is St Nicodemus. There is a pilgrimage to it every year on the feast of St Nicodemus. Everyone who is cured at the well leaves a rag or a cross on the bush beside it. The water of the well is a cure for sore eyes. The people who attend at the pilgrimage say five "Our Fathers", five "Hail Marys", five "Glorias" and go round the well seven times on their knees on pebbles, for penance. If a person wants to be cured, he or she must bathe the eyes seven times. The men and women offer the same thing which is the aforementioned rag or cross.

A woman who could stop bleeding with a prayer[6]

I knew a woman, and a poor woman she was too, and she had a prayer for stopping the blood, but she would not give it to anyone at all as she said that it was not the right thing to do with it. She said that she got it from a man, and he got it from a woman, and she said that when she would be dying that she would give it to a man if God left her in the state of health, that she would do so. I know that woman to be offered plenty of money for that prayer and still she would not give it away at all. She said that that prayer should never be said only when there was great need for it, and it should never be ill-used at all. She said that she knew of a person that fell in for an awful stroke of bad luck because they used that prayer when there was no necessity at all for it; and the prayer itself was no use at all any more after that. It would not stop blood if a person was to die.

6 Collected by John Butler from John Aylward of Foulksmills, a labourer aged 84, in 1939. IFC 608: 272–3.

The home, children and crafts

Lore about clothes[7]

The only phrase I ever heard when new clothes were first worn was: "Well you may wear, and soon you may tear", but sometimes the last part – "soon you may tear" – was left out.

New clothes were usually worn first to mass, or to a wedding, or some great event, like; and the moment the wearer came home he immediately changed into his old clothes, for fear of soiling the new ones. Among the poorer class new clothes were a great treat, because, as often as not they had to buy second-hand articles of wear, and couldn't afford new ones.

Up to about fifty years ago tailors went from house to house making men's and boys' clothes. They never made women's or girls' clothes at all. The dressmaker made some of the women's clothes and the women themselves made other articles of clothing. Boys' clothing was made by the tailor, for boys from the age of thirteen upwards. Before this age they were made by the dressmaker. Pedlars did a great trade in olden times. The pedlar was nearly always certain of getting rid of some of his wares in every house.

Homespun wool was used in every house. Every house had its spinning wheel, and some had a weaver.

The only dye ever used was the juice of elderberries, mixed with the juice of blackberries, which gave a blue-black dye. But generally underclothes were never dyed, but worn in their original colour, which was generally a dirty white. The only bought material I ever saw used was calico, and was in colour a dirty yellow.

People always went into mourning for at least three years, and sometimes longer. Women used never strip their heads. The whole townsland would cease work on the day of the funeral, and there would not be a dance in the same townsland for at least three months. The relatives would not attend a

7 Collected by Thomas Carey, teacher, of Adamstown, from Denis Kane of Courthoyle, a farmer, whose informant was his mother. IFC 750: 133–49, written in 1940.

dance or a game for a couple of years. The family of the deceased was very particular about giving the clothes away for the dead; because the old people always said that "if the clothes were not given away, the soul would be naked in the next world".

Salt was always carried, tied in a paper, in a person's pocket. It was believed that, by carrying the salt, the carrier would not be molested by anything evil.

Most of the children's clothes were made by the *bean an tí* [woman of the house] from flannelette. Red petticoats, white pinafores, and differently coloured frocks. The clothes were worn down to the mouths of the boots, which came up half way on the legs. Boys were dressed like girls up to the age of ten, and sometimes longer, but the boys' hair was cut at the age of six. The children used always show off their new clothes, and mothers used talk a lot about them to others.

Shifts were made from flannel. The well-off women wore calico ones. They were all white in colour. Under-petticoats were also flannel, always white. They were fastened down the front with buttons or with hooks and eyes. They were very tight, with high necks and were boned downwards. They all had short sleeves, and very wide neck-kerchiefs were greatly used. They were knotted under the chin, except a few people who used knot them at the back of the neck. They were never bought ready-made. People used buy the material, which was a spotted red, by the yard, and made the neckerchiefs themselves.

Skirts were usually made from wool and navy blue in colour. They were dyed by the elderberry or blackberry juice. They were very wide, and were kept wide by hoops which were inserted in the tail, and could be taken out if desired. They had a border of white calico. The bodice was always worn over the skirt.

Hood cloaks were worn greatly in this district. They were big loose shapeless cloaks of navy blue, or of black colour. They were made by the dressmaker. They were gathered in about the neck, and there was a band put on all around to the front where it was fastened with one hook-and-eye. The whole cloak depended on this one fastening. There was a hood, the head of which was attached to the cloak and could come down over the head to the eyes, but it was usually thrown back out of the way. A white cap made from fine linen was worn under the hood. It was frilled all around with homemade lace, but was usually covered by the hood, so that only a strip of lace could be seen across the forehead. The white cap used not be taken off, except when working at home. When visiting the cloak would be taken off when entering the house, but the cap would be left on. There were no hats worn then.

The poorer people wore plaid shawls and the more well-off ones wore shawls made from something like serge, but it wasn't the real serge. The general colour was brown with a faint white stripe for the "big people" and plain black for the poorer people. They were doubled corner-wise and pinned across the chest. There were never ribbons nor combs worn in the hair, to my remembrance.

Bonnets were worn in later years rather than the hut cloaks. They were made from plaited rushes and were dyed black. They were small and close-fitting, and the shawls were worn over them.

Straw hats were worn in summertime. They were something in the shape of an umbrella, because they were so wide. They had a small crown just to fit the head, but had a great big wide leaf. The hats were kept on by a string under the chin, because with any gust of wind the hat would fly off, it was so wide.

Elastic boots were always worn in olden times. The elastic was inserted in the boot from the "mouth" down to below the ankle. There were no toecaps on the boots. The leather would meet the elastic from the toe; then there was only one joining around the elastic.

The favourite colours were pink, red and blue. Pink or red for a little girl; blue for a boy. Green was considered very unlucky – "Green for Grief".

New clothes were generally bought in May. Usually worn first time at Mass. The children would be sent to a neighbour's house, or a nearby relative to show off the clothes.

Tailors went from house to house to make men's clothes. They never make women's clothes. Tailors made boys' and men's clothes.

MORE LORE ABOUT DRESS [8]

Men's dress in olden times   More than sixty years ago the styles in men's clothes or mode of dress were mainly two. *Sunday and "state occasion" style*: the knee breeches of frieze and corduroy, more generally the latter; the long-swallow-tailed coat; the white linen shirt with high peaked collar; the stout boots called "pumps"; white or blue "blossom" stockings; the "beaver" hat or the "half-beaver". *Working clothes*: these consisted of the corduroy breeches and the flannel bainín, old "pumps" and stockings (but clean), an old hat and sometimes a fur or a hand-knitted cap.

The corduroy knee-breeches had three brass buttons in the lower end of each leg on the outside. The swallow-tailed-coat was made of blue frieze made from the wool of the sheep on the form. Three brass buttons ornamented its

8 Compiled in 1940 by Mary B. Dunphy, retired National School teacher, of 69 The Irishtown, New Ross. IFC 750: 164–84.

straight front. It was cut across straight at the waist and then straight down to hips where it swept out in a curve, making a big long tail which gradually narrowed till it reached the "gams" – where it ended. "The brass buttons shone like 'goold' " so my informants expressed it. "The tail of the coat seen on a man on horseback was 'a sight'," they said; "it stood straight out and up according to the velocity with which he was travelling." The shirt was made of linen spun from flax grown on the farm; the front was made of finer spun linen than that in the body; the collar was attached to the shirt, and as high as to tip the ears, "two front points standing out like a cow's horns, as high as the man's mouth and out inches beyond it," said my informants.

All menfolk were immaculate in trousers and shirt on Sunday. The women prided themselves in turning out the men to mass on Sundays in spotless shirts and corduroys. To this end the wash tub was ever busy in the home and the "beetle" at the wells and streams. A wide black silk tie "bowed" kept the high collar fastened. This was called the cravat." The "pumps" were stout boots or rather something between a boot and a shoe as far as the "uppers" were concerned – not quite so high as a boot, and not quite so low cut as a shoe – and they were tied with leather laces called "fungs". The long stockings were home-knitted from wool carded at home by the women of the house. They were either the natural white of the wool, or a pale blue called "blue blossom" dyed at home. The beaver hat, and the "half-beaver", called in these parts "a Newtownbarry hat", was a tall hat that stood almost a foot high and gave its wearer a very commanding appearance. Though it looked quite heavy, it was nothing of the sort – being made of the finest materials; the "hatter's plush" which we know and appreciate so much would be coarse and cheap-looking beside the material used in "the beaver hat" of almost a century ago.

"A bold peasantry – their country's pride." The men coming from mass in any rural district in these parts sixty to eighty years ago were a grand sight. Can you not imagine them! Hundreds of tall beavers, snow-white shirt fronts and breeches, gleaming brass buttons returning the glitter of the morning sun – and all carrying on lively conversation and banter. Not infrequently politics are being discussed and as these were stirring times fraught with many (considered then) revolutionary movements – the "anti-tank-gun" to the various Coercion Acts of the British – feeling ran very high and glorious patriotism oozed from every pore!

Some of the outdoor dress of women in olden times "Paletot" (Palletó) [was] the name given to the long overcoat of any style worn by women; any old coat was called a paletot. A "Dolman" was a half cape with "paw" holes and sometimes half sleeves – this garment was made of a light material, cashmere often, and trimmed with frills and lace. The hooded cloak was very commonly worn in these parts fifty to seventy and more years ago. Yards of lovely cloth went to make it. Cloakmakers did a good trade. A black satin apron and gloves completed this picturesque costume.

Women's dress in olden times   This consisted of an inner white linen or calico garment called a "chemise" by the more refined, and a "shift" by the working classes (a loose garment); a bodice made of calico and stiffened by whalebone or more often by "sallys" and buttoned down the front with strong white bone buttons (this was the predecessor to the corset); two flannel petticoats, one white, the other dark blue; a tight-fitting white calico bodice; a jacket fairly loose made of "linsey"; a skirt of "linsey" also. Over all these she wore a neckerchief, plain grey and sometimes shepherd's plaid, and a check apron. She wore the neckerchief cornerwise and tucked the two corners in front, right under the belt of the check apron.

The cape cloak, called also the Corporation cloak, was worn in these parts too but was not as popular as the hooded cloak. It was like the hooded cloak without the hood and with the addition of a cape which came to the hips.

The shawl was worn cornerwise – one corner down the middle of the back about eighteen inches from the ground, the other two corners hung down in front same length. The shawl was worn from the shoulders. The head-dress was either a smaller shawl (headkerchief) worn also cornerwise, or a straw bonnet. Both shawls and bonnets were home-made.

The frilled cap   Beautiful white caps with very fine frills were worn on the head, and women vied with each other in the making and laundering and ironing of them. There was a special iron for them called the "tally iron" and sometimes again called "the dolly". The poorer woman, who had not this iron special for the frills, worked in her frills with her three middle fingers and the flat iron.

The age at which the cap was worn   Marriage, not age governed its wearing! Married women wore the frilled cap, and to prove that they donned it at a very early age; the writer knows for certain that her own grandma, who was noted for her beautiful caps, died at the early age of thirty-two years. The cap was made of fine muslin and its chief object seemed to be the *insignia of marriage*. The frilled cap and hooded cloak had to be donned by all girls after marriage, so my oldest informant tells me.

Wool and flax were the products of the farm and they were manufactured in the home. It is truly amazing to hear the tales of the fireside industry that was carried on by the women during the nights, especially the long winter nights in addition to their long daily household tasks: they carded and spun the wool and flax and made the thread into woollen and linen cloth, and "linsey". Then their scissors and needle got busy and they made all the wearing apparel for their children and themselves. They made the beautiful white linen shirts and the long stockings for their menfolk, and into the latter their deft fingers wove the most beautiful patterns.

The rabbit contributed dinner as now, but the older housewife knew how to "cure" the skin, and convert it into a comfortable work-a-day cap for her husband or grown son.

Rockets and Gally Gaskins Strange as it may seem, little boys were not tucked into trousers sixty to eighty and more years ago, till they were seven or eight and even nine years of age. They were tucked into a short little "drawers" made of red plaid, a couple of petticoats and an outer dress. The red plaid drawers was called a "Gally Gaskins" and the outer loose dress was called a "rocket". The Gally Gaskins, petticoats and rocket were worn by boys until seven years and longer of age.

Tailors were numerous in old times but they were not noted for fitting, nor were the people exacting in that respect. "Ballyverneen where they hanged the tailor" is a Co. Kilkenny expression. This townland is situated nine miles west from New Ross, on the Kilkenny side of the river. The story goes that he made the clothes so badly, and "fitted" so slovenly, even for these unexacting times, that his customers hanged him.

Handy women on the needle abounded and "earned their bread" by sewing either at home, or in the houses of their patrons. These women never "served their time", as the saying goes, but they ripped the old worn clothes and took the pattern from them.

The spinning wheel turned out the natural colour of the wool. This was dyed black with logwood; brown with copperas; blue with indigo. Each home had its dye pot, a necessary corollary of the spinning wheel. Every woman who could spin could dye – and that was every woman in the countryside. The logwood, copperas and indigo were sold in the grocers and hardware shops and quite a quantity could be obtained for a trifle. There were no bright colours in dress of women or men in these old times, and so a congregation was only brightened up by the sparkling whiteness of the shirts and "corduroys" of the men.

School children's wear Boys up to 14–15 and 16 years wore short trousers and a "jacket" with no collar or lapels. A white collar similar to what nurses on duty wear now was worn over this jacket. Long ribbed stockings and stout boots with a large "catcher" of web at back and hooks in front. A "Scotch" cap completed the outfit, and the boys' outfit was homespun and homemade – homemade by the women of the house. Schoolgirls wore very loose fitting pinafores then called "bibs" – the better class wore ones made of linen, "diaper" (a lovely linen with a small diamond pattern) or Scotch holland (a strong hard linen something like that used in window blinds to-day) – the poorer class wore ones made of a cotton check.

DYEING BONNETS AND SILK [9]

Chip and straw bonnets may be dyed black by boiling them for four hours in a strong liquor of logwood adding a little green copperas [ferrous sulphate] occasionally. Let the bonnets remain in the liquor all night; then take them out to dry in the air. If the black is not satisfactory, dye again after drying. Rub inside and outside with a sponge moistened in fine oil. Then block.

Bleaching straw bonnets: wash them in pure water, scrubbing them with a brush. Then put them into a box in which has been set a saucer of burning sulphur. Cover them up so that the fumes may bleach them.

Silks dyed yellow: take clear wheat bran liquor (fifteen pounds) in which dissolve three quarters of a pound of alum; boil the silks in this for two hours until the colour is good.

How starch and soap were made

STARCH [10]

The way they used to make starch long ago was to grate the potatoes and put them into a basin with water on them and leave them resting for a time. Then the water was drained off and a white substance remained at the bottom called starch.

Long ago the people would not buy the starch. They used to make the starch with potatoes. The people used to get potatoes, cut them and put them in a dish of water for about two or three weeks, and every second day they steeped them and put clean water on them. Then about the end of the week they

9 Informant: Peggy Morris, Drinagh, of St John of God Convent School, The Faythe, Wexford (Sister M. de Sales, teacher), in 1938. IFCS 881: 432–3. 10 Two recipes from pupils of the Christian Brothers' School, Wexford (Brother Healy, teacher), 1939; the first was collected by Edward O'Toole of Commercial Quay from Pat Tierney of Commercial Quay, aged 66; the second was collected by Nicholas Saunders of 23 Green Street, Wexford, from Mrs Lacey of 5 White Mill Road, aged 84.IFCS 881: 222–3.

would be as white as snow and then the people used to starch the clothes with starch.

SOAP [11]

About forty years ago most of the big families round Ballycanew made all their own soap. The following receipt was used in "Springmount", Ballycanew: 7 lbs clarified fat; 1 lb caustic soda; ½ gal. water.

Method: Boil fat in water. When cold, lift and scrape off sediment from the bottom. Put water in earthenware vessel. Add soda and stir with stick till dissolved. Have grease and soda at same heat, that is, just lukewarm. Slip fat into caustic soda water. Stir till thick as honey. Have ready box lined with calico. Pour contents into it and cover and stand in warm place till set. Cut in bars and stand a couple of weeks.

Beliefs about a clean hearth, dirty water and salt [12]

The hearth is swept clean before going to bed; dirty water thrown out, and clean water left in, because "the Good People (the fairies) like to find it so".

You may borrow salt from a neighbour but it is never lucky to return it. If you spill some, throw it over your left shoulder. You should never "help" anyone to salt, that is, put it on their plate, "for if you help them to salt, your help them to sorrow".

How they built houses long ago [13]

First they used to cut out square pieces of rock and clean them until they were free from dirt. Then they got liquid and mud and mixed it with gravel and then they put the mud and gravel into moulds. Then they used to put the tops on the moulds and put them into a big oven to set. After three days they were taken out and left on the ground to dry. These mud bricks were put at the bottom of the house and then a kind of cement was made to stick the blocks together; this cement was made of powdery chalk and gravel mixed

---

11 Collected by Caitlín Maybury of Gorey, a teacher in Ballycanew School, Gorey, in 1938. IFCS 890: 12.   12 Narrated by Seán Ó Broin of Gorey, a teacher in Castletown School, in 1938. IFCS 888: 196–7.   13 Account written by Thomas Nolan of 31 Hill Street, Wexford, in 1938. Thomas was a pupil of Brother Healey in Wexford Christian Brothers' School; his informant was Mrs Redford of Clonard, Wexford, aged 79. IFCS 881: 270.

with water. Then the bricks and squares were cemented together. The roof was made of the bark of trees.

Descriptions of old houses

FROM TAGOAT [14]

The houses had no windows but instead of them there were small holes in the walls; and when a storm came on the holes were stuffed with sacks. The floors were usually made of yellow clay but sometimes cobble stones were embedded in it. Every house had a half door with a whole one inside it, and many have them still.

Turf, beanstalks and faggots were used as fuel.

Dips supplied light; they were made by dipping a cord in grease and letting it dry; and dipping it again and again until it was sufficiently thick. Buachalláns, small hand lamps and home-made candles were also used as a means of giving light at night.

Old houses were built of mud with thatched roofs. The thatch was made from oaten straw by those who were rich, the thatch being obtained after the threshing of the oats. Those who had no straw thatched the roofs with reeds and rushes which were obtained plentifully in the bogs and marshes. When the straw thatch was worn, it was thatched over with heather which was obtained in Ballycrane, Tagoat.

There was a kind of bed beside the fire in every house called a shakedown. This was folded up as a table in the daytime and it served as a bed at night. Sometimes people lay down on it when taking their "entete",[15] which was about two hours rest after dinner. The fireplace was usually at the gable end of the house and sometimes in the middle of the floor.

The front of the chimney was made of bricks and sometimes mud and stones.

FROM BREE [16]

Some of the old houses long ago were thatched. The thatch was got from straw, or reeds that grew by the River Slaney. Most of the old houses had a bed in the kitchen. It was placed by the fire and could be closed up like a box

14 Collected by Peter Carroll of Streamstown, Tagoat, a pupil of Tagoat School (Patrick Colfer, teacher), in 1938. His informant was Mrs Catherine Colfer of the same address. IFCS 879:126–7.   15 Probably from the Old French verb *entoitier* "to shelter (indoors)". Dinner was, and is, the midday meal – lunch.   16 Collected from William Rossiter and Mrs Ellen Rossiter of Ballyhogue, Bree, in 1937, by Mrs Margaret Cahill, teacher. IFCS 902: 228–9.

or a table in the daytime. It was called a settle-bed or a box-bed. The fireplace was usually at the gable-end of the house. Many of the old houses had no glass in the windows. Boards were used instead of glass. Sometimes a kind of little door fastened with a hook was used to cover the window-spaces. The walls were made of clay and stones and were very thick. The floors were made of clay. Half-doors were very common at one time, and some can be seen still. They were used for keeping out chickens, pigs and hens. They were handy for people bringing in turf or sticks. Turf and sticks were burned in the fire. Turf was got in Kearns' field of Tinnakilly; the field is still called the turf bog.

Furniture[17]

Half doors were very much in vogue eighty years or so ago. They are very few now and getting fewer every day, even in the countryside.

Half-boarded-up windows (shop windows) used to be seen in shops here and there throughout town and country seventy and eighty years ago.

Tables hinged to walls were and are still in vogue where space in kitchens is small.

Wooden fans for blowing the fire were in vogue over sixty years ago. Some are still in use here and there throughout the country.

Three-cornered presses may be seen in many of the old-fashioned houses in town and country. Their diamond-shaped glass panes are very quaint-looking. They are hung at right-angled corners and are the real sign of the "good old times".

Home-made toys[18]

Dolls were made out of white cloth and stitched up in the form of a doll. Then sawdust was put in it. It was marked on the face with red ink or blue for

17 Notes collected by Mary B. Dunphy of The Irishtown, New Ross, in 1940, from Brigid Turner, aged 103, of Lacken, about four miles from New Ross. IFCS 618: 7.   18 Written by Bridget Doyle of Nash, a pupil at Gusserane School parish of Tintern, in 1938 (Mrs Corish, teacher). IFCS 872: 177–81.

the purpose of making the eyes nose and mouth; then half way up the legs for shoes and stockings.

Rattle-horses were also made out of seven rushes and a stone put in the middle of it to make the rattle.

Necklaces were made out of daisies. You got one daisy and put a hole in the stem of the other daisy through it and so on until you had it long enough to go around your neck. Necklaces were also made from Johnny Magoreys [rose hips] by putting a hole in the gorey and then putting thread in the holes and so on until it's long enough.

Cars were made from a box with polish boxes under it for wheels.

Whistles   The way to make a whistle is get a piece of a sally stick and hammer it until the skin moves on it. Then pull the skin off and cut three holes in the middle of the stick. Put on the skin again and cut a hole in it and the whistle is made.

A Turnip Man is made from a big turnip. Cut the turnip in half and scrape it clean. Then cut two holes for the eyes and one for the nose. Cut a long line for the mouth and then put a candle inside to make it bright. Then it is made.

Lanterns were made of tin which was pierced with holes with one panel of glass to show the light.

A hooter   Get a tailor's reel and scoop out a hole. Have it broad at one end; at the other end of the hole stick a little piece of tin like a reed. When you blow through it, it will make a funny sound; then you have a nice hooter made.

Dancing masters were cut out of wood. His arms are shaped out. There is wire at his knees so that he can bend them freely. His eyes are marked with a red iron.

Rocking horses were cut from wood, the legs and neck and head joined on to the body and bolted on a board with rockers under it.

Jack in the box   A square box was made with a clasp on it, a head was stuck inside and when the box was opened out jumped Jack in the box.

A potato-pig was made from an oval-shaped potato, the mouth was cut on one end of the potato and the eyes nose and ears were also shaped; four matches were stuck in the flat side of the potato to act as legs; a half match was put in the remaining end of the potato for the tail. Then the pig was made.

Games I play[19]

A blindfold game   This game which I am going to describe is not very common, but at the same time it causes fun and amusement. Only two players are necessary. It is an indoor game. Two handkerchiefs, a spoon, and some eatables are required.

The two players are seated on two chairs opposite each other, but a few yards away. One of the blindfolded parties is presented with a spoon on which is put a sweet. Now this child is asked to try and put the contents of the spoon into the other player's mouth without ever moving out of their position or ever speaking to each other.

Colours   Twenty or thirty children are needed to play this game. It is an outdoor game. A devil, an angel and a captain are selected.

The devil is put a fair distance from the other children, who are standing in a row, and the angel likewise. The captain calls each child in turn and gives her a colour like blue, black, green, brown, etc. No child should know her neighbour's colour.

When every child has got a colour, the captain says, "Who's there?" The angel answers, "The angel with the golden hair." The captain now says, "Walk in and point me out the blue." If the angel cannot point to the girl who represents blue, the captain says, "Go back and learn your abc's." The devil does the same.

If the angel or devil points to the right person, she goes to the one who points to her. Whoever gets the most children wins the game.

Sardines   Sardines is an outdoor game. Any number of children can play it. The children are put in a line and the person that twenty falls on must go off and hide.

When he has hidden, the others go look for him, and the first that finds him stays with him until the others find them. The person who finds the

19 Accounts furnished by Ena Murphy, Mary Redmond, Henry Cullen, John Tierney, Louis Rossiter, John Cahill, Edith O'Byrne, John Rowe, pupils of Lady's Island School, in 1938 (G. Ó Murthuile, teacher). IFCS 878: 208–21.

hidden boy first goes off the next time and the others go to look for him and so on like that.

Stooping tig   A number of boys is selected and put standing in a line. One boy is picked out and says, "T.i.g. tig you have the old Irish stooping tig." The boy on which "tig" falls has the tig. The other boys commence to run while the boy with the tig follows them. When the boy with the tig draws near, the other boys stoop down. While in that position the boy with the tig cannot give them the tig. But if he is able to catch them while running or standing upright, he can give them the tig. Any number of boys can play this game.

Ball in the hat   This game provides great sport. First of all, a number of hats are put in a row. Secondly the players stand at a distance away from the hats and one of the children throws a ball towards one of the hats. They do this one by one. Whoever puts the ball in the hat first has to put a stone in it. This is continued and the person who has twelves stones in his hat first is chased and hit with the ball. He also wins the game.

Bird catching   Every Sunday afternoon, I go to see my friend, Jim Murphy. Sometimes we play games, and one game we often play is birdcatching.
    The articles we use in catching the birds are a slate, three twigs and some oats. Each person selects a spot which he thinks is frequented by the birds. Here he digs a small hole, just large enough to contain a fat tom-tit, and puts some oats in a conspicuous place in it. First one twig is fixed firmly in the hole from side to side. Another is then balanced on this but not touching the sides of the hole. Lastly the third twig is put standing on these two to hold up the slate. If the middle is touched, the whole structure collapses and the slate falls, completely covering the hole.

Skittles   Any number can play skittles. A ring should be drawn on the ground, 1½ ft in diameter. Small blocks called skittles are placed about 4 ins apart around this ring. The skittles should be about 3 or 4 inches in height and should be cylindrical. Each skittle is numbered. The numbers are 1, 3, 4, 5 and 10. Ten is called "possible". The players use what are called "lobbers" or blocking wood and those are also cylindrical. Three "lobbers" are used. The players stand about 8 yds from the ring, and each player fires three times. When the first player has fired, he adds the numbers on the skittles which he has knocked out of the ring. The others do the same when their turn comes. A game of 20, 30, 40 or any big number can be played. If a player required three to win, he must hit the three or the one three times. If he hits more than three, he loses the game. Whoever scores the required number first, wins.

Rounders   First of all girls are collected and two captains selected. Each of those calls her team and having done this they "toss up" to see which team will have the ball first. The field is then marked with four stones – one at the top, one at the bottom and one at each side. The team at the top of the field throws the ball to the opposite team. If they succeed in getting the ball without letting it fall to the ground, they come to the top. If they let it fall, they stay where they are and the girl who threw the ball runs from one stone to the other. If the ball hits her while she is running, she is out and one of her partners must try to get her in again by running around without being hit. The game is continued like this until one of the teams scores twenty. Whoever scores 21 wins the game.

Hide and seek   My favourite game is hide and seek. It is an outdoor game, and any number can play. A player is selected to count. The player on whom 20 falls turns his back while the others hide. When they are hidden, they shout out "cuckoo", and the person in the den tries to find them. If anyone is caught before he reaches the den, that person has to "lie" next time. If no one is caught, the last person in must lie.

An indoor game   I like a wet day because my brother and I have great fun playing a game. The game has no particular name but we call it "Hiding the thimble".

We toss a penny to see who is the first to hide the thimble. The boy who is not hiding it shuts his eyes. When the other boy has hidden the thimble, he says "Ready". The other boy then looks for it. If he finds it, he hides it and the other boy must look for it. If he doesn't find it, the other boy hides it again.

Prisoners' base   Prisoners' base is a very exciting game, which we often play in school. A large number is required to play, and the children are divided into two groups with a captain for each group. There is an even number with each captain. The lower end of the playground is used as one base and the top part is used as the other. When the game begins children from one base come up more than halfway to the other base. Then the children from the other base run out and try to catch them. When anyone is caught, he is kept as a prisoner by the children of that base. The children of the other base try to catch the prisoners back again. Whichever base has caught the most prisoners when the time is up, wins the game.

Buying and selling[20]

Shops were not common in olden times. People had to go to the nearest town to make purchases. Buying and selling was carried on after Mass. It is not carried on now. Boots, stockings, dress, bread and butter etc. were sold. Money was not always given in exchange for goods. Markets were held in former times. They were held in Waterford and New Ross. The market is held there still. There are accounts of hucksters, pedlars, and dealers who visited the district and were buying feathers and rags. Some coins and types of money have gone out of use. Fourpenny-pieces are gone out of use. They do not come still.

My mother told me this.

Shops was not common in olden times. People used to go around with baskets on their arms to sell groceries. They used to give rags and bottles instead of money for goods.

My father told me this.

Means of transport: the trap[21]

Almost every household in Bannow has a "trap" – a rather wide, flat, light spring car with very wide laces. The car is drawn by a pony which invariably trots at great speed – often carrying five persons. Donkeys draw smaller traps. The occupants of the traps sit with their legs hanging outside – even girls and women. In wet weather the women sit in the body of the trap, which invariably has a fine bed of dry straw covered with a rug.

Spinning and weaving[22]

The old people were great experts in many kinds of handicrafts, namely spinning and weaving. There was a spinning-wheel in almost every house which was used by the women and girls of the family for turning out their own cotton thread and worsted. Cotton thread was got from flax and worsted was woven into coarse tweed which was worn by the men and boys in those days.

20 Two accounts, the first by Bridie Molloy of Whitechurch, New Ross, a pupil at Aclare School (M.E. Campbell, teacher); the second by Patrick Fitzgerald of Piltown, New Ross, a pupil at the same school in 1938. IFCS 873: 345–6.   21 Supplied by Thomas Walsh, teacher at Bannow School, in 1938. IFCS 876: 27.   22 Related by Ita White of Heavenstown, Cleariestown. She was a pupil of Mrs Christine Byrne at Cleariestown School in 1938. IFCS 873: 245.

A kind of material called "linsey" was spun from the cotton thread. This was probably another name for linen which was also woven from the flax into under-clothing and other coarse cloth.

The Lace School at the Carmelite Convent, New Ross[23]

This lace school – discontinued these thirty years – was a most up-to-date one under the supervision of the Carmelite Nuns. "Point Lace" and "crochet" were executed in the school. The fame of the New Ross lace resounded through the world. It won prizes at all exhibitions. The beauty of the design and the perfection of the execution in fragile thread were the marvel of the lace world.

At the Chicago Exhibition in 1886 workers from this famous school plied their needles in the presence of huge admiring crowds. Lady Aberdeen was in charge of them. Many Royal orders came to the school through her and through Baroness Burdett Coutts.

When the old lace workers died, there were none to take their place. It was too tame an occupation for the younger generation. Besides, it was not a very money-making occupation considering the amount of time and care it demanded.

Miss Margaret Fitzharris was the premier "point lace" worker. She represented the school at the Chicago Exhibition. Other lace workers included Miss Bridget Howlett, Mrs Eliza Wherry Roche (the premier "crochet" worker) and Miss Anty Whitty.

The making of baskets and churns[24]

In olden times Francie Kehoe of Rathimney, Gusserane, New Ross, Co. Wexford, who was my grandfather, made baskets and beehives. He made the baskets out of sallies. He put the sallies in and out through each other. He had smaller sallies for the middle of the basket and one big sally for the mouth of the basket. He put two handles in it; he did this by getting a few thin sallies and twisting them around each other. Then he fastened them to the big sally at the mouth and the basket was complete. All the farmers in the district

23 Written by Mary B. Dunphy of The Irishtown, New Ross, a teacher at St Leonard's School, Ballycullane, in 1938. IFCS 871: 123. 24 Written in 1937 in Gusserane School, parish of Tintern, by Mary Kehoe of Rathimney. Mary was a pupil of Mrs Brigid Corish, and her informant was John Kehoe, aged 72, of the same address. IFCS 873: 401–2.

bought baskets from him. They used them for carrying the lime to the kiln to be burned and for gathering potatoes.

He made the beehives out of wheaten straw. He got bunches of straw and arranged them; then he sewed them together. Briars cut in two were used for sewing them; this was done like darning. He continued that until he had all the bunches of straw sewed together. Then he got a big bunch of straw and he sewed it around the top. Then the beehive was complete.

James Kehoe and Paddy Kehoe of Rathimney made churns and keelers out of wood. They earned their living by making these because very few could make these in olden times. These two men were called "The Coopers".

Candlemaking[25]

About eighty years ago a certain man named Ned Daly lived where Gregory Furlong is living now. He was a relation of Luke Daly, the hedge schoolmaster who taught at Katty's Rock, Boley. He was a tallow-candle maker by trade; he made them for the people of the district.

He made two sorts of candles; one sort was made from bog-dale [bog deal] and the other was made from tallow liquid which was got from the fat of the sheep. This was boiled in a large pot; then the pot was taken up; he cut thin cord in foot lengths and dipped them in the pot of tallow, one at a time and let them dry. He repeated this until the candles were thick enough, then he sold them to the people.

Bog-dale candles   The dale was taken out of the log and cut into lengths which were left by the fire until they were seasoned. Then they were cut into thin foot lengths. They used flint and steel and brown paper steeped in salt-petre to light them. They struck the flint and steel together and lit the brown paper. It was from this the dale candles were lit.

Nailmaking[26]

About forty years ago two men named Nicholas and William Scallan made "hob" nails in a small forge adjoining their home.

The iron from which the nails were made was bought in town. It was

25 Written by Mary Kehoe of Rathimney in IFCS 873: 403. See above. Mary's informant was Peter Kehoe, aged 56, of the same address.   26 Related by Martin Fortune of Kilmannon, Cleariestown, a pupil of Mrs M. McGrath, Forth School, in 1938. IFCS 873: 312.

called "nail iron". Each was triangular in shape and about a quarter of an inch thick.

To make them, one end of the iron was put in the fire which was red hot. When taken out, the top was sharpened. A piece about half an inch long was cut off and placed in a "shape" or mould. This was a block of iron with a cavity the size and shape of the nail to be made.

The red hot iron was hammered into this mould. When quite cold, the nail was taken from the shape.

The Whitechurch forge[27]

There are two forges in my parish. The name of the people that are working them are Bill Brien and Matt Bowe. They have been smiths since their fathers' time. Bill Brien's forge is in the village of Whitechurch. It is near a cross-roads. It is a small forge. It has a slated roof. The door is divided into two parts. There is one fireplace in the forge. The bellows is made of timber and leather. It is beside the fireplace. The bellows was made locally. He uses a poker for stirring the fire. He uses a tongs for taking the red iron out of the fire. He uses a hammer to make the iron the shape of the horse-shoe. The smith shoes horses and asses. He shoes the horses and asses outside the door.

Poteen making[28]

The making of poteen is an illegal practice. It is made in very few places in any part of Eire, except in the West.

It was made in this district, at the foot of the Blackstairs mountains in Carrigeen Grange up to the year 1922.

The house in which it was made is situated, near the source of the River Boro, and the Blackstairs mountains are at the back of the house.

For the making of poteen it is necessary to have the still near a river, as running water is required. Poteen is made from barley. The barley must be steeped for nine days until it starts to bud. Then it is left to ferment for some

27 Related by John Hearne of Ballykelly, New Ross, a pupil of M.R. Campbell at Aclare School, in 1939. IFCS 873: 326.   28 An account written by an anonymous pupil of Rathnure School, parish of Killanne, in 1938 (Catherine Bolger, teacher). Thomas Coady, aged 85, was the informant. IFCS 900: 215–17.

days. When it has fermented, it is put into a large vessel called a "copper" and boiled. There is a coiled pipe called a "worm" going from the "copper" into the river. The steam from the "copper" passes through the "worm", and it is necessary to have it in running water, so that the vapour will become liquid quickly. This liquid is the poteen, and it is far stronger than any "spirits". A few spoonfuls of this liquid when it is diluted makes the equivalent of a five-naggin bottle of whiskey. Very little of it would make a man drunk unless he was accustomed to taking it. A great many of those who manufacture it consume a great deal of the liquid without making them drunk. Sometimes it is called "The Mountain Dew".

The "still" and "worm" belonging to the poteen-maker were seized on by the Civic Guards, Enniscorthy, in 1922. There were some Irish Republican Army boys "on the run" hiding in the mountains. The Guards got information, and went on their track. They happened to go into the house to make a search, and caught the daughter boiling the "copper" over a big fire. They seized on all, arrested the poteen-maker, and brought the "still", and "worm" to the Civic Guard Station, Enniscorthy. The man was heavily fined, and since that time no one in this district ever attempted to make poteen.

Food

TWO MEALS A DAY [29]

The people of olden times only ate two meals a day. They always did a great deal of work before their breakfast. In the mornings they used to eat porridge and milk, and for their dinner they had potatoes and salt. Goat's milk and potatoes was the staple food.

The table was placed on the centre of the floor and the people sat around it. The bread was made of yellow-meal. Meat was seldom eaten except at Christmas.

BOXTY BREAD [30]

(b) Boxty bread is made in the following manner. A number of raw potatoes are procured, and grated. The raw pulp is then left on a damp cloth and all the moisture is pressed out. Some boiled potatoes are crushed on the losaid [kneading tray] and the raw pulp and a pinch of salt and soda are added. The mixture is then kneaded into cake form and cut into squares. These are spread

29 Collected by an unnamed pupil of Loftus Hall School, parish of Templetown (The Hook), in 1934 (Brigid O'Hara, teacher).IFCS 870: 28.   30 Collected by Mary Walsh, a pupil of Ballycullane School (John Doyle, teacher), in 1937.

on the floured griddle and baked for half an hour. They are then taken up, spread with butter and eaten while hot.

SOWANS [31]

In olden times the people used to steep oaten meal in water and leave it for some time. Then they stirred it and put it through a sieve. The juice that came through was a whitish colour, this they used with porridge when milk was scarce in winter.

31 Collected by Betty Doyle, St John's Road, Wexford, a pupil of St Mary's Convent, Wexford, in 1938 (Sister Brendan, teacher). IFCS 881: 321.

Farming lore

Farming methods[32]

Years ago the people had a very different and slow way of doing the work on the land in comparison with the way they do it now.

They used to get up very early in the morning about three or four o'clock.

The corn used to be sown in what were called ridges, the whole length of the field and twelve sods in breadth. From baskets on the men's backs, the seeds would be put in the ground and the furrows would be dug and shovelled up on the ridges. When the harvest time came, all hands in the houses would be up about three o'clock in the morning and they would keep cutting the corn until about eight o'clock in the morning. The weather used to be so warm then that they could not work at it in the daytime and that they should cease at that hour until evening. They would start in the evening for a few hours again. It had all to be cut with the reaping hook and every latch had to be caught in the hand. When the cutting was finished, the corn would be drawn into the haggard and put into stacks of about four horse loads. Then the threshing would start coming on to Christmas. One stack would be put into the barn and one man would be left to thresh it with a flail consisting of two sticks joined by leather and a swivel made from leather also. When they would get a fine day and a good breeze, the corn would be taken out in the haggard and it would be kept tossed up against the wind to blow the chaff and the dirt.

32 Related by Margaret Walsh of Aclare School, Horeswood, to teacher M.E. Campbell, in 1938. IFCS 873: 207–9.

Making butter[33]

Early-rising The farmer and his staff were afoot generally about 4 a.m. or, as one old man put it, "when the stars were still on the sky."

Milking Began by those who had charge. This was done into *pails* (A). These pails when full, were carried on the head. No one could do that now.

Care of the milk This was "set" in what were called *keelers* (B), shallow wooden vessels which used to be scrubbed scrupulously clean. When the cream came to the top, the keelers were skimmed.

The dairy The dairy was filled up with "stillions" or stands all round the walls on which rested the "keelers".

Skimming the cream tub The "keelers" were skimmed with a wooden *skimmer* (C) like a plate and the cream was put in the cream tub.

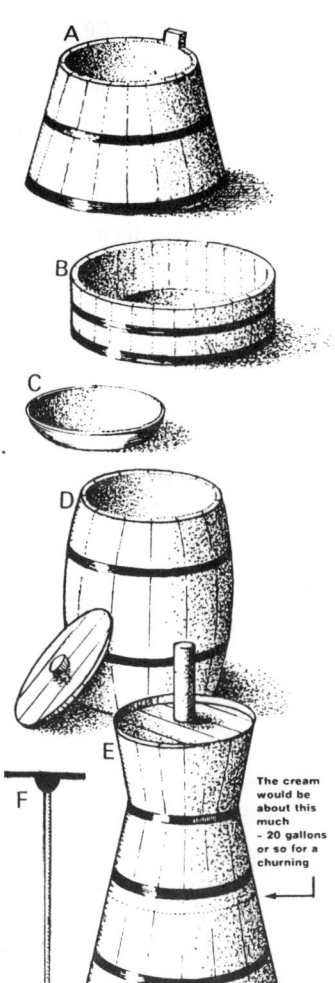

The cream would be about this much – 20 gallons or so for a churning

The old "dash" churn Where there were large herds, churning was done every day or every second day at least, and the butter put into *firkins* (D). These firkins were then taken to the nearest butter-market to be sold.

Butter buyers came from all parts to the butter markets and purchased the firkins of butter.

The "dash" churn (E). Anyone who entered the house while the churning was in progress had to take a hold of the dash to help with two or three strokes: otherwise it was believed the butter or some portion of it would be stolen by that person - or the "good people".

The cream would be about this much – twenty gallons or so for a churning.

(F) = A sketch of the instrument used long ago to test firkin butter

33 Related by Mary B. Dunphy of The Irishtown, New Ross, in 1939. IFC 577: 300–2. Her informants were William Kelly, a native of Ballykelly, a farm labourer, who in turn got his information from his parents, who went from farm to farm, following the work; and Neddy Curran, aged 87, address not given. The illustrations are based on Mary Dunphey's drawings.Farming methods.

How the buyers tested the butter long ago   They carried an instrument like an augur with which they pierced the lid of the firkin and then pushed it down to the bottom of the firkin. The butter filled the cavity of the instrument and the buyer had a sample (in the cavity) of the butter in the firkin.

The firkin and the old "dash" churn have now been superseded by the modern butter box and end-over-end churn and later by the rapidly growing creameries all over the country.

Early-rising has disappeared with the pail and the reaping hook.

The cooper has also disappeared with his noggins, firkins, pails, keelers, tubs, "dash" churns, and the thousand and one wooden vessels which were needed in olden times.

Faggot cutting [34]

"All the old faggot [35] cutters are dead and gone," said an old man (Neddy Curron, 87 years) to me not long ago. Ask him "How did they cut 'faggots'!" and he became reminiscent.

All the old men kept their own "gear" and generally made them themselves. The gear was (1) a leather glove made of horseskin for the left hand, and (2) a "cuff" for the bill-hook. The cuff was made of "uppers" of old boots or other such stuff. The leather glove and the cuff protected the hands from prods of thorns. The bill-hook was adjusted to the right hand by a strap which kept the "cuff" and the bill-hook from slipping. A good faggot cutter would cut 100 faggots a day.

The night of the threshing day was always a merry night given to dancing and singing in most houses. Beer used to be given at threshings in these good old days: barrels, half-barrels, and quarter-barrels being put in according to the size of the threshing. With successive great temperance drives, helped by the more expeditious steam power, beer disappeared from the threshing day menu completely.

The potato crop [36]

We usually sow a half an acre of potatoes. The ground is prepared by means of a pair of horses and a plough. We sow them in drills and when the drills are

34 Also related by Mary B. Dunphy.   35 Faggots: sticks, usually ash, cut for fuel.   36 Related by Kathleen Forristal of Killesk School, Horeswood, to her teacher, Margaret Sutton, in 1938. IFCS 873: 64.

made we spread the manure and then split the drills over the potatoes to cover them. The people in our district usually sow the potatoes with their own help. When the potatoes are up over the ground, the plough is run on the furrow to take the weeds out of them. Some farmers dig their potatoes by means of a plough but the greater part of them dig them with a digger. They are picked into baskets or buckets and put into cars and are then put into pits in the haggard, or into a potato house. There are different varieties of potatoes. The British Queens, and the Kerr Pinks are the most common. The Golden Wonders are an early sort and the best potato for early digging.

Reaping the corn[37]

Reaping the corn in the olden days was a slow job. The hook was a man-killer. The teeth on this hook are like the teeth that are now on a bread-knife, and it was not every man that was able to sharpen these. When a man starts to cut corn at first with a hook he is bound to cut himself, and it is an old saying that you must cut yourself three times before you are a reaper. In the big farmers' places I often saw ten men reaping and there would be about five of them, five of the best, in front. The man leading them would be the best man in the place, and he would be called the leader, and then the man next to him would be called the "neck hook". There were names on them all, but I cannot think of them all now. Each man would take off a space of about two feet, and what he would cut with one movement of the hook would be a handful, and three of these would be a sheaf. It was generally women that used to bind the corn, and three or four of them would be able to bind as much as ten reapers. There was a man one time telling me that he was working in a place, and he never knew whether the dwelling house was thatched or slated for two months. He used to get his breakfast early in the morning, and his supper late at night, and he never saw the house in the day for the first two months.

Harvest home in the 1890s[38]

Bringing in the corn forty years ago was a very exciting job.
    The men were always up very early and they put on their Sunday clothes

37 Collected by Kathleen Walsh, Ballyverogue, a pupil of Aclare School in 1938 (M.E. Campbell, teacher). Informant: Robert Power, Curraghduff, Campile, aged 84. IFCS 873: 144–5.   38 Written by Emma Owens of Lambert Terrace, William Street, Wexford, in 1937. Her teacher was Mrs Victoria Sherwood, St John of God's School, The Faythe. Her informant was Mrs Sherwood of Parnell Street, aged 76. IFCS 880: 195–6.

and their best boots, and had a good wash and shave, which was not a daily occurrence.

The men and sons from the farms around always came to help. Before they could come into town with the corn they had to hire sacks and bring in a sample.

They had to be up and ready by six or seven o'clock. All the sacks were sewn the day before and then, when everything was ready, the horses were yoked and they drove off.

When they came into town, the cars were lined up in a certain place and they went off to sell the corn.

When the work was done, the farmers went into an eating house and made merry and had a good time before going home.

They then did their shopping and when it was dusk the farmers went home.

It is very different now; the lorries go out and they bring in all the corn and the farmers have no fun.

At that time forty years ago or so there was a prosperous distillery in Wexford owned by Devereux.

It was situated on what is still called the Distillery Road. The remains of the building have now been turned into part of Pierce's foundry. There was also a brewery - owned by Wickhams - but it too is now closed.

The barley is sold to the maltsters who ship it to the big distilleries and breweries. All round the town may be seen the malt houses and during the winter the smell of malting is one of the characteristic smells of Wexford.

How barley was brought into Wexford in the old days [39]

The barley was not brought to Wexford forty years ago the same way as it was brought today. It was brought in carts and spring-carts.

The day the barley was brought in was a day out for the farmers. They used to get up very early and put their best clothes on.

They then put the big sacks with the barley in them on the cart and yoked up the horse and drove into town. They then employed some men to carry the sacks into the malt house. When dinner time came, they went to an eating-house and ate a good dinner.

After dinner they went down town and with the money got for the barley

39 Written by Pat Short of St James's, The Folly, Wexford, in 1938. Pat was a pupil of Mrs Victoria Sherwood at St John of God's School, The Faythe. Pat's informant was Bartholomew Coursey, of 1 Lambert Terrace, William Street, aged 92. IFCS 880: 197–8.

they bought their winter supplies. Oil and coal were the main things bought. They went home in the evening well satisfied with the day's work.

Threshing with a flail[40]

Long ago the people used to thresh with a flail. The flail was a piece of long stick with leather in the end of it and another piece of stick joined to it. The people used to thresh in a barn and the barn was a thatched house with a level stone floor. The people used to leave the sheaves in the barn and then thresh it with the flail. When the people used to have a lot of corn they were often months threshing it. After the flail came the horse machine. The horse machine was brought from house to house to thresh, and at night there would be a great dance in the house.

The cultivation of beans[41]

Years ago when beans were grown plentiful this was how the people prepared the fields. First they ploughed the field with a wooden plough or dug it with wooden spades. Then they harrowed it with pieces of wood with long nails driven through them. When they had all the weeds and grass out of it, they would plough it again and then they would keep harrowing it till it was fine enough to make ridges in it. When all the ridges were made, manure was put in them and the beans put on top of the manure and then with some rain and sun they would soon be above the ground. When the time came to pull the beans, many people were got to do the work. When they were pulled, they were tied into sheaves and when they would be dry they would be drawn into the haggard and then the great day would come at the threshing of the beans. The beans were threshed by two men with flails. Then the people would sell the beans and they would burn the stalks.

I remember that when the public road was made from Carrig to Bannow, beans roasted, potatoes and salt was the food of the workers. I remember the road being made and I often saw the men roasting the beans. In olden times beans were sown largely through the country. The ground would be managed like for corn. They would be sown broadcast. They would be cut with a mowing machine, tied into bundles, made into a stack and threshed.

40 Written by Mattie Banville of Barry's Cross, Taghmon, a pupil at Caroreigh School (James Kelly, teacher), in 1938. Mattie's informant was Bessie Banville, Shanoule, Foulksmills. IFCS 883: 73. 41 Collected by Bridie Davey of Grange, a pupil at Bannow School in 1938. Her teacher was Thomas Walsh and her informants were Catherine Dake of Grange, aged 97, and Thomas Morris of Newtown. IFCS 876: 67.

Seaweed as manure[42]

Seaweed (locally called "woar" [from Old English *wār*) has been always used extensively as manure in the district of Bannow and on this account the rents of the holdings in the district were much higher than for similar land in other districts, especially inland. The weed is taken from the beach without any attempt at selection and is regarded as specially suitable for root crops: it is never used for corn or meadow or grassland. Its value lasts for the one crop; hence there is great labour owing to the continual drawing of the woar for use in growing mangolds (always referred to locally as "the mangold"); it is spread in the drills before closing. For turnip crop it is spread on the stubble or red ground and ploughed into the land in late autumn or early spring. For the potato crop it is spread on the stubble and ploughed in, and when land is drilled farmyard manure is added. As a manure for the beet crop it is better to have it ploughed into the soil at winter ploughing. It is specially good for cabbage and is just spread in the drills before closing.

Woar from the various beaches in Bannow School District was confined to the tenants of the Boyse Estate (Boyse family, Bannow House, being land-lords). The woar was to be drawn only from sunrise to sunset and any breach of the rule was reported by the man in charge of the woar for the landlord. Cases were brought to court in Duncormick and offenders fined. Owing to the great value of the weed and the restrictions on the beach, there were often disputes and fighting. A farmer in trying to bring an extra heavy load often got held up, and as passages were narrow the way would be blocked and no others could come in or get out. That would cause a very severe fight. Even to delay talking or smoking would cause trouble. The woar was filled with a three "tag" sprong, and this sprong was made locally in the forge. In winter time the weed was drawn to the headlands in the fields and was repeatedly turned. Sometimes sand was mixed with it. After harvest, before ploughing the stubble or lea, the woar was spread. In May it was drawn and put directly in the drills for mangold crops. There were various places for filling the woar and each tenant had to go to his own special place. Where "bank" (local name for land beside sea)" was high, "gaps" were cut in cliff or bank to the beach. "Barry's Gap", "Harper's Gap", "Wade's Gap" are still to be seen, but several are worn away at the beach and others are in disuse.

---

42 Lore collected by Thomas Walsh, teacher at Bannow School, in 1938. IFCS 876: 31–2.

Lime kilns[43]

About fifty years ago the farmers in our locality manured their land with lime which they burned in old kilns. They had to go to the limestone quarries in Dunkit in the Co. Waterford and bring it by boat to Campile. Then the farmers had to burn the lime in kilns, and leave it burning there for a week. The fire was put out then and the lime taken away and spread on their land.

Our farm animals

OUR ANIMALS [44]

The horses, cows, cattle, sheep, pigs, dogs, cats, ferrets, are the farm and domestic animals at home. The cows' names are: Rosemount, Whitney, Whelan, Carroll, Franco, Kelly, Sutton, Black, and Buzzer. When driving the cows home from a field, I say, "Chew up, chew up," and when calling the calves I say, "Suck, suck." The sowhouse is a long slated building with a slanting concrete floor and a passage before the cow's heads to enable us to feed them without being injured. It also has three doors and twelve separate stalls. It is called a byre. The cows are tied around the neck with a chain tie. In case of a roguing cow, she has to be tied from the horn to the fore leg. Some people tie them with jute ropes. St Benedict's medal is hung in our sowhouse so as to bring luck on the stock.

The horses' names are: The Hunter, Bigbelly, Nellie Lyndy, Tom the Tug, Mollie Bawn, Fleshie, Castlewrath, Agadir, Brighter London, Kyle's Son, Comet and Pollie. When calling the horses we say, "Come, come." The stable is a slated building with a loft overhead, two half doors, and a shuttered window, with a sack and manger to feed the horses out of; the floor is paved and cemented; the horses are tied with a head collar. The fodder consists of hay, oats, and mangolds and they are bedded with barley, oaten or wheaten straw. The horses are clipped when the ploughing season comes or when they are housed for winter and again in the spring. The only famous horse we know of in this locality is Captain Stafford's of Dunmain House, Co. Wexford. He was able to jump a high iron gate with his owner on his back and a child under his owner's arm.

When calling the hens we say, "Tuck, tuck."

---

43 Collected by Baby Colfer, a pupil at Killesk School in 1938. Her informant was her mother; her teacher, Margaret Sutton. IFCS 873: 37.　44 Written in 1938 by Margaret Larkin, The Kyle, Gusserane, New Ross. Her informant was her father; her teacher, Mrs Brigid Corish of Gusserane School. IFCS 871: 384–5.

CARE OF THE ANIMALS [45]

We keep many animals on the farm at home such as cows, pigs, sheep, horses, fowl, and an ass. The cows have got names. These are Judy, Lill, Peggie, Nancy, Eclipse, Dot, Norah and Poll. When driving the cows in or out we say, "Chew on" or "Chew in." When calling calves we say, "Suck, suck." There are a number of stalls in the cowhouse, a stall for each cow. The chains for tying the cows are made from iron. Horses are also tied in stalls; a horse shoe is usually nailed on the stable door. When calling hens we say, "Chuck, chuck," and for ducks we say, "Lute, lute," and for turkeys "Bia, bia." It is said that goats can see the wind. When giving eggs for hatching, it is not lucky to give them for nothing, as this is said to be giving your luck away.

Spades [46]

In an old forge in Ballina, spades and shovels of every description were made.

Pratie spades were made out of a piece of iron about a foot and a half long and about six inches wide. The smith would cut down along the piece of iron about an inch in from the edge down to about six inches. Then he cut the iron across at the five-inch mark and turned down the sixth inch and that formed a step. When that was done, he put three holes an inch wide in rotation in the bar that was left. Those were called "pratie spades".

"Step-spades" were made thus: A piece of iron about eighteen inches long and about six inches wide was procured. Then a set was put in the two sides about six inches from the top. The two edges were then turned in from the cut up, and a block of wood was then wedged between the two bits that were turned in. These were called "step-spades".

Unlucky days to plough [47]

Old customs are still in existence in the townland of Ballygow; it is considered unlucky to plough on Saturday afternoon.

This custom is still in existence, and tradition exists that if this old custom was broken the people would lose their stock-horses, cows, etc.

---

[45] From Nano Harte of Campile, a pupil of Margaret Sutton at Killesk School, in 1938. IFCS 873: 75.   [46] Collected in St Brigid's School, Blackwater (Diarmaid Ó Súilleabháin, teacher), in 1937. The informant was John Cash of Inch, aged 70. IFCS 886: 44.   [47] Collected by Peter Murphy of Bellgrove, a pupil at Duncormack School (P.S. Ahearne, teacher), in 1937. IFCS 877: 34.

The origin of this custom goes back to the time of public penances that were imposed on the townsland a couple of centuries ago.

It is also considered unlucky if a person comes into a field where another man is ploughing and steps across the beam of the plough; so the ploughman unyokes and ceases to work for that day.

It is unlucky too when a person comes into a field and fails to say, "God bless the work."

Protecting animals from the evil eye[48]

Long ago a great many people would tie a little bit of red thread around a beast's tail, so that it could not be "overlooked". There are some people that do it still. Some people up here used to do it. It was done about ten years ago, whether they do it still or not. They made out that when the bit of red thread would be on the tail, no one could overlook the beast (put the evil eye on it). There was great power in the bit of woollen thread, according to them. Of course, there is no mistake but people used to do things like that long ago. Like taking [stealing] butter, and crops, and overlooking animals – that was done; and no mistake.

48 Collected by Thomas Carey from Edward Fitzgerald of Ballinaboola, New Ross, in 1938. IFC 577: 69.

The sea and sailors

Wages and diet on the Wexford schooners[49]

The Master of the schooners had four pound ten or five pound a month, the Mate had three pound fifteen, the A.B. [able-bodied seaman] had three pound ten a month, the Ordinary Seaman or Second Boy had two pound ten and the Boy had a pound a month. They were dieted from the time they left Wexford Quay, but when in Wexford Port they had to supply their own food. These were home-trade wages.

There was no regulation diet for the schooners. There were lashings and leavings of food to be got from the shipping company, but the Masters, as a rule, did not believe in giving too much to the men. There was full and plenty.

Devereux's ships were very well victualled. Devereux's were the biggest ship-owners in the town and had foreign-going barques as well as schooners. There was no check on anything. Devereux's had a yard where the Custom House is now and you went up to this yard with a hand-barrow and got all you wanted of pork and beef. The meat was brought aboard and put into harness casks, into pickle. All this beef and pork came from Devereux's own stock, which he reared and killed on his own land at Ballinagee, about two miles out the Distillery Road. There were two harness casks, one for beef and the other for pork. Every voyage these casks were replenished.

For breakfast there were cold-meat from the day before, tea and ships' biscuits, called "blahs" [from the Irish, *bleathach*]. These were big coarse biscuits, something like the modern cream-cracker, but much harder and tougher.

Dinner: we had meat, cabbage and potatoes for dinner.

Tea: we had meat left over from the dinner and tea and biscuits, for tea.

49 Collected by James G. Delaney from Richard Delaney, aged 80, of Wexford town, in 1954. IFC 1344: 419–21.

There was no supper officially, but we could always get something unknown to the skipper.

Some of the skippers were very mean about food. They were the only ones aboard that had loaf-bread, and after every meal they'd put a mark on the loaf, when they were finished, so that the Boy wouldn't steal any of it. Some of them wouldn't allow you meat for the tea. The feeding of the crew depended entirely on the individual skipper.

Old Joe Cousins was master of the *Mary Agnes*, one of Devereux's schooners. He had just joined Devereux's. He had previously been sailing out of Carne in the *Samuel Dixon*, a small vessel belonging to Hutchinsons, I think. She was about eighty tons burden. Barry had come into the Devereux property at this time, through marriage. I was Second Boy of the *Mary Agnes* at the time.

Anyhow, Joe Cousins started to buy foreign meat, instead of taking the meat from Devereux's yard. One day Mr Barry came up the quay in his horse and trap and Joe Doyle driving him. He must have heard about Joe buying the foreign meat. He came aboard and asked for a sample of the meat out of the cask. He brought it home and boiled it.

The next day he came back aboard and kicked up a terrible row.

"Who authorised you to bring such meat aboard this vessel?" he asked the Captain. The Captain was left speechless and quaking with fear. Mr Barry told him he was to get his meat from their own stock from Ballinagee, as they always did before, and not to attempt to give meat like that to the men again.

The faithful sailor boy [50]

On a cold and stormy winter's night when the snow was on the ground,
A sailor boy stood on the quay, his ship was outward bound.
His true love standing by his side shed many a bitter tear,
And as he pressed her to his heart he whispered in her ear,

"Farewell, farewell, my own true love, this parting gives me pain,
You'll be my own true guiding star till I return again.
Me thoughts on you will be, me love, when storms are raging high,
So, farewell, love, remember me, your faithful sailor boy."

50 A song, collected by James G. Delaney from Thomas Murray, a labourer from Kilmuckridge, aged 77, in 1954. IFC 1344: 341–2.

'Twas in a gale our ship set sail, the lass was standin' by,
She watched that vessel out of sight and the tears stood in her eye,
She prayed to Him, in heaven above, to guard him on his way,
And parting words from his own true love did echo o'er the bay.

The ship returned and sad to say without her sailor boy.
He died at sea while on his way and the flags were half-mast high,
And his comrades came on shore and told her he was dead,
And in a letter he had sent the last lines sadly said,

"Farewell, farewell, my own true love, on earth we'll meet no more,
I hope we'll meet in heaven above, in that bright and happy shore,
I hope we'll meet in heaven above, that land beyond the sky,
You never will be parted from your faithful sailor boy."

Sailing and fishing lore [51]

Yawls and cots   The commonest boats in Kilmore fifty years ago were the
cot and the yawl. The cot is still used around the Wexford coast but very few
of them are in Kilmore. Before the turn of the century they were very common and varied in size from about twenty feet in length to thirty feet. There
were all double-ended and clinker-built and all equipped with oars, usually
three, as there were generally three of a crew; and sails a stay foresail, mainsail and mizzen. They were usually built in Rosslare and sailed around to
Kilmore.

The yawl was a bigger boat with a keel, whereas the cot was flat-bottomed
with a centreboard, which was put down in the centreboard casing when sailing on the wind. The yawl was double-ended also and carvell-built usually.
They were made in Wexford town by Simon Lambert, who set up his own
boatbuilding establishment, when the Wexford Dockyard closed down.

In October 1898 there was a great storm which wrecked many of the fishing boats at Kilmore Quay. Only one escaped damage; this one that escaped
belonged to a man named Power, who lived in Ballyhealy and was not a native
of Kilmore. Lady Fitzgerald of Johnstown Castle and the gentry of South
Wexford made a collection for the fishermen and any boats that were not too
badly damaged, they got repaired. Along with that, they built three new yawls.
These were built at Simon Lambert's yard in Wexford and launched in Wex-

---

51 Collected by James G. Delaney from Jack Devereux, a fisherman from Kilmore Quay, in
1954. IFC 1399: 197–200C.

ford Harbour near the old dockyard and then sailed to Kilmore. Each yawl, with full equipment of oars and sails, cost fifty-two pounds. Two of these yawls are still in the little harbour at Kilmore Quay.

Herring fishing For about fifty years there was little or no herring fishing in Kilmore, but about two or three years ago the herrings came back and they have been fishing them ever since. About fifty years ago there was a great haul of herrings made. They caught so much they couldn't sell them and the herrings were heaped up on the pier. The farmers were drawing them away in car-loads and there were so many that the farmers used them to manure the land. After that there was no more herring fishing, and the herrings deserted the sea around Kilmore. The old people said that the scarcity after that was a curse sent by God, because of the waste of herrings on that occasion. They tried for herrings after that but got none, and the impression was that it was unlucky to be fishing herrings. The only way they ever fished herrings up to recently since the big glut of herrings was to throw out a net at the back of the East Pier at the spring tide. Last year and this year they began to fish the herrings regularly again and made good catches.

Curing of herrings The people in the district used to salt down herrings and have them for Lent. They placed the herrings on the floor of a barn and sprinkled salt on them. Then they were turned over with a shovel. This was called *huddling*. They were left on the barn floor for a day or two; then they were put in a barrel and salted again.

Cod and bream – Ballyhealy fishers Bream and cod were always very plentiful around Kilmore and they were fished with a line and hook. Nearly all the farmers in Ballyhealy had cots, and they landed the cots on the shore in the fine weather. They never started fishing till the eleventh of June, the same day as the Fair of Scar [near Duncormac] and they would pull up the cots on the beach above the high water line about the first of October. All the Ballyhealy fishermen, or nearly all, owned land as well.

Curing of cod fish The cod fish used to be salted for the winter. The fish were first put in pickle and left there for three days and three nights. They were then taken up and dipped in a bath of fresh water and the surplus salt washed off of them. Then the fish were tied in pairs by the tails and they were hung across a line out in the haggard and a bit of furze bush was placed between them to keep them separated. They were then taken down and placed on very dry hay or withered ferns. They were put out in the sun on the dried hay or fern and let dry out thoroughly. Before the dew fell in the evening, they were taken in. They were then packed in a barrel, or tub, first a layer of fish and then a layer of hay or dried ferns, then another layer of fish and so on. They were then stored in a dry place.

Oil   The livers of the cod were rendered down and the oil taken out of them. The oil was used in the lamps for lighting at night.

Wreck of the John A. Harvey   The *John A. Harvey* was a three-masted barquentine, a new ship, and she got caught off Kilmore on a lee shore and couldn't get away again. She had a load of yellow corn. She came close in shore and stood out to sea again. The coastguards were signalling to her from the shore. Whether they misunderstood the signals or not, they got caught on a shoal or rocks as they stood out to sea and the vessel was wrecked. The crew cut the masts out of her and the masts fell overboard on the leeside. They did not cut them clean away so that the masts and rigging were hanging over the lee rail and the lifeboat could not get year the ship.

The lifeboat from Carne came by road, but the Carne men wouldn't put to sea. Father O'Gorman asked for volunteers and the first to volunteer was a Kilmore fisherman named John Madden. Other volunteers were John Monaghan, Nicholas Rochford, Anthony Morgan and Laurence Clarke. The coxswain from Carne went with the Kilmore men and he took the tiller. But he nearly upset the boat as they got out into deep water, either by accident or design. The Kilmore men were going to heave him over the side. Madden then took the tiller. The ship was only a couple of hundred yards off-shore and when the lifeboat went out to them the crew wouldn't come off the ship. The volunteer crew then came home. The next day the storm had eased a good deal and the Carne men went off in the lifeboat and took the crew ashore and got all the credit. No lives were lost.

J. Devereux heard this account from his mother, who was a native of Kilmore.

Reclaiming of the sloblands at Kilmore   From Kilmore (or Ballyteigue to be precise) as far north as Sarshill and on to Baldwinstown and Richfield, where the land is now, was all a lough. Boats used to put in there. They would come in over the Bar of Lough. There is a place near Boxwell's of Sarshill, still called "the dock", though it is now several miles inland.

The land where this big lough was, was reclaimed in 1847. It was one of the Public Works. The landlords of the time (Bruen was one of them) opposed the reclaiming of the lough, which was locally known as the Broad

Water. The reason they opposed it was because it would destroy the fowling and fishing, for which the place was famous. It was supposed to be one of the best places for fowl and fish in the British Isles at that time.

Vessels (schooners up to sixty tons burden) used to come into a place called Lackan, about a mile on the Kilmore side of Cullenstown. All the vessels were locally owned and their main cargoes were coal, coke, culm and slates, from Bangor, North Wales. When the vessels came in, there would be upwards of a hundred lighters taking the coal out of them and distributing it around the shores of the lough, which are now called Inish and Ballyteigue Slobs. Inish was an island at that time. At present the remains of these old coalyards are still at Moate, Ballyharty. There is a canal from Leafield (near Duncormac) to Bridgetown.

The canal from Seafield to Bridgetown was built when the slob was to be reclaimed. The woodmen, working at this canal, got two-pence halfpenny a day and a pound of yellow meal. By the bridges over this canal small docks were built for the discharging of the coal etc. from the lighters.

Some of the old men from around Kilmore have worked on the canal. They used to stay away from home all the week, as it was too long a journey on foot to do every night and morning. When they would be leaving home on a Monday morning they would bring a can of buttermilk with them and a cake of bread, made from the yellow meal. They used to bury the yellow meal bread in the damp clay they'd be digging and so they kept the bread fresh. They slept in barns near the canal they were digging.

There is a man in Kilmore at present and he is called the "male man". I thought for years that his father had been a postman. It was not till a short time ago I heard the reason why he is called the "male man". His proper name is Mike Walsh but his father and grandfather before him were also called the "male man". They came from Gibberwell between Rathangan and Duncormac. An old man told me that Mike Walsh's grandfather was in charge of giving out the yellow male and he was called the "male man" from that. The name was then given to the son and now the grandson is called by the same name.

Kilmore boats and further fishing lore [52]

The fishing cot and yawl   There were two main types of boat used in Kilmore Quay – the fishing cot and the yawl. The cot is sometimes called a Rosslare

52 Further lore of the south Wexford coast collected by James G. Delaney (whose notes are included in the text) from Bill Blake of Kilmore Quay, aged 74, and from his son, John Blake, in 1954. IFC 1399: 201–20.

herring cot, because it was used extensively in that locality and also because the cot was often built there. The cot was clinker built and double ended, that is, the bow and the stern were both sharp-pointed, but the sharp-pointed stern was not always adhered to. Some of the cots were square-sterned. They were all flat-bottomed and so suitable for shallow water, as their draught was not deep, varying from about four inches to six inches. Each cot had what is called a leeboard casing in the centre, running fore and aft and varying in length, from about twenty-one inches to thirty inches depending on the length of the cot. A cot of about twenty-two feet, would have a leeboard casing of about twenty-one inches. The casing was just wide enough to allow the leeboard or centreboard to sink down into it. The leeboard is about three feet six inches long or longer, according to the size of the boat. The leeboard was pushed down into the leeboard casing when the boat was sailing "on the wind", that is, when the boat was tacking against the wind. When the wind was fair, there was no necessity to use the leeboard and then a tight-fitting wooden cover or lid was placed over the casing to keep the water from coming up and into the boat. The idea of the leeboard was to keep the boat from going too much to leeward. If the leeboard were not used, the boat would be blown as much to leeward [same pronunciation as the French town Lourdes: JD] as she would go forward. The pressure on the leeboard is very great when the boat is sailing "on the wind". If you put down the leeboard and the boat sailing before the wind, it will spring up again.

The boats themselves, that is, the cots were usually built in Rosslare or Carne. There was up to a year or two ago a boatbuilder in Carne named John Ennis. Carne is on the south coast about three miles from Lady's Island, in the Barony of Forth.

The frames of the cot are made of oak and the planks are usually larch.

The cot rig: the usual cot rig consisted of a stay foresail, jib, mainsail and mizzen. The bigger cots had a jib, stay foresail, a fore and aft foresail, mainsail and mizzen. The bigger cots around Kilmore Quay all had gaff sails, and were raised and lowered with halyards. These had reef points, a double row usually, about six inches from the boom, the first row and the second row being about twelve inches from the boom. With these reef points the sails could be shortened in bad weather. Another method of reefing was to lower the fore and aft foresail on the big cots and use only the jib, mainsail and mizzen.

The bigger cots carrying stay foresail, jib, fore and aft foresail, mainsail and mizzen were three-masted cots and about thirty-five feet in length.

Then there were two-masted cots with stay-foresail, mainsail and mizzen.

Some of the smaller cots used a sprit [pronounced "spreet": JD] sail. These had no gaffs. The sprit was a long pole, about an inch and a half in diameter which was placed in a loop [called a "crindle"], made of rope, which was sewn on to the peak of the sail. Another rope with a loop on it was placed around the mast about two or three feet from the step of the mast, that is, the socket at the bottom of the boat into which the mast fitted. This rope was adjustable. To raise the sail, the sprit (which was pointed at both ends to fit into the loops), was first placed in the loop in the peak of the sail. Then the peak was raised up and the other end of the sprit was fitted into the rope about the mast and it was adjusted till the sail was tight. The boat was put into the wind to do this.

To reef the cots with the sprit sail, the sprit was taken out and the peak of the sail lashed to the mast to keep it from flapping about. In some of the sprit sails there was a thin line of rope sewn into the sail and passing diagonally from the head of the luff to the clew, thus stiffening the sail and making it easier to reef when the sprit was taken out.

The sails and their care   The sails were made of duck. There were two kinds of duck, cotton duck and light duck, or calico. The sails were made by the fishermen themselves. They cut them out first on the pier and then got some brown stuff, like pitch, called kutch. This kutch was boiled in salt water or pickle and it dissolved completely. Then this mixture of brine or pickle and kutch was put on the sail with a scrubbing brush. The sails would be real brown then and would be preserved from mildew. This kutch was some kind of brown pitch.

In the town of Wexford for the schooner sail and for the big fishing boats' sails they used a mixture of this kutch and tallow, boiled together and spread on the sails. It gave them a rich brown colour as well as preserving them. [This information about the tallow and kutch I got from R. Delaney (aged 80), master mariner, who remembers mixing the kutch and tallow when he was boy: JD.] Each cot big or small had three oars.

The yawl   The yawl is a keel boat, much deeper than the cot and bigger in every way. They were made by Simon Lambert of Wexford. When the boats at Kilmore were wrecked by a storm in October 1896, Lady Maurice Fitzgerald of Johnstown Castle made a collection among gentry and people, and repaired the boats that were not beyond repair and had three yawls built by Simon Lambert of Wexford. Fully equipped with oars, sails and so on. They cost about fifty-four pounds each.

The yawl carried a jib, stay foresail and mainsail, but no mizzen. She also carried three oars. Whether yawl or cot was used, the crew always numbered three – the skipper, who was also the owner, and two hands.

The sails on the yawl were made and treated as those on the cot. The yawl also carried a main topsail in fine weather. It was fixed to the gaff of the mainsail and sometimes called a gaff-topsail.

Maintenance   Every Saturday the old men would haul up their boats on the strand and scrape the bottoms of them and put on fresh tar. There was no paint used on the boats that time above the waterline, but sometimes the boat was tarred even above the water-line. The sails needed to be coated only every two or three years. They had to be kept aired, though. Periodically the sails of the boat if not in use would have to be loosened out and aired. If they were kept furled too long, they would get mildew and rot.

Ballast   The usual ballast used in both cot and yawl was stones. The stones were just laid in the bottom of the boat, properly trimmed, so that she sat well in the water. There were no platform boards in the boats fifty years ago, just the bare stones with no covering. Metal, like pig-iron, makes bad ballast, as it takes the life out of a boat and makes her sluggish and heavy. Sand is not much good either, especially when it gets wet, because the sacks in which it is held will then last no length of time and the sand will get all around the boat and stop up the vents. The stones are the best and they can be easily taken out and replaced. William Blake also said that the air gets down between the stones and makes the boat more buoyant than iron or sand would.

The carriage of animals to the islands   The cots, that is the biggest ones, were big enough to carry a beast to the island. They drove the horse or cow down on the strand (the small harbour strand) where the boat was hauled up. The after part of the cot would be full of straw. Two planks went from the strand to the after part of the boat. The beast was then thrown on its side and its front feet securely tied and then its hind feet. It was placed on the two planks and pushed up along the planks and so into the bottom of the boat on top of the straw. There were rings in the side of the boat on the inside to which the fore and back legs of the beast were also tied to prevent its kicking and staving in the planks. Cattle and horses gave little trouble. The men were so expert at it that they would have the beast in its side, tied up and aboard the cot in no time. Sheep were the most troublesome and the hardest to keep quiet. Parles, who owned the islands at that time, were used to this work and very expert at it.

One of these Parles was a powerful man and could carry two twenty-stone sacks of meal, one under each arm. William Blake says he often saw him doing it.

The mare that was used to the island   Peter Parle of Ballyhealy had a mare that had been on the Saltee Island for years. It was used to the passage in and out. One day he brought the mare down to the strand for a load of sand. There was a cot drawn up on the strand. The mare went over to the cot, when she saw it, and stretched herself out beside it. She thought she was going in on the island.

Fishing at Kilmore   In the winter time they used to haul up the yawls on dry land, within the small harbour opposite Sutton's public house, and then they would use the cots instead of the yawl. There were about eight or nine cots at the Quay at that time. The reason for this was they could have the cot up every night if they wanted to, and in the winter time they would have to be prepared to draw up the cots at any time. It took very little trouble to do this. It needed a big number of men to haul up a yawl on dry land. So the cot, because it was easier managed, was used in the winter time.

Fishing grounds off Kilmore   The East Bank is one of the best fishing grounds off Kilmore. It runs from the Black Rock off Carnsore Point West sou'west for six miles. The time for fishing off the East Bank is from February to October. The Bank is six miles wide.

   The landmarks at night time are the Tuskar [pronounced in south Wexford by sailors and fishermen "Teskar": J.D.] and Hook lighthouses, mainly. "At night-time when you get the flash of the Teskar in the Black Rock after lavin' the Quay," shoot your nets, that is, when the Black Rock and Tuskar are in line. The boat is then westward of the Black Rock. In the daytime you can go north east of the Black Rock and fish there.

East of the Ship   This is another shoal like the East Bank or Black Rock Bank. The "ship" means the Coningbeg lightship [locally pronounced "Conny Beg": JD]. There are a great many shells on this bank. The *Isolde*, the Irish Lights tender, was bombed off the Coningbeg lightship during the war and sunk. She is sunk right in the passageway and hundreds of nets have been caught on her and lost.

   Between the Coningbeg and the Hook lighthouse is also a good fishing ground. Only ninety-five fathoms of rope are needed for trawling on this bank. The bridles of the trawl must be three times longer than the depth of the water on the fishing ground.

Trawlers   Trawlers never came in to Kilmore district. The 1914 War started the trawlers coming in. The fish were very plentiful those years. I had a motor boat at that time but was getting only thirty gallons of oil a month for her. It was a motor-car engine, though I had a fairly big boat, that's why I only got thirty gallons. It was no use to me as it lasted only three days. There was never any trawlin' done in Kilmore till that time. Before that it was all line fishin' (from William Blake).

Blessings at night   How would you find your way home if you were fishing on one of the Banks at night? You'd know what part of the Bank you'd be on and as well you'd know your course from wherever you'd be on the Bank to St Patrick's Bridge. [St Patrick's Bridge is a causeway running under the water from the strand a few hundred yards east of Kilmore. Away to the Great Saltee Island. At low water you can see it running out into the sea for hundreds of yards, disappearing under the water; then it rises again from the sea as it approaches the island. It is a very dangerous place and old men tell me that the water over the submerged causeway boils like a pot of water: J.D.] When you'd make St Patrick's Bridge you'd know the course then into the pier. You could not do it without a compass. The older men never fished at nighttime as they would not be able to get in in the depth without a compass and they had no compass.

Compass adjusting   You have to be very careful with a compass, as the least thing affects it, especially the metal of the engine. The compass we carry we can shift it about as it is not fixed in a wheel-house. When steering for a certain headland we would know the course of it and we'd watch the compass to see if it was right. We'd check the compass by shifting it about on the deck until we'd get our course on the compass the same as the course we'd be making for the headland. We'd have the compass then in that position and we would be able to depend on it.

To signal to other boats at night: if a boat gets into any difficulty at nighttime, the fishermen signal to their friends in the other boats by lighting a bit of rag. The others know then that there is something wrong and come to their aid. In the daytime no signal is necessary as they would know by the boat itself if anything was wrong.

Lobster pots   The lobster pots were made at home. Every fisherman made his own pot, of sallies, fairly closely woven like a basket. Nowadays the young fishermen have improved on this old-fashioned pot. The modern pot is made almost entirely of netting wire. The top and bottom are made of sallies, but then this frame is covered over with netting wire. It has two main advantages over the old-time pot. The lobster can more easily see the bait through the netting wire. In the old, all wickerwork, pot, the sallies were so closely woven together that it was not so easy to see the bait. The second advantage is that the wire pots are not so easily lost in a storm.

The old fishermen used to put stones in the pots for ballast. Now a neat piece of cement is prepared and the bottom of the pot is covered with the cement for ballast.

The old fishermen used to use one buoy line for each lobster pot. Now they use ten pots together and only two buoys for the ten pots. They tie the ten pots together, with rope, leaving ten fathoms between each pot, and then they put a buoy at each end pot. The pots are now hauled by winch.

Around the Saltees is the best place for lobsters, in under the cliffs, though it is a dangerous place, and there is also the danger of losing pots. Ninety pots were lost in one storm off the Saltees.

Now the lobster fishing starts in April. The old fishermen never started before the eleventh of June.

Shooting the pots   The pots are shot in the day-time and left all night and then hauled the next day. They are left about twenty-four hours. Any kind of fish would do for bait, a piece of mackerel, cod, etc. There is no particular time to finish the lobster fishing. It depends on the weather. The weather usually finishes it.

Making of lobster pots   The dearest part of the gear for lobster fishing is the rope. The rope at present is two shillings and two pence a pound. The rope is tarred before it is used, to preserve it. The sallies for the lobster pots are not got in Wexford but are ordered from Carrick-on-Suir from a man named John Shanahan. They cost twelve shillings and sixpence per bundle. There are about five hundred sallies in each bundle. They are sent by train to Bridgetown Station.
Before the fishermen made their own pots, they used to get them from Bannow. A man named Grace used to make them. John Walsh, of Ballyhealy, father of John Walsh of the Burrow Restaurant, Kilmore Quay, was a fisherman and basket maker. He also used to make lobster pots. The pot is about two feet high and about fifteen inches in diameter at the bottom. There are five stand-ards or uprights. Those standards are made of strong wire, five-gauge. The round opening of the pot at the top is made of sally and the bottom also, but the bottom is not closely woven because a small round block of cement, like a pancake, is fixed on to the bottom of the pot and completely covering it. This

is the ballast that sinks the pot to the bottom. This frame is covered with netting wire, with a two-inch mesh and the wire is fine seventeen-gauge.

Baiting the pots   The bait is put on twigs of sally and placed inside the neck, close to the neck, between it and the outer frame. The bait must be fairly small or otherwise the lobster might be able to reach it from the outside. Therefore the bait is tied to the neck, and all around it. When the lobster sees the bait, he goes into the pot after it, sinks to the bottom and then crawls up along the inside wire to get it. He can easily get out of the pot if he wishes. Therefore enough bait is put in to keep him there till the pots are hauled twenty-four hours later. The best bait is gurnet, but a lobster will not go after fresh fish. The gurnet therefore is salted at least a day before being used as bait. A whole gurnet will not do, as it would be too big and the lobster might be able to reach if from the outside. What is done is to split the gurnet down the back in half and then place the bait all around the neck inside the pot.

If you use fresh fish, you'll get nothing but crabs in the pot. The crab is not so fond of salt fish. The lobster doesn't mind.

Cost   Every owner of a fishing boat has from anything from eighty to a hundred lobster pots, which cost about £1 each to make. If you got someone else to make them, they would cost much more.

J. Bates lost ninety pots one year in a storm, sixty that he had shot and thirty that were on Kilmore Quay. The seas swept over the pier wall and the pots were all carried out to sea and lost. Last year he lost about forty. The maintenance of lobster pots runs to about £100 in the year.

Often after a storm you'd take up the pots and there wouldn't be a bit of the sally wicker-work left on them and they'd be all battered out of shape. It is more trouble to mend one in such a condition than to make a new one.

The old fishermen years ago never could cope with any more than forty pots.

Wexford Bay herrings[53]

A lot of herring fishing goes on in Wexford and we might not have it, had it not been for the Danes. When the Danes brought fishing to Wexford, the

---

53 Account of Emma Owens, 3 Lambert Terrace, Wexford, in 1937. Emma was a pupil of Victoria Sherwood, who taught at Forth Convent School (St John of God's). IFCS 880: 201–2.

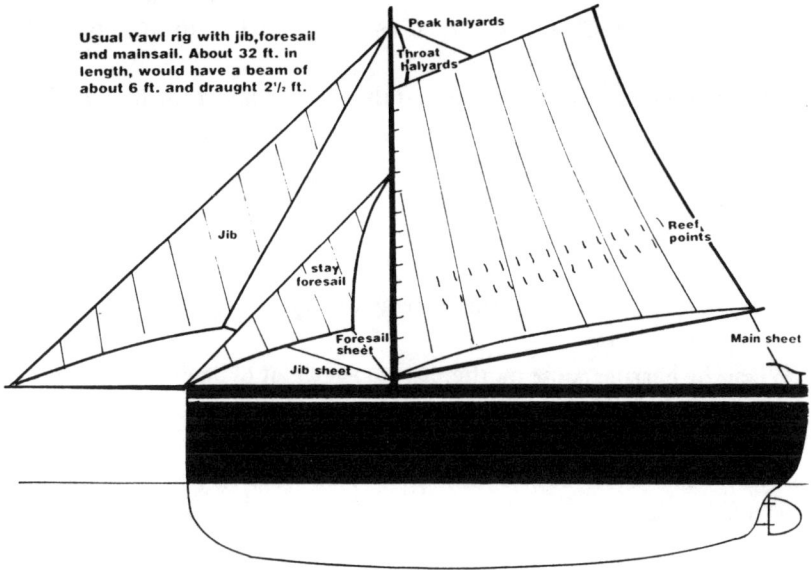

Usual Yawl rig with jib, foresail and mainsail. About 32 ft. in length, would have a beam of about 6 ft. and draught 2½ ft.

Peak halyards

Throat halyards

Reef points

Jib

stay foresail

Foresail sheet

Jib sheet

Main sheet

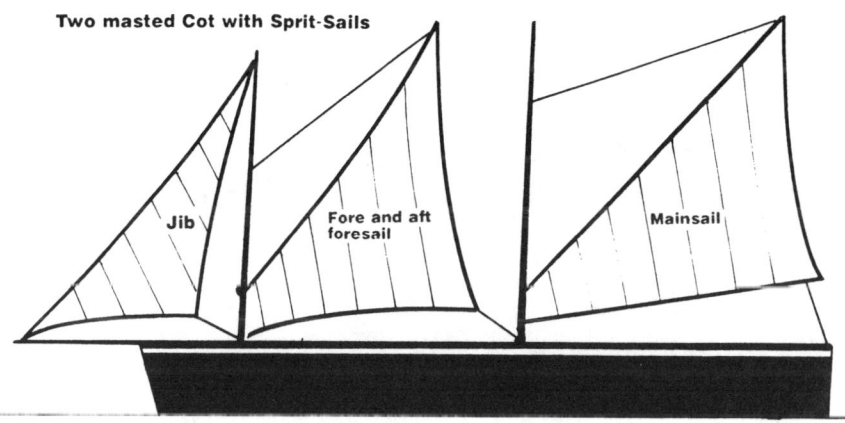

Two masted Cot with Sprit-Sails

Jib

Fore and aft foresail

Mainsail

town was very different from what it is now. The fishing people lived mostly up in the Faythe and William Street, and it seemed a different part of the town.

Now the people have spread out but they have not lost the herring fishing which is a very good thing. The fishers go out every night almost, during the season which lasts from October to January. During a good season the herring are sometimes as cheap as sixpence a dozen. When the herring are brought in at night, they are very nice to look at; they are like a lot of coloured glass stuck together.

You can always tell if a herring is fresh or stale: if it is stiff, it is fresh, and if it is stale, it is limp.

When the herring come in, there are always a lot of hawkers' carts waiting to hawk them around the town.

There are sometimes lorries waiting to take the herring inland. "Fresh Ross-lares" is one of the well-known cries of Wexford and it may often be heard many miles away too.

Swapping fish for other goods in Bargy [54]

When I see so many persons, even mere children, flying on bicycles to the shops for various articles for domestic use, I sometimes recall their forebears of forty years ago. It was then a common sight to see two or three men or perhaps women walking along with little sacks on their arms. They had pickled cockles or other shellfish and would call to the various houses on the fast days with them, not selling them, but exchanging them for a plate of wheatmeal here, some flour there, perhaps a bit of butter or even a packet of tea.

The baby's caul: a token of good fortune [55]

When some children are born, the thin piece of skin that covers them before birth often remains on them and they are born with it and this particular covering is called the baby's caul. There is a great charm attached to this caul and whenever a child is born with it the mother will always treasure it as some people would give any money at all for it. Sailors, although they are all divil-may-care sort of fellas, will give their last penny for a baby's caul. They

54 Collected by Thomas Walsh of Bannow School, from John White, a merchant from Bannow. IFCS 876: 57   55 Lore from James Banville, a labourer aged 70, from Cullenstown. Collected by John Butler at Foulksmills in 1938. IFC 553: 152–8.

say that if they have one of them on board a ship it will never be sunk and I could tell you a tale that I overheard from a sailor himself. This sailor was on the water all his life and he said that the ship that he travelled on was never without a baby's caul only on one occasion, and they were very near all drowned on that trip. They were travelling along by the Bay of Biscay and as a rule it is always an awful stormy place and an awful storm arose and they were all in dread of their lives that something was going to happen. They had no baby's caul on board and that was the reason why they were in such a state, as it was their first time on board without a caul and they thought that it was on account of that that the ship was so unsteady. They said that they wouldn't mind in the least if they had the caul with them as it was the firm belief of all sailors that, when a caul is on board a ship, nothing whatsoever is going to happen to them. Anyway they just happened to get clear of the storm and they were delighted to get out of it without it doing them any harm, and they vowed that whatever it cost them they would never again be caught on board a ship again without the baby's caul.

The next time that the ship was sailing they made sure to have the caul with them, and one of the sailors told me that he had awful trouble in getting one. However, they succeeded in getting one and they set sail once more, and when they were passing by the stormy Bay of Biscay they didn't mind in the least as they had the baby's caul with them, although the sea seemed to be as rough as ever it was. The fact of the matter was that when they actually knew that they had the safeguard with them they didn't mind in the least although the sea was as rough as rough could be. That certainly goes to show that when the sailors really and truly believe in this as a protection, it will prove a friend to them when they need it.

I have heard another tale in connection with this baby's caul. A ship went off and it had a baby's caul on board and of course it was considered real safe, and everyone on board said that they were real safe to themselves, when they had been told by the sailors that there was no danger whatsoever of anything happening to the ship. Well, on that trip this ship saw several others going down, actually going down, and she didn't go down herself, and what was more they all on board believed that she wouldn't go down. So you see that there must be something in a baby's caul. It is very hard for sailors sometimes to get this particular covering as mothers don't be in a bit of a hurry selling it, and sometimes they must pay an awful price for it before they can get it at all. For when people know that they are really in need of it, they will not sell it for some time but wait until they will get a good price.

Some women too are very superstitious as regards this caul and will not part with it on any account at all; and they certainly will believe that it is a very lucky thing to have in the house. They believe that in the event of sickness it will keep the whole house from sickness or death and there is a certain way of keeping this thing preserved. It is only a very thin piece of skinny stuff and when it is left as it is when it is taken off the child it melts away and after some time there is nothing seen only water. But even then that water is treasured and kept in the house. I heard an old woman saying once that she had seven children and five of them were born with cauls and she said that she never realised that there was any importance in them at all and used to dispose of them as quickly as ever she could. It was after some time that she began to find out that there was any real value in them and for the last two that she had she got a good price.

It is very hard for to preserve these cauls and there was a person telling me that salt, saltpetre, pepper and some hot water must be put on them in order to keep them properly. This must be repeated every year and then the caul will get the very same as a calf-skin and will be real hard, and it will last for several years.

A Ross sea captain and his strange adventure[56]

Old Captain Curran of Irishtown, New Ross, had a notable adventure on one of his voyages. In mid-ocean he came on a vessel that did not return the usual marine salutation of the time, that is, in or about eighty-five years ago. He thought this very queer and studying with his glass the behaviour of the vessel came to the conclusion that something was wrong aboard. He decided to steer nearer and find out. He did so, and after exhausting all means known to mariners to establish communication, failed. He came to the conclusion that the crew were sick and needed help. Hoving to, himself and one of his crew got into their boat and rowed for the queer ship. They boarded her.

Everything was in perfect order but there was no trace of the crew. He searched the whole ship for traces or clues of what had happened, but none were to be found. Having no time to delay, he set out for his own ship, held a meeting of his officers and crew and appointed his own mate captain of the mystery vessel. A volunteer crew was given him, and the two ships proceeded in the ocean, each manned with half a crew. Both arrived in port safe and sound and the Board of Trade gave great praise and a large reward to Captain Curran for his prompt action.

---

56 Recorded by Mary B. Dunphy, teacher, of The Irishtown, New Ross. She collected it from James Power of The Maudlins in 1938. IFC 618: 66.

The Banks of Newfoundland[57]

Newfoundland, Talamh an Éisc, the fishing ground, is mentioned in many songs sung along the Wexford coast. A rich fishing ground it was, and in the 18th century a great tide of emigration flowed towards it from the south east of Ireland. Some fished and came back with their cargoes of salted cod; others remained, and their descendants speak an English reminiscent, in terms of both accent and vocabulary, to that spoken in today's Wexford.

Will anyone join this merchant ship
    That lies in Liverpool docks?
Beware of your monkey jacket
    With your oil skins on your hands,
Beware of the cold north-westerly winds
    [two lines missing]
    On the banks of Newfoundland.

Last night as I lay in my bunk
    I had a pleasant dream.
I dreamt that I was in Liverpool
    And I walking down Park Lane,
A nice young girl by my side,
    A bottle of rum in her hand,
But when I awoke my heart nigh broke
    On the banks of Newfoundland.

We had one Irish girl on board,
    Jane Walsh it was her name.
Her passage was paid out to New York,
    From Dublin town she came.
She tore her flannel petticoat up
    To make mittens for our hands.
She could not see her true love free
    On the banks of Newfoundland.

Now we're coming round Sandy Hook
    Where stormy winds do blow,
Our gallant crew are all on board

57 This song was collected by Mary B. Dunphy, who taught in St Leonard's School, Ballycullane, in 1938. She heard it from Mrs Furlong of Coolroe, Ballycullane. IFCS 871: 208–9.

A-shovelling of the snow.
We'll wash her down and scrub her clean
    With scrubbing stone and sand,
We'll bid adieu to Jane Walsh, my boys,
    On the banks of Newfoundland.

Van Dieman's Land [58]

The place we had to land on
Was a dismal barren shore.
Convicts swarmed around us,
We could count them by the score.
They swarmed all around us
And bade us understand
'Twas only snakes and tyrants
That ruled Van Dieman's land.

The bed we had to lie on
Was built of sods and clay,
With old mown grass to sleep on
We dare not one word say.
We were beaten and ill treated,
They sold us out of hand,
Then put us to the braces, boys,
To plough Van Dieman's land.

Last night as I lay on that bed
I dreamed a happy dream.
I thought I was at home again
Walking by a silver stream.
My little girl was by my side,
We were strolling hand in hand.
When I awoke my heart was broke:
I was in Van Dieman's land.

58 Collected by Mrs Brigid Corish of Gusserane School in 1937. A note in IFCS 871: 362 says that "it was composed by a hedge schoolmaster when serving penal servitude, and it found its way home by some unknown channel, probably by somebody who was either liberated or escaped". Mrs Corish got the song from Murty Walsh of Dunmain, Gusserane.

The Rosslare Lifeboat crew

One of the most daring lifeboat rescues in recent memory was that of the crew of the tanker World Concord *which broke in two when hit by mountainous seas in the winter of 1954. The heroic rescue was given world-wide publicity. The following ballad was composed by Leo Carthy of Lady's Island.*

On the twenty seventh of November, in nineteen fifty four
A storm it struck the Irish coast and the mighty seas did roar,
An S.O.S. flashed to Rosslare saying 'Our ship is broke in two',
It was answered by the coxswain of the Rosslare lifeboat crew.

He sent up a signal and assembled all his crew,
And out through the Carrigs to the Liberian ship he flew,
Though the tide it ran against him and the winds at gale force blew,
It was fifty miles of hardship for the Rosslare lifeboat crew.

Before they reached *World Concord*, it being the dead of night,
There is no need for to tell those sailors' dreadful plight;
Exhausted by the frosty wind and soaken by the ocean spray,
Says the Coxswain, 'We can't rescue until the dawn of day.'

It was early the next morning as the daylight did appear
After a night of fearful hardship for the wreck sure they did steer,
By a great feat of navigation Coxswain Walsh drew by her side
And soon had those poor sailors safe on board the *Douglas Hyde*.

God bless you, Jack Wickham, a sailor of renown,
And likewise Richard Hickey from dear old Wexford town,
Not forgetting Billy Duggan and his young son Dicky too,
The eighteen year old hero of the Rosslare lifeboat crew.

To Jim Walsh and Jack Duggan the best of praise is due.
They volunteered like heroes and a great job they did do.
Of all those gallant lifeboat men no one knew their fate:
They were brave like their forefathers were in seventeen ninety eight.

Long life to Coxswain Richard Walsh, may your courage never fade,
And your fearless boys of Wexford who with you history made;

Throughout the wide and weary world your equals are but few:
May God forever bless you, and your gallant lifeboat crew.

Emigration[59]

THE PARTING SPREE

[*A note by the collector*]   Most of them emigrated to friends and because
there was a better living in America. My informant had never heard of the
term "American Wake". He called it a "Parting Spree". He had been at some
of them. They were held usually on the Sunday night before the emigrants
left. There were dancing, music and singing at any of the sprees he attended
and also plenty of drink. The party started at about seven in the evening in
Winter, but later in the Summer. It was held in the house of the intending
emigrant, and he supplied the material for the party. There was a supper,
consisting of tea, bread and butter. Drink also was given out. All the friends
and neighbours attended, as well as the workers on the farm. There was no
distinction made. The party went on till about two o'clock in the morning.
Matthew Rowe never knew of more than one person going at a time.

AN ANECDOTE

An old woman, Catherine Somers, had three sons in America. They had gone
out around the [18]80s. She could not read nor write and she used to ask a
neighbour, Jim Brien, to read the letters for her. Jim could not read either but
he used to pretend he could.

He'd make up the letter as he went along, telling of the weather and the
conditions in America. The old woman would get impatient. "Which of them
is it from, Jim?" she'd say. Jim, of course, did not know, and he'd evade the
question by saying he had not reached the end of the letter yet. By this time
his inspiration would begin to fail and he'd begin to stammer.

"Oh, I know which of them wrote it," the old woman herself said, when
she heard Jim stammering "It's from Terry, he always had a stoppage in his
speech."

59 Collected by James Delaney in 1955 from Matthew Rowe, Wygram, Wexford, aged 87, a
retired farmer who once lived in Ballymore, Killinick, barony of Forth. IFC 1408: 192–3, 261–
2 and 288–90.

The Kilrane boys

The biggest exodus at one time in south Co. Wexford happened in 1844. There were twelve men and one woman. The woman was the wife of one of the men named Whitty and they were not long married. The men were all young and the sons of farmers in the district. This ballad was made about them by a man named McCormack. One of these 'Kilrane boys' was Murphy of Haysland, Kilrane, who became very rich and successful. It was he whose children came home to be educated in London and spent their holidays in Kilrane.

I

On the thirteenth day of April in the year of '44,
With the bloom of Spring, the birds did sing around green Erin's shore,
The feathered train in concert their tuneful notes did strain
To resound with acclamation that echoed through Kilrane.

II

Twelve matchless youths I see approach, most splendid they appear.
They leave farewell with all their friends, their neighbours and parents dear,
As usual to their bosoms flew some mirth for to display,
They cried, "Adieu, God be with you; we're bound for Amerikay."

III

My darling boys, what is the cause or reason you must go.
To leave your native country for a shore you do not know,
Where you'll profess the Holy Faith, from which you ne'er did stray;
Ah, what dull news have you induced to wild Amerikay?

IV

Foul British laws are the whole cause of our going far away;
From the fruits of our hard labour they defraud us here each day.
To see our friends in slavery tied with taxes for to pay,
Ere we'll be bound to such bloodhounds we'll plough the ragin' say.

V

There's Bill Whitty and his bride, their names I will first sound,
John Connors and John Murphy from Ballygeary town,
Mick Kavanagh and Tom Saunders, two youths that none can blame,
James Pender, Patrick Howlin and four from Ballygillane.

VI

To Wexford Quay the thirteen, there were many to bid farewell,
They stayed conversing with their friends till the sound of the last bell,
Then gave three cheers for Ireland, that echoed with hurray,
And one for Dan O'Connell; they boldly sailed away.

VII

Ah, now, they're on the ocean, may the Angels be their guide,
And send them safe through angry wave, o'er rock and welling tide;
That we may live to meet again, in health and wealth and store,
God send them safely to their friends, the blooming Kilrane Corps.

Nature lore

Weather lore

SIGNS [60]

The sky　If there was a halo around the moon it would be a sign of the weather.

> The farther the circle,
> 　　　The nearer the rain.
> The nearer the circle,
> 　　　The farther the rain.

Red clouds in the east at sunset foretell the rain is going away from us. A yellow sunset foretells fine weather. Red clouds in the west at sunset foretell rain.

The wind　When the wind from the north would be blowing, we would be going to have cold weather.

> The north wind doth blow
> 　　　And we shall have snow
> And what will the robin
> 　　　Do then, poor thing?

If the wind from the south was blowing, we would have rain. The west wind foretells a storm. The east wind foretells cool weather.

The birds　When the swallows are flying high, the warm strata is in the air.

---

60 Collected by Mary Egan, Boley, Ballycullane, from her mother, in 1938. Mary was a pupil at Ballycullane School, taught by John Doyle. IFCS 870: 295–6.

That is a sign of fine weather. When the swallows are flying low, it is the sign of rain. The seagulls will come in on the land if we were going to have rain. When the robin would sing in the butt of the tree it, would be going to rain.

The animals   The dog would eat grass if it was going to rain. The sheep and cattle would go to the shelter. The cat would sit with her back towards the fire.

Landscape   If it was going to rain, the mountains and hills would appear nearer. If we were going to have fine weather, the mountains would appear far away. A rainbow is for bad weather.

> A rainbow at night is the sailor's delight,
>   A rainbow at noon is the sailor's doom,
> A rainbow at morning is the sailor's warning.

When the dust would rise off the road, it would be a sign of rain. The sea would look black if it was going to rain. When the fog would get heavy, it would rain.

The insects   The crickets would chirp if it was going to rain,
                   The cricket too how sharp she sings,
              Puss on the hearth with velvet paws
                 Sits wiping o'er her whisker's jaws.

The smoke   The smoke would go to the ground if it was going to rain. If the smoke went up straight, we would have fine weather.

ANOTHER ACCOUNT [61]

When the wind blows from the hill of Tinnock it is the sign of rain, and [another sign is] when there is a rainbow at morning. When the shadow of the sky reflects in the water and also when bubbles rise on the sea, and the flies fly about very much [rain is coming]. When we see soot falling it is a sign that we will soon have rain, and when we hear the ducks quacking, and when we see the cat turning her back to the fire. To see wild geese flying inland is another sign of rain, and when you hear the summer goats bawling, and to hear an ass braying and to hear the sound of a bell over a long distance. To see a dog eating grass is another sign of rain.

61 Collected by Nano Harte of Tinnock, Campile, a pupil at Killesk School (Margaret Sutton, teacher) in 1938. IFCS 873: 26–7.

If you see smoke from the fire going up straight, and if you see a rainbow up in the evening it is another sign of fine weather. When the morning looks bad, and if you see a blue piece of sky under the sun it is a sign that it will make a fine day. If you see the distant hills looking far away it is a sign of fine weather.

If you see blue blazes in the fire, and when you see the stars glittering in the sky is a sign of frost. When we see the sky spotted like mackerel it is a sign of frost.

Bird lore[62]

The wild birds common in our district are the robin, thrush, blackbird, starling, cuckoo and the swallow. The robin is a brown bird with a red breast; she is called the robin redbreast because she tried to take the nails out of Our Lord's feet when he died and a drop of Blood fell on her breast. The blackbird is of a black colour with a yellow bill but the female blackbird is of a dull brown and her bill is bright. She builds her nest in bushes with mud and lays four or sometimes five blue eggs. The water-wagtail is an unlucky bird because she has three drops of the devil's blood in her head.

The swallow, the cuckoo, and the corncrake are called migrants. They are called this name because they emigrate to other countries over the sea in winter and return in spring. The wren is known as the devil's bird because she betrayed Our Lord. When the soldiers were looking for Our Lord, they asked the wren did He pass this way. She told them He went this way. Then the soldiers arrested Our Lord.

Herbs[63]

The most harmful weeds growing on our farm:

Praiseach   This is a very harmful weed on the farm because it spreads rapidly and it makes the soil poor. It usually grows in corn and in green crops.

Fairy flax   This grows in fairly good soil. It spreads rapidly in potatoes.

Soft thistle   This grows in poor land.

62 Lore from Baby Colfer of Killesk and Nellie O'Connor of Knockea, pupils at Killesk School in 1938. IFCS 873: 45–6.   63 Lore collected by Nellie O'Connor, and another, unnamed pupil of Killesk School. IFCS 873: 69–70 and IFCS 872: 77–8.

Geosadán This only grows in very rich soil. You never see it in poor soil. It is a big green weed with yellow blossoms on it.

Glúnach This leaf has a tint of red on it. The tradition that is connected with this is when Our Lord was nailed to the cross on the hill of Calvary, this weed was beneath the cross and a drop of Our Lord's Precious Blood fell upon it. It is usually found on the hilltop.

Ribleaf This cures cuts. Chew the leaf up and put it to the cut and it would be cured after a couple of days.

Dock-leaf This cures nettle stings. Rub it on the stings.

Comfry This is only found in a few places. It cures sprains.

Milk-leaf This leaf is found in good soil. It cures the itch. Boil it in a small quantity of milk and when boiled drink the juice of it.

Giolcach is a weed, with a yellow flower; when boiled, it is a cure for erysipelas. This plant is not common. It grows like a tree on the top of a ditch and is used for making brooms. *Ribleaf* is very good food for young turkeys. It grows in most places and its leaves are lance-shaped. It is to be found where there is a lot of grass growing. *Chicken weed* is harmful as it spreads over the land.

There is an herb called *soft thistle*. It has three red spots on its leaf since Our Lord was dying on the cross. This herb was growing at the foot of the cross and three drops of blood fell on it and ever since it has three red spots on its leaf. The *nettle* is used as a cure for rheumatism. It is boiled and taken with milk as it is supposed to purify the blood. Nettles are also given to turkeys as a food. They are cut up and boiled in stirabout. This is given to turkeys when they are getting the red heads.

Blackberry picking [64]

The blackberry grows most plentifully and lusciously all over Co. Wexford, and a feature of the county in September is hordes of children with sweet cans and baskets and every kind of container, all out picking blackberries; the poorer children picking them to sell to merchants in Wexford, who buy them

64 Recorded by James G. Delaney, full-time collector, in 1954. IFC 1795: 303.

for export, the better off ones picking them for their mothers for jam-making. It was always a part of our September, when I was at home in Wexford, to go blackberry picking, and I have gone year after year, when in Wexford, even after I had left school. But this is by the way. In no other county I have worked have I seen this tradition of blackberry picking, nor have I seen the same prolific crop in any other county or the same lusciousness of the fruit. But it has been discovered from a scientific survey of Bord Talúntais, that the Wexford soil and conditions of climate etc., but particularly the soil, are peculiarly suited for the growing of soft fruit, in which category, I presume, blackberries would take their place.

Poaching and animal lore [65]

Fish   They used to do an awful lot of poaching after salmon around this place long ago. They do it still, but not quite so much now, as about thirty years ago. They used have a torch and a spear after them. The torch was made from a straight piece of deal timber, and a bag wound around the end of it, with plenty oil in it. The river there under Tinnycarrig, any amount of salmon come up there to spawn in the winter time. There was a crowd of fellows there at the Bridge of Ballynaboola one night and the peelers came on 'em. But faith they didn't catch them. They threw the two of them in the river and then hooked it; and they were never found out. Then they used make weirs in the river: build up across the river with stones; and they leave a gap in the middle of it. Then they'd put a net across the gap, and they'd try and hunt the trout down into it. Then they used have another plan. They'd get a bag and put a round hoop on the mouth of it, and a long handle out of it. Then they would put it in by the bank; and one fellow would have a long stick and start prodding in under the bank, trying to hunt the trout into it. Then they used throw lime into the water in order to kill trout – but 'tis seldom they used do that. Well, about the month of July and August a whole lot of fellows used make dabs, and go dabbing for eels. The way they used make the dab was, they'd get a big lump of worms and sow thread in and out through them. There would be no hook at all used. Then they'd have a line out of that, tied on top of a long stick. When they'd leave that down in the water, maybe you'd get two or three eels each times the thread used get caught in the eel's teeth and he couldn't let it go. Then another way for catching eels, was what they called "niggling" – "niggling for eels". A fellow would fix a hook on top of a

65 Lore collected by Thomas Carey from Edward Fitzgerald of Ballinaboola, New Ross, in 1939. IFC 631: 80–6.

stick, about five feet long. He'd go along and he'd prod that in under the bank, and into little holes and corners. Often I seen damn fine eels caught that way. I saw them one time, down in Campile, and what I seen them fishing with was a snare on top of a stick. They used manage to work the snare in over the trout's head. Then one whip and out he'd come. I saw any God's amount of them caught that way. They used snare pike around here.

Hare   I used do a lot of hunting one time. Meself and a few more around here, we used be out damn near every night, netting hares. We used want them alive, you know, for coursing. We used get four or five shilling a piece for them. Well, 'tis a strange thing about a hare. We'll say there was a hare here, and she had a path on straight the way of Cushinstown; well, if I caught her; and in about two months time another one came along. She'd have the very same path as the first one had. They all have the same road, like. Well, the quicker you'd be out after nightfall the better, if you were catching hares. You'd get them near the place. We always found that out when we used be after them. As soon as they start out, the first thing they do is go and get a feed. So if the feeding ground is any way near at all, you'll surely find them at it. Then after they feed they ramble around, I suppose.

Fox   Isn't it a strange thing about the fox? If you happen on a nest of young ones, and you kill them, and leave them thrown around, the ould one will come along that night and she'll take every one of them away and bury them. I've seen that happen above in Bennett's place. The fox came here one day and took a hen, and hid her below in the moor. I seen where she hid her. One of the Bennetts told me to bring a young fox up (a dead one) and leave it near the hen and to have a trap set. I did, but the dickens ever the fox came back for the hen, or the young one. She was that cute she never came back. I saw five foxes one morning down in Stephenson's field. The ould one and four cubs. Well, the devil such flittering up and down a furrow as they had. One would run a bit and lie down, then another one would come after him, and make a drive at him; and the ould one training them in. They say that when a fox comes along to a badger's burrow, and he wants to hunt him, the fox makes his dirt at the mouth of the hole, and then the badger will leave. The badger is supposed to be a very clean animal; but the fox is really rotten.

Rabbit   They say that a rabbit skin is a right socket to put in a boot (insole) to keep the feet warm in winter time. Several fellows use them. Some people say that a bit of straw, or hay, is better.

Weasel And I used always hear that an eel skin is the master to make a "middle band" for a flail. Long ago they used do all the threshing with flails; and they used say the eel skin was the best of all for the middle band. And I often heard, if you could get a purse made from a weasel's skin, that 'twould never be empty. There would always be plenty money in it. There were two fellows living here one time – Johnny Doyle, and Paddy – two brothers. They were down in the field one day mowing a meadow, and they happened on a weasel's nest with four or five young ones in it. They took the young ones out of the nest and left them out on the ground. The ould one was on the ditch watching them all the time. And over at the headland there was a jug, with some milk and water in it. They had it there to take a drink when they'd be feeling dry. When the ould weasel seen them taking out the young ones, she went on over to the jug, and she started spitting into it. After some time she came back to the nest, and she found all the young ones back safe and sound. They never meddled with one of them. Back the weasel goes to the jug again and she kept nosing and pushing it until she spilled it. She didn't want them to get poisoned when they didn't harm the young ones. A weasel, they say, is very spiteful if you meddle with her young ones.

They also say that the weasel's spit is poisonous. Long ago when they used be curing skins, such as rabbit skins, or foxes' skins, they used nail them out on a board, and shake alum water on them. The fur would never fall off the skin after that. That the way they used preserve them.

Frog They say if you catch a frog and put it in your mouth three times that you'll never get the toothache.

Newt And if you get a newt and lick its belly, you will be able to cure a burn. Any burn you'll lick after that you will cure it. 'Tisn't everyone would like to do that, though. You'd damn nearly rather suffer the burn.

Birds About thirty or forty years ago, I remember, fellows used be shooting crows, and gulls, and starlings. They used get three halfpence each for crows; and they used get from fourpence to sixpence for gulls (seagulls). And the Blackstairs (starlings) you'd see flying around you'd get a penny, or threehalfpence each for them. I don't know what they used want them for. Whether 'twas the feathers they wanted; or to make car grease out of them, I couldn't say. But you wouldn't be safe with your life out that time. Everyone that had any kind of an ould "Repeater" would be out in the fields blasting at them. And there was a great price for woodcrests (woodpigeon). Down about Carnagh they used get wheat and steep it in whiskey and leave it out for the woodcrests. The woodcrest would come along and ate a mighty feed of that. You could kill them with a bit of a stick or anything then, for they'd be all dazed after the whiskey. They used do that up in Carnagh about forty years ago. Whiskey was plenty at that time. There was plenty of it, and poteen too to be had.

Lucky and unlucky things

FROM BALLYKELLY [66]

It is said to be unlucky to throw out ashes on Monday because the luck would be thrown out for the week. The ashes are left in the kitchen until Saturday. It is also unlucky to sweep out through the door on Monday because the luck would be swept out for the week. It is unlucky to change houses on Friday. Long ago a cock was killed on St Martin's Day to bring luck for the year. It is also unlucky to yoke horses on St Stephen's Day. It is unlucky to see a black hare on Monday.

My mother told me those.

FROM WEXFORD TOWN [67]

If you break a looking glass, it is said that you would have seven years' bad luck.

If you hear the banshee, it is a sign that someone in the family is going to die.

If you would walk under a ladder, it is said that you would not grow any taller.

If a cat is seen washing her face, it is said that there is a stranger coming to house.

If a knife falls off of a table, it is said that there is a man coming to the house.

A singing in your ear is a sign that there is a soul in Purgatory calling for a prayer.

A black cat entering the house is a sign of good luck.

Crossed knives is a sign of a row.

66 From Peggy Cooney of Ballykelly, a pupil at Aclare School, New Ross, in 1938. Her teacher was M.R. Campbell. IFCS 873: 285.   67 From Philip Sinnott of St Brigid's Boys' School, Wexford (M. Gould, teacher), in 1938. IFCS 880: 3.

FROM FOULKSMILLS [68]

Eggs   They say small eggs is lucky. When the hen would lay a small egg – you know the real small ones, about the size of a pigeon's egg – you should stick it in the thatch; and they say the house would never be burned. There's about a dozen of them stuck here and there in the thatch in this house. Long ago when we were young when we'd find a real small egg like that they used say, " 'Twas a cock layed that." Sure the young lad here, young Jim, he thought for a long time that the dog used lay. There was a pet hen here and she used always lay there under the table and the dog used be lying there, and we used to tell him 'twas the dog was laying and he believed it for long enough.

When you'd see a little round bit of froth floating around on top of your pint, that's a sign of money. Well, if you take a sip and if the froth come towards your mouth, you'd get it, and if it went away from it you wouldn't get it at all.

If you were sitting right behind a person, they say, if you kept gazing at the back of their head for a certain time that the person would look around. 'Tis only one out of twenty that wouldn't look round, they say, if you did that. But you should keep the eyes fixed on them all the time, never take them off. I suppose the power of the gaze that does it.

They say that, if you had pains, goose grease is the best thing at all for it. Long ago they used always keep a supply of it in case a person would need it.

ABOUT FISHING [69]

They say it's not lucky to see a fox if you were going fishing. That's a fact. I was going fishing the other night, and I seen two foxes below under Culleton's house, well, I caught nothing only two or three little sprats, and I lost some of the finest of trouts, and they say you should never bring a dog with you fishing.

There's an ould fellow down here, a rale cranky ould fellow. Well, 'tis the greatest sport of all to see him at it. If you could slip down to the bank and hide when he'd be at it, you'd hear some of the awfulest curses you ever heard in your life. A trout would be nibbling at it and Johnny would give a great pull, and miss, "The curse of Jasus on ye, you'll take it the next time, ye whore ye!" "I'll put on a worm now and ye'll take it, be Jasus ye will!" Well, it bet all to hear him; and no one at all with him, you know. They say you should always kill the first fish no matter how small he'd be. I know I often threw in the first fish that way, when he'd be small, and the divil a thing I'll get after. I

68 Collected by Thomas Carey from James Whitty of Foulksmills, formerly of Knockroe, in 1938. IFC 520: 203–4.   69 Thomas Carey from the same informant. IFC 520: 190–2.

was down there one evening. There was a grand fresh in the river. The very first offer I made I caught a little small thing, and I threw it in again. Well, I was the whole evening after and I could get nothing, and all the rest of the fellows around me cutting the face off me with trouts, I brought some of the finest of trouts to the top of the water and they'd fall off again.

The devil's own lot of salmon comes up here in the winter time, and a lot of fellows goes out after them in the night with the spear. One man struck the spear in a big salmon above the bridge of Cullenstown one night and the minute he stuck him the salmon made a plunge and brought him with him. The salmon went off up the river the length of two moors and he spraddled across him. He fell off there and the salmon was nearly bet, so he kept going up after him, and he got him above in the shallow water. He was a devil of a big fish all right. Another man stuck a fish another night in the same spot and he pulled him up along the river and got away on him. "Be Jabers," says he, "he was seventy pounds weight." I often heard 'tis good to spit on the worm, the trouts would take it better.

Special times

Certain calendar dates [70]

> He who bathes in May
> Will soon be laid in clay.
> He who bathes in June
> Will sing a merry tune.
> He who bathes in July
> Will dance like a fly.
>
> A shower in July is worth a plough of oxen.
> A dry summer never begs its bread.
>
> Swithin's Day [15th July] if thou dost rain,
> Forty days it will remain.
> Swithin's Day if thou be fair,
> Forty days 'twill rain nae mair.

August   August needs the dew as much as men need bread.

70 Sayings, collected by Molly Fortune, Ballinaslaney, Oylegate, a pupil of Seán Breen's in Oylegate School, in 1938. IFCS 886: 245.

After Lammas corn ripens as much by night as by day.
A thick fog on an August morning betokens rain.
All the tears St Swithin can cry
St Bartholomew's mantle wipes dry.

On Bartholomew's Day [24th August] take the honey away.
If a cool August follows a hot July, it betokens a hard
    winter.
A warm, dry August betokens a snowy winter.

September   September blow soft,
Till fruit be in loft.
On St Matthew's Day [21st September]
Shut up the bee.
Never eat a blackberry after
Michaelmas Day, for the devil
Spits on them.
(The meaning, of course, is that blackberries are not good to eat late).

October

If the hare wears a thick coat in October, lay in a good store of fuel. October
has always twenty-one fine days.

Many hips and haws
Many frosts and snaws.

If foxes bark much in October, they are calling up a great fall of snow.
When birds and badgers are fat in October, expect a cold winter.

November   If on the trees the leaves still hold,
The coming winter will be cold.
If there's ice in November that will bear a duck,
There'll be nothing but sludge and muck.
You can't blow away a November fog with a fan
At St Martin's Day [11th November] winter is on the way.

December   A green Christmas makes a fat graveyard.
A wet December empties the granary.
If the milky way in December shows clear,

You may safely count on a fruitful year.
Cock crowed "Christus natus est."
Raven croaked "Quando?"
Rook cawed "Hac nocte."
Ox mooed "Ubi?"

On *New Year's Day* [71] the children go around from door to door with the daisy. They get a small match-box and put a few daisies in it. They then go around from house to house asking a penny for the daisy.

St Brigid's Day (1) [72]   In ancient times the people had great devotion to St Brigid. The following custom was kept by every family. Before supper the youngest boy or girl knelt on the threshold holding a bundle of fresh rushes. He knocked three times and repeated in Irish "Kneel down and let Brigid in." Those inside answered "Brigid is welcome," and the rushes were carried in and laid on the table. Each member of the family got a share of the rushes and made them into Brigid's crosses. These were kept to be blessed on All Saints' Day.

At supper in place of the usual meal of barley or wheaten bread they had rice pudding sprinkled with currants. No customs are kept on that day now.

St Brigid's Day (2) [73]   The boys get a large doll and dress her up in ribbons and papers. Then they dress themselves up in bright colours and go from house to house with the doll and some play music while the others dance with the doll. They then collect money.

In all the houses they make a cross with rushes and put it in the ceiling to keep away sickness and fire.

Hansel Monday (1) [74] Long ago when the people would open a new shop, the first man or woman in was to "hansel" it. Another thing is that if a person bought a new bag or a new case or a new purse bag, the person that would have bought it for another person they would always put sixpence in it for good luck or for a "hansel" because it was an old custom that when anybody would be giving a present of a purse it was the custom that they should put something in for luck.

71 From a pupil at the Christian Brothers' School, New Ross, Brother Kennedy and Andrew Kielthy, teachers, in 1937. IFCS 897: 90.   72 From Kathleen Caulfield, a pupil at Templetown School, Charles Hearne teacher, in 1937. IFCS 870: 346.   73 From Eileen Moran, Woodville, New Ross, a pupil at Mercy Convent, New Ross in 1938. Sister M.F. Ní Mhaoldomhnaigh, teacher, IFCS 897: 181.   74 Collected by Danny Lawlor, Swan View, Wexford, from his mother in 1938. Christian Brothers' School, Brother Healy, teacher, IFCS 881: 125.

Hansel Monday (2)[75] "Hansel Monday" is the day before "Shrove Tuesday". This is what happens on that day: A person gives a friend a sum of money and the friend gives it to another person and so on until that night. Then whoever has it keeps it. This is how it started: A noble man who was a native of New Ross was out walking one day when he met an old woman who was believed to be a fairy. She had a new shawl on her and she asked him to "hansel" it. He gave her a shilling and she gave it to her son, and he gave it to his friend and it went on like that until that night a young boy got it and he did not give it away. That is why the person who gets it at night keeps it.

It was an old custom long ago with tailors to put either a penny or a half-penny in the pockets of the suit he would have made. Some say it was to hansel the suit. Others say that the person that would wear the suit would always have luck. Some used to put a halfpenny more in each pocket. They used put a half-penny in one pocket and a penny in another pocket and so on like that. Many people used not go to a tailor that would not put something in the pockets of the suit.

Shrove[76] is the Tuesday before Ash Wednesday. It is called Shrove Tuesday. People made it a great feast day of pancakes. A ring was put into each cake and whoever got it was said to get married in that year. Pegs were also put into them and whoever got a peg was said to be an old maid or bachelor. All the young boys and girls in villages went to one house and they danced and sang.

Lent long ago[77] It was very hard to live in Lent long ago although people did not realise that when they had to go through it. Now I'll tell you what we had to do long ago. We'd get up in the morning, and not a bit would we get to eat until eleven o clock, and that time we would have as much work done at eleven o'clock as some of the fellows would do now in a week. What we would get then would be a mug of buttermilk, and a piece of bread. Then we would have to work on that all day, and not another bit until night, and that's what we would get for the day.

Easter customs[78] It has always been a habit amongst the old people here, to get up early on Easter Sunday morning to see the rising sun dancing.

75 Collected by Evans Byrne, 2 Colbert Street, Wexford, and Thomas Whitty, 8 Emmet Place, Wexford. Same source: IFCS 881: 226–7.   76 Lore from Mick Dempsey of Mount Ego, New ross, a pupil of Ballykelly School, New Ross, Pádraig Mac Uadáin, teacher, in 1938. IFCS 873: 261.   77 Collected by M.E. Campbell, teacher at Aclare School, parish of Horeswood, from Robert Power, Carraghaduff, Campile, a farmer aged 86, in 1938. IFCS 873: 145–6.   78 Told by Kitty Gaffney, a pupil of Aclare School, M.E. Campbell, teacher, in 1939. Kitty heard her father 'talking of it in his time'. IFCS 873: 189–90.

Another custom here is for people to get something new to wear on Easter Sunday morning. A very old custom which is beginning to die away now is this: A whole crowd of young people used to band together on Easter Sunday night and go around from house to house gathering eggs from the people. Sometimes there would be about forty, maybe, and they would go to every house in the neighbourhood and outside of it too, asking eggs at every door.

At some houses they would get maybe one, two or three as the case might be, and maybe six, but they would seldom be refused even if they got bad eggs, as sometimes happened.

When the crowd were tired collecting, they went into some house or barn and cooked the eggs and ate them.

This very old custom was kept up in this place until about thirty years ago. Some of the boys got so well-up that they began to sell the eggs, and that ended the sport. People would not give eggs any more.

The May Bush[79]   It has always been the custom here to put up the May Bush on May morn – the first of May. A fair-sized bush is got and it is decorated with pieces of coloured paper. The May bush is then placed at the gate or outside the dwelling house.

May Day[80]   The people long ago never white-washed in the month of May, and the farmers would not give any milk to the people around the place because it would not be lucky.

The girls used to go to the fair on May Day to be hired by the farmers for a year.

The children used to get May bushes and decorate them with flowers and dance around them on the cross roads.

The people around Taghmon used to kill a cock and sprinkle the blood on the out-houses to keep disease away.

St John's Eve,[81] 24 June, it was the custom in former times to light bonfires on that night. The young people used to gather together and then dance around them. But this custom has died out in this district.

On Sts Peter and Paul's Night,[82] 29 June, a bonfire was lit. A barrel or two of

---

79 Lore from Nellie Shannon of Ballymaclare, a pupil of M.E. Campbell's at Aclare School in 1938. IFCS 873: 190–1.   80 Collected by Matt Murphy of Cleariestown School from James Murphy, aged 79, of Cleariestown, in 1938. Matt's teacher was Mrs Christine Byrne. IFCS 876: 235.   81 From Catherine Bolger, teacher at Rathnure School, parish of Killanne, in 1938. IFCS 900: 307.   82 Lore from Margaret Burke, teacher at Carne School, Barony of Forth, in 1938. IFCS 879: 22.

coal and a half a cask of tar would be burned all night. Boys and girls danced all night on this occasion and the best step dancers got porter or two or three ounces of tobacco.

St Martin's Night [83] St Martin's Night falls on 11 November. Some years ago some fishermen went out to fish. In the night a storm arose and drowned most of the fishermen. What was left of the fishermen told the following story. When the storm was at its height they said they saw St Martin and he riding on a white horse. So ever after that night fishermen are afraid to go out on St Martin's night for fear of getting drowned.

A Martinmas custom [84] On the vigil of St Martin a fat goose would be killed every year. The mother of the house would kill the goose herself and then she would take the head of the goose and throw it over the house. On the Feast the goose would be cooked and when this was done the broth would be divided and put into jugs; then she would divide the goose. Then she would call each of her children and give them a jug of broth and a slice of the meat to carry to each poor neighbour in the district. This was all done in honour of St Martin.

Another ancient custom is described by Miss Flusk, who says, "When the harvest was over and the wheat ground into meal, my grandmother made a nice loaf in a pot oven beside the fire. This was the first loaf made from the new meal. That evening before supper was served the man of the house, taking the loaf, went outside the door, and striking the door three times in the name of the Three Persons of the Blessed Trinity prayed that hunger and want might not enter the habitation during the year. Then his wife opened the door, and coming into the kitchen the man of the house broke a piece off the cake and ate it; breaking off a piece and giving it to his wife and his children he thanked God for the new food, and finally placed himself and his family under the protection of Christ and his blessed Mother during the coming year. Then the loaf was cut into slices and the family sat down to supper." This old custom used always take place in her grandfather's home in Glandoran.

Hallow Eve or Colcannon Night [85] Potatoes, cabbage, parsnips, onions, mashed up with "pot stick", a dash of pepper and salt was eaten on Hallow Eve. There was a ring, thimble and button put into colcannon.

83 Lore from James Bright and Peter Crosbie of St Brigid's School, Wexford (M Gould, teacher) in 1935 IFCS 880: 84.   84 Related by Mrs Aine Doyle of Cranford School, Gorey, in 1938. IFCS 889: 135–6.   85 From Margaret Burke, teacher in Carne School, 1938. IFCS 879: 23.

Dipping for apples: They dipped for apples on Hallow Eve in Carne long ago. They also roasted beans on a fire. They had a "barn brack" for supper with a ring in it. They also had "Game of Three Saucers" – clay in one saucer, water in another and a ring in third saucer. A person was blindfolded; if he put a finger in water, he would cross the sea, if in clay, he would die, and if he put his hand in the saucer where the ring was, he would be married.

All Souls[86] It is believed that anything you throw out on All Souls' Night will come back into your face.

One All Souls' Night a woman by the name of Fagan threw out some ashes The moment she threw out the ashes a great whirl of wind came and blew all the ashes back into her face and she was blind for some time after it. People say that God did it, for the wind stopped as quick as it had come. It is now the firm belief of the people that anything you throw out of an All Souls' Night will be dashed back into your face.

On All Souls' Night in former times in this district, the people lit candles in the windows of the houses, to show light to the poor suffering souls, as they believed they passed from Purgatory to Heaven on that night. All people remained in their homes on that night, as they were afraid to be out during the night. It was the belief that ghosts and fairies were to be seen. This custom is now dying out in the district. In very few houses now the lights are to be seen in the windows, and several dances and other amusements, such as card-playing, are now held during that night.

All Souls' Day, 2 November: on that morning there are three Masses said in the Chapel, and the people of the district assist at those Masses for their deceased relatives. They also make nine visits to the church between noon on 1 November, All Saints' Day to noon on 2 November, All Souls' Day, and offer prayers for the suffering souls in Purgatory. New Year's Eve, the last day of the year, the people of the district make preparations for New Year's Day. They send cards and gifts to their friends.

On *St Stephen's Day* [87] boys go around from house to house with a wren on a bush; these are called Wren Boys. They usually recite a piece of poem about the wren such as this:

---

86 Lore from John Fagan, a pupil at Castlebridge School, P. Breen, teacher, in 1937. IFCS 885: 173. Further lore from teacher, Catherine Bolger of Rathnure School, in 1938. IFCS 900: 310–11. 87 Lore from Kathleen Forristal, Knocklea, Campile, in 1938. Kathleen was a pupil at Killesk School, Margaret Sutton, teacher. IFCS 873: 73.

> The wren, the wren, the king of all birds,
> St Stephen's Day, she was caught in the furze.
> Although she is small her honour is great,
> Cheer up, old lady, and give us a treat.

Then the people of the house usually give the Captain of the boys some money. When all the money is gathered, the Captain divides the money equally among them, but he is allowed to get more than the rest. On St Patrick's Day everyone wears a sprig of shamrock to honour him. It is the custom to make pancakes on Shrove Tuesday on Easter Sunday it is the custom to go around gathering eggs. On Halloween eve the children put a number of apples in a tub and try to catch them with their mouths.

The Wexford carols

In 1684, Luke Wadding, in the first year of his office as Catholic bishop of Ferns, published in Ghent a little book that had a far-reaching influence on the spiritual lives of the people of his diocese which included the entire county of Wexford. The book bore the title A SMALE / GARLAND, / OF PIOUS AND GODLY SONGS / *Composed by a devout Man, / for the Solace of his Friends and / neighbours in their afflictions, / The Sweet and the Sower / The nettle and the flower / The Thorne and the Rose / This Garland Compose.*

It contained some religious 'posies', some poems written for the disinherited gentry of Co. Wexford, and some verses relating to the Popish Plot. It also contained what was to become the foundation of a tradition of carol singing in the county, eleven Christmas songs, two of which are sung to this day in the village of Kilmore.

Luke Wadding's carols became very popular, and the *Smale Garland* was reprinted in London in 1728 and 1731 for a James Connor, a Drogheda bookseller.

The bad days were slow in passing, but carol singing was given a new impetus by Father William Devereux, who, on returning from the Irish College in Salamanca because of ill-health in 1729, composed a garland of carols. This he called *A New Garland Containing Songs for Christmas.* He was appointed parish priest of Drinagh, and he had no chapel; the Register of Popish Priests of 1731 gives the information that he said Mass in the corner of a field.

Manuscript copies of Devereux's Garland multiplied, and astonishingly they were still being transcribed in Kilmore until very recently.

For over three hundred years they have been sung there during Christmas by choirs of six men, divided into two groups of three. Tradition has it that the little choir must contain a member of the Devereux family.

To hear the carols sung during Mass can be a very moving experience indeed, and those of us who have had the pleasure of being in Kilmore church before a misinterpretation of the spirit of Vatican Two led to them sharing the

altar with songs that have their base in American trash-culture, could understand the sentiments of the man who was quoted in a letter to *The People*, a
Wexford newspaper, in January 1872: "I have stood", he said, "within many
of the grandest cathedrals of Europe and under the dome of St Peter's itself,
but in none of them did I ever feel the soul-thrilling rapturous sensation that
I did as a boy listening to six aged men on a frosty Christmas morning sing
the carols beneath the low straw-thatched chapel of Rathangan."

They are no longer sung in Rathangan, but the attachment of the people
of Kilmore to their very special tradition is as strong as ever. Long may their
beautiful songs survive.

For Christmass Day is by Luke Wadding: it is not sung in Kilmore. *On St
Stephen's Day* is also by Wadding: it is still sung in Kilmore. *On the Circumsision
New Year's Day*; also by Wadding, it is sung in Kilmore to the tune of *For
Christmas day*. *A Carol for Twelfth Day* is from Devereux's *Garland*; it is still
sung in Kilmore.

The texts given below are taken from *The Wexford Carols*, by Diarmaid Ó
Muirithe, Dublin, 1982. The music was transcribed by Professor Seoirse
Bodley from the singing of Jack Devereux, a fisherman, the leader of the
carol singers. Those wishing to know more about the ornamentations, grace
notes, tempo etc. of the performance should consult Professor Bodley's *Notes*
in the book. It is scarcely necessary to add that the quaint spellings, punctua-
tion and capitalisation reproduced here are those of Wadding's book and of
the 1803 MS that was in the possession of Jack Devereux.

For Christmass Day
(To the tune of, I doe not Love cause thou art faire)

This Christmas day you pray me sing
My Caroll, to Our new born King,
A God made man, the Virgin's Son,
The word made flesh, can this be don;
Of me I pray noe more require
Then this great mysterie to admire.

Whom Heaven of Heavens cannot containe,
As scripture doth declare most plaine,
In a pore stable is born this day
Layd in manger wrapt in hay.
Of me I pray no more require
Then this great mysterie to admire.

Heavens great treasures are now but small
Im'ensity no extent at all
Eternitie's but one day Old
Th' Almighty feeleth the winter cold
Of me I pray no more require
Then this great mysterie to Admire.

On St Stephen's Day
(*To the tune, Neen Major Neal*)

This is St Stephen's day
His feast we solemnize
From him we learn to pardon
And love our enemies
He's the first Christian Martyr
Who pass'd from earth to heaven
By suffering hate and envy
And Injuries of men.

More Just than the Just abel
This Prince of martyrs dy'd
His blood not for revenge
But for God's pardon cry'd,
For fury and for rage
He did remission crave
For mallice he had mercy
And Love for hate he gave.

This souldier of the Cross,
Arm'd not with Iron but faith
Doth not Assault but suffer
All that men doe or saith
On bended knees with hands
And eyes fix'd on the skies
With humble heart he prayes
For murthering enemies.

He clos'd not up his lips
Whilst he enjoy'd his breath

To gaine for them a pardon
Who did procure his death
Pardon good God thin rage
This holy saint doth pray
Lay not unto their Charge
What e'ere they doe or say.

This Champion of the Cross
To conquer death doth dy
Suffrings are his triumphs
Death is his victory
The stones like showers of haile.
Which Jews on him doe cast
Become pure Crownes of Pearles
And Palms which ever last.

He saw the heavens all open
His throne of glory drest
His saviour Christ prepared
To place his soul in rest
Then let us daily pray
For those who us offend
That with Saint Stephen we may
Enjoy a blessed End.

On the circumsision New Year's Day
(To the same tune of Neen Major Neale)

This first day of the year
Jesus to us doth give
His pure and precious blood
That we in him may live
A most rare new-years gift
A greater none can have
A gift more rich and precious
None can desire or Crave.

This gift brings us great Joy,
And makes us all admire,

A CAROL FOR TWELFTH DAY

Now to con-clude our Christ - mas mirth With the
news of— our re - demp - tion We will
end our— songs on our Sav - iour's birth With —
one that de-serves at - ten - tion.

Three great won - ders fell on this day— A —
star brought kings where the In - fant lay,—
Wat- er made wine in Ga - li- lee,— And —
Christ bap- tised in — Jor - dan.

It proves His love for us
To be all flames and fire
And for our sake this day
Jesus is His sweet name,
A name which cost him deare
His bloods' spilt for the same.

This name doth cost him deare
By Circumsision knife
For it this day he bleeds
And after gives his life
Coverd with costly Red
In his own blood He lies
Prepared to give the rest
When on the Cross he dyes.

Both heaven and earth admire.
And doe adore Jesus
To Himself this day severe,
And mercyfull to us
As soon as he's made man
And being but eight dayes Old
For us he gives his blood
More precious than all gold.

But how can Circumsision
With Jesus's name a gree
The true marke of a sinner
To saviour Joyned be
If circumsis'd how saviour
If saviour why circumsis'd
Why should this marke of sinners
To saviour be apply'd.

What's done on this great day
By circumsis'd Jesus,
Is comfort and delight
Wonder and Joy to us
Who never had beginning
He by whom all begun

Begins this day the worke
Of our Salvation.

Bless'd be this new year's day
Bless'd be this name Jesus
Bless'd be this day of grace
And mercy unto us
Let's all put on new hearts
To give to our Jesus
No other new years gift
Doth he require from us.

A carol for twelfth day

1st

Now to conclude our Christmas mirth,
For the news of our redemption,
We end these songs on our Saviours birth
With one that deserves attention
Three great wonders fell on this day
A star brought Kings where the Infant lay,
Water made wine in Gallilee,
And Christ baptized in Jordan.

2nd

Those Kings must have known what Balaam of old,
Said of a star that would rise
In Jacob's land when he foretold,
The comeing of the Messias,
Jaspar, Melchior and Balthasar,
Set out when they saw the new bright star,
Leaving their eastern Kingdoms far,
To find the new born Jesus.

3rd

They bent their course to the Jewish Court,
Jerusalem renowned,

Where to find him they did not doubt,
But met with a stranger crowned,
They tyrant Herod shocked at The news,
To hear of a new King of the Jews,
In dread the usurped crown to loose,
Ordered a bloody slaughter,

4th

But for amends in this surprise,
Those straying Kings could visit,
The temple made by Solomon the Wise,
The world had nothing like it,
There the Ophir gold they could see,
There Diamonds rich and Ivory,
Imbroidered silks and tapestry,
From both sides of the Indies.

5th

Yet nothing rich nor rare in art,
Not finding him could please them,
The're told of Bethlehem and depart,
No court toys could delay them,
Their guiding star again did appear,
And to that city straight did steer,
Till over the house resting most clear,
Thus bid the monarchs welcome.

6th

Amazed to see the cottage poor,
The stall perhaps where he was born,
Leaving their retinue at the door
Though great they entered without scorn,
The blessed babe and Mother found,
Laying their crowns and scepters down,
Adored him prostrate on the ground,
And might have spoken as follows,

7th

Thou King of Kings here in disguise,
Whom stars obey and Angels serve,
Who Wealth and grandeur you dispise,
You have given us more than we deserve,
Our beds are gold and Ivory,
Our garments rich embroidery,
Set with stones and pagantry,
Whilst you lies in a stable,

8th

Here's gold and myrrh and frankincence,
Not for to inrich you we bring,
But to honour thee O! heavenly Prince,
As god as man and as King,
Incense to thee as god is due,
The gold shews kingly powers too,
The myrrh keeps corpse long sweet and new
We have heard how you must suffer,

9th

And when the grand affair is done,
The world from hell redeemed,
When God have glorified his son,
At length by men esteemed,
Let our poor pagan nations in,
And thy happy sheepfold bring,
That free from blindness and free from sin,
They may in truth adore thee,

10th

What else might passed you may conceive,
In this fond converssation,
They bid farewell taking their leave,
Homewards to their habitation;
Farewell good christians farewell too,

Many a happy Christmass I wish you,
With a blessed end hence to ensue,
Through the merits of sweet Jesus. FINIS

Birth and death

Christening lore

FROM WEXFORD TOWN [88]

When a baby is born, it is not christened until the following day. If it is a wet day or if the people are wealthy, the baby is brought to the church in a motor car; but if the day is fine, the baby is brought to the church by the nurse, who walks accompanied by two sponsors.

If the baby cries when the water is poured on its head, it will die; if it does not cry, it will live. If a sponsor stands for two children in one year, it is believed that one of them will die. Sometimes the sponsors ask some request of God for the child and their request is certainly granted.

When the party returns from the church, there is usually a feast and the people present drink the baby's health. When the neighbours come in to see the child, they bring presents such as coats, caps and dresses. The sponsors put silver into the child's hand.

It is considered a very unlucky thing to put the first child in a new cradle, and it is said that the father or mother should not buy a cradle but that one of the relatives should provide it.

Children born on Christmas day have power to see ghosts.

FROM NEW ROSS [89]

In the words of one of my old informants, "Musha, there was no nonsense about bringing babies to Baptism in the old days like there is today, with their laces and flounce." The mother had a plain little outfit made with her own hands out of the homespun linen. There was no nurse with her uniform, neither was there a motor. The baby was wrapped in its little homespun and

88 From Eily O'Donnell, 137, The Faythe, Wexford, a pupil at St John of God's School (teacher, Sister Columcille), in 1936. IFCS 882: 85–6. 89 From Mary B. Dunphy, Irishtown, New Ross, retired teacher, in 1938. IFC 750: 188.

then wrapped up in the shawl of the "handy-woman". The whole party (father, "*gossips*", as the godfather and godmother were called in old times, and the *handy-woman* with her precious burden in her shawl) all drove in a dray-car to the chapel. The women folk were comfortable sitting in the heart of the car on about half-a-hundredweight of lovely clean straw fresh from the rick, and for a rug they had the best patchwork quilt in the house. It was they that were snug, far snugger than in a stuffy motor.

Death foretold[90]

There are a great number of tales told in this county of Wexford regarding the signs of death.

There is such a thing as a person's fetch [ghost, spectre] being seen before his death. I often remember my grandfather saying that he saw one on a certain occasion, aye and in broad daylight too. He said he was coming home in the middle of the day and it was spilling rain and he was rushing along for fear of catching cold. He met this fella and he was travelling also at a very heavy pace and he didn't wonder at that either. He spoke to him and the other man spoke also and they passed on and he didn't put any more *suim* [interest] in him. My grandfather went home and got his dinner and he never told my grandmother anything about what he had seen for he didn't think that it mattered much. He stayed at home for that evening and worked away at home as he was a carpenter, and at about half past three in the evening he went out in the yard to see if the day was going to be fine; and what did he see coming down towards him only a man and he running for all his worth; and he never stopped until he came up close to where my grandfather was and says he, "Do you know that Tom Doran is dead, he died about half an hour ago and I want a couple of men to lay him out." My grandfather looked at him and says he: "How long is he dead?" "About half an hour, I said before," says the man to him. "How long is he in the bed?" then said my grandfather to him. "Oh," said the lad "the poor fella is only in the bed a couple of days." "He wasn't out today then?" said my father. "Oh no, he never got out of the bed since he got into it the day before yesterday." My grandfather then told him his story and the lad wouldn't believe it at all and they came to the conclusion that it was the dead man's fetch that they had seen.

Another man was inside eating his breakfast and he was living down a long lane and he happened to look down the lane and he saw a travelling man

90 Narrated by John Butler of Foulksmills in 1938. His informant appears to have been his father. IFC 548: 97–108.

coming down it and he knew him very well; and he came on down to the house and passed on by it, down the lane by the house, and he went within ten yards of the lad and he saw him quite plainly. About half an hour afterwards he heard that the man had been dead and had been in the bed for over a week. He couldn't believe it all but he swore that it really happened. It is rather strange that all these "fetches" are seen in the daylight. None of them are seen nowadays, but it is certain that they were seen years and years ago.

Another sign of death is a black raven appearing a few nights before a person dies. At the old church of Bannow there are plenty of ravens seen before a death. Nearly every time before a person dies down near Bannow, the raven will be seen and heard on one of the old walls of the church and he will go along the top of the wall and make some of the most awful noises that ever you heard. That raven is there for years and years.

In Bannow also before a person is drowned a woman is heard screaming on the shore. It is said that this woman was drowned herself and she always comes back to let people know that there is a danger. There was a family in Wexford town and whenever any member of the family was going to die, a black dog would appear to some member of the family. They used to dread the appearance of this dog coming around. He is described as a very big dog with large feet and almost as big as a calf.

It is always said in this county that when the head of the house dies some animal is bound to die also. It generally happens that the animal will die a couple of days before the man or woman. It is always proper to say when any animal dies "All our hurt and harm go with it." All these things of course will follow certain families. There is a family here in Wexford and their name is Walsh, and whenever any member of it is about to die, a robin will come into the kitchen or parlour. There was a family of Walshs lived in Carrig-on-Bannow and there were six brothers of them in it, and there was none of them married, and they were getting fairly old; and they didn't know what to do. Begor they said that the best thing they could do was for one of them to get married. So the youngest of the family said that he would get a woman and so he did. Not long after that one of the old men of the place began to get sick and he had to take to his bed. He was about a week in the bed when one morning a robin came into the house and the woman put no *suim* in him as she never could believe in the like of them at all. Begor the very next day the old man that was sick died, and one of the brothers said that was the reason why the robin came into the house. He said that a robin always came in their house before a death. It happened he said when his own father was dying. This woman that married that man buried him and five of his brothers, and every time before a death the robin was sure to turn up. One time when they were all dead a robin came in and she got an awful fright as she did not know but it was her own turn that had come. She lived on for a few weeks after that and she heard nothing at all, and then, begor, a letter came to her saying that her husband's brother had died out in America.

Some people are able to tell by the way the grease or the wax on the candle falls off it that there is going to be a wake somewhere in the locality in three spaces of time. That would mean three days or three weeks or three months. In the parish of Clongeen three or four people noticed these "blankets" on the candles at the same time and a person was found dead the next day.

There is a very historic spot in the parish of Glynn and battles were fought all around it in the troubled times: in Cromwell's time and during the '98 period. This place is also a fairy rath and there are three old sceachs [brambles] growing in it, and it is said that they are there for hundreds of years and if a person touched one of them sceachs or dug the ground all around them he would die. There is a story told of a man who went into this place and broke a piece off one of these sceachs and he took an awful pain and died.

There was a farmer living in the parish of Glynn and one year when the potatoes were coming up he noticed that there were two misses in the drills. That is, there were two drills that had been sowed and there were two spaces in them that hadn't been sowed and of course they weren't noticed until the potatoes came up over the ground. Anyway he was one day scuffling these drills and an old man came into the field and he was looking at these drills; and he saw the misses in them and he waited until the man came back down the field to the headland. And he says to him: "What did you do when you were sowing the potatoes that you had the misfortune to leave a couple of misses?" "No harm in that," said the other man. "Oh, wait until you see," said the other, "what harm that is in it". The very next year his father and his mother were dead. It is said that when a miss is left in a drill some member of the house is going to die before that year is out.

There was a woman lived in Duncormick and she was married and had a big family and she met with a lot of trouble. Her husband died and all the children, and strange to say she was always warned beforehand of the approach of death. Her mother appeared to her one night when she was in bed and she swore that she was looking at her in over the end of the bed. Her mother appeared to be in trouble also, and she seemed as if she wanted to say something but couldn't. The poor woman in the bed was greatly troubled when she saw this and waited on without speaking for a long time and her mother's vision died away; and a few days after that her husband died. Then one by one the children died also, and the poor woman met an awful lot of trouble, and everytime that anyone of her children died her mother always came to her beforehand, and then the poor woman would know what was in store for her when she would see the vision at the head of the bed.

It happens sometimes that some people get the idea into their heads that they are going to die; and there was one man lived in the parish at Glynn and this morning he got up: it was a Sunday morning too, and he put on his good clothes and did himself up just as usual, and brushed his hair, and trimmed his nails, and was about to go out to mass when all of a sudden he said to the wife that he didn't think he would go. The woman asked him what was wrong with him and he said that there was nothing the matter, only he didn't feel like going. He took a good breakfast and all, and appeared in the best of form and all that. The woman wondered what was the matter with him and said nothing but went off to mass herself, and when she came back there he was in the bed, and he told the wife in a very strange voice to go for the priest as he was sure that his end was near. The poor woman got an awful fright when she heard this, and the thought never struck her that her husband was going to go as quickly as all that. The priest came along anyhow and prepared the man for death and told the wife that it could happen any time. When the priest had gone, the wife went up to the husband and says she to him: "Johnnie, is it possible that you are going to leave me after all the happy years that we have spent together?" He said that it was the case, and he also told her that he knew from the beginning that he was going to die. Something told him when he was about to go out to mass that he was going to die. Something told him that beforehand.

A Kilmore funeral custom[91]

This custom has been commonly practised at Brandycross, Sarshill and Tenacre all in the neighbourhood of the old churches of Kilturk, Tomhaggard, and Kilmore and also at Bannow in Wexford. In all these places the pieces of wood remaining over from the boards out of which the coffin has been made were fashioned into crosses a couple of feet high and painted in various colours. These were then carried by the chief mourners and placed on or at the foot of a hawthorn or ash tree convenient to the crossroads nearest to the graveyard towards which the funeral wends its sorrowful way.

91 Written by an unnamed pupil at Kilmore Convent School (Sister Lorcan Ryan, teacher) in 1934. The child's informant was Thomas Doyle, of Ballyask, Kilmore. IFCS 877: 134.

Wakes and wake pastimes

WEXFORD TOWN WAKES [92]

The wake was the local name; the term "corpse house" was never used. If the person died before twelve midnight on Monday, for example, he would be waked Monday night and Tuesday night and buried on Wednesday, but if he died after twelve o'clock midnight on Monday, he would be waked on Tuesday night and Wednesday night and buried on Thursday.

The people were not invited but came voluntarily. In fact a wake was a godsend to many of them, as they could look forward to a night's sport with plenty to eat and drink. About two or three hours after the person died, people began to assemble for the wake. They'd give them time to prepare the corpse and the wake room and so on. Women and old people visited the wake in the daytime as a rule. Children would be sent home at night-time. Women attended the wakes at night-time also, but they wouldn't stay all night except those who would be giving a helping hand to the people of the house. The women would be mostly in the wake room and the men in the kitchen, though sometimes some of the younger women would be in the kitchen also in the earlier part of the night and would take part in the games, particularly in the games of forfeits.

A person who never attended wakes was not thought any the worse of on that account, neither were there any adverse opinions of one who never missed a wake.

A big crowd was welcomed as it showed the popularity of the family and the deceased person. It was considered a mark of respect to the family and the deceased to attend the wake.

There were no particular customs or beliefs about visiting or leaving a wake.

Everybody who went to the wake entered the house and went into the wake room first of all, where the corpse was laid out. Each person on entering knelt down by the side of the corpse and said some prayers, usually a Pater and Ave. After saying the prayers, the person then sprinkled holy water on the corpse and then shook hands with whatever relative of the corpse would be in the wake room and sympathised with the words, "I'm sorry for your trouble." Everybody knelt and prayed but it was not the general custom to touch the corpse, though the old women would sometimes touch the clasped hands of the corpse. There is no explanation for this. There was no welcom-

---

92 Collected by James G. Delaney from Henry Keyes, aged 67, a labourer, of King Street, Wexford, and from James Kelly, a baker from South Main Street, aged 79, in 1954. IFC 1399: 243–59.

ing by the relatives. They just thanked the person for sympathising and then generally said something about the last hours of the deceased, the time he died, how long the agony was and so on.

It was not customary for anyone to stand in the wake room. There would be seats all around the room and if they were all occupied when others arrived, some of the occupants, usually the men, would rise and give their seats to the newcomers. Then they themselves would go down to the kitchen where the biggest crowd would be. The men did not stay very long in the wake room. It was usual for them either to stay a short time in the wake room or go immediately to the kitchen after sympathising with the relatives in the wake room.

There was no custom which forbade anyone to sit or stand between the corpse and the door. The neighbours lent seats and chairs and whatever else was needed for the wake. The women usually remained in the wake room, but did not sit apart.

Before leaving it was customary to sympathise again with the relatives, shake hands with them and ask could you help them in any way, fetch water from the pumps or well, or do some similar service. Most people would be eager to do all they could for the relatives at a time like that. No work was done in the house by the people of the house. All cooking and similar work were done by the neighbours, who came for that purpose. The grave also was dug by the neighbours. All the household duties were done by neighbours.

Wake candles   Three, four or five candles were lighted. The number had no significance. Holy water was also placed on the table beside the candles and a crucifix. The candles were placed on a small table, covered with a white cloth at the head of the corpse and to the side. The candles were placed about the crucifix. The ordinary household candles were used and brass or glass candlesticks. They were borrowed from the neighbours if there was not a sufficient number in the house, and were lighted immediately the corpse was laid out by the people who laid out the corpse, and they were kept lighting during the whole course of the wake. There were no beliefs about the manner in which the candles burned, and no curative or other properties were ascribed to them. The candles were burned in the fire after the wake.

The women brought flowers to the wake and left them at the foot of the corpse. These were placed on the coffin at the funeral and then placed on the grave after the burial.

Blessed clay was got from the clerk of the chapel and put in the coffin before the burial.

Wake pastimes   The time was spent telling yarns, jokes and stories about characters in the district, arguments about different topics, stories about hurling and dogs. The general tone of the wake house was one of levity, and it did not matter about the age of the dead person, though where the person was old with none or few to mourn him, the tone of the wake would be more hilarious, though it was never sad. Of course, in the wake room itself where the relatives would be, the gathering would be more decorous and becoming. There were plenty of jokes and chafing going on and one person would try to outdo another in telling jokes. The following is an example of the jokes told: "A woman had a husband who was very fond of drink. Nearly every night he'd come home drunk. At last she went to the priest to complain and ask his advice. The priest told her to get a sheet and put it over her head and wait for the husband and he coming home drunk some night. So she went to a lonely part of the road and waited for the husband and he coming home. The priest told her to say she was the devil, if the husband spoke to her.

The husband came along the road and he well oiled. When he saw the white figure and heard it groaning, he said, 'Who are you?' 'I'm the divil' she cried. 'Well,' says he, 'I'm married to your sister.' "

There was no storyteller especially invited and no storytelling, only jokes by different members of the company.

There was no singing at the town wakes nor no dancing nor mumming, though there was a set of mummers in nearly every street in the town at that time.

The games   Supper was given out about eleven o'clock or more usually the supper began after the Rosary which was said at midnight. The beer would be given out after the Rosary before the supper began. Everyone would get a bottle or two of stout or minerals, if you didn't take stout; whiskey was seldom given to the casual visitors. The games have finished for about fifty years or more although there have been instances of games being played as late as thirty years ago. They were not played at all wakes. It depended on the people who attended the wakes. They seem to have been played at the wakes of the working-class people, mostly. The same thing obtained in the country districts. In the town the games were played in the kitchen, where the bulk of the people assembled, especially the men, though some women took part in the less boisterous ones. The people of the house never took part in the games and never objected unless they became too rowdy. It was often known for the people of the house to put those out who were playing the games, particularly if they played the game "The Dry Barber".

The games began after supper, that is, about one o'clock in the morning and lasted for most of the night or until the people got tired or until the fellows who played the games were put out. My informant tells me that the "Dry Barber" was usually the finish of the games and that it was so rowdy that "they were usually fired out of the house" after it by the angry relatives of the corpse.

The clergy never objected to the games.

The following is a description of games played at wakes in town. [93]

(1) *The dry barber*   Any number of people could play this and it was often played when fellows were getting tired of the wake and wanted to be sent home.

Lots were cast to see who would sit in the barber's chair and who would do the barber. Numbers were placed in a hat. Whoever got the highest number had to sit in the chair to be "shaved". The person drawing the second highest number acted the barber. The person to be shaved sat in the chair and the "barber" then donned a woman's apron and prepared to shave the man in the chair. Before the shaving started, a big jug of water was brought in and everyone taking part in the game took a mouthful of water and kept the water in his mouth. Then the barber, of course, had a mouthful of water and also the man in the chair. Everyone then stood around the chair and waited for the game to begin. The barber with an old shaving brush and any kind of soap began to lather the man in the chair. He did his best to try to make the man laugh. If he laughed, and swallowed the mouthful of water, that was the signal for all hands to squirt their mouthfuls of water on top of the man in the chair. The sport was mainly in the attempt to keep the water in one's mouth and not to swallow it or lose it by bursting out laughing, and the pleasure derived from squirting the victim in the chair. The kitchen would be in a terrible mess after this game. Hence its unpopularity with the people of the house.

(2) *Who've the button*   Any number of people could play this. One was appointed to act as leader in the game. Everyone sat around with the two hands held out and cupped. The leader of the game went around the room once or maybe twice, saying, "Who've the button?" He placed a button or some other small object into the cupped hands of one of the players. Then he asked one of the players who had the button? If the person asked could not tell who had the button, he had to pay a forfeit. [According to James Kelly, to pay a forfeit in any of these games meant actually giving something like a ha'penny or

93 *Collector's note*: For numbers 4, 5, 7, I am indebted to James Kelly, aged 79, baker, South Main Street, Wexford, but I have put all the games together. Henry Keyes, who gave me all of the above information about wakes and wake usage, could only remember nos. 1, 2, 3, 6.

some object of small value. It never meant performing any task. These forfeits were given to youngsters who might be at the wake. It was customary for some mothers to bring their children with them to a wake, when they would be too young to be left on their own at home. If they got too sleepy they'd put them to bed in the house of the wake: JD.]

(3) *"Hide the finger"* This was simply the hiding of some object, by a person chosen to do so. He might hide it in another part of the house or in the room where the game was played. If in the latter the other players were expected to close their eyes and not to watch. When any particular player was near the object he had to be told that he was "warm". As he approached or receded from the hidden object he was told he was getting warmer or colder. Whoever found the "finger" then had to hide it and so the game went on.

(4) *The crooked crabtree* Any number of people could play this game. It was played in the following manner: a leader was chosen to give out the rhyme. He took a bit of stick and handed to the first person. Everyone sat around the room for this game. On handing the bit of stick to the first person, the leader said these words, "This is the crooked crabtree." The person taking the stick repeated the sentence and then handed the stick to the person beside him. It got more difficult every round. The second round went thus, "This is the crooked crabtree that grew in the crooked grass that grew crooked around the crooked crabtree."

The third round: "This is the crooked apple that grew crooked in the crooked crabtree, that grew in the crooked grass" etc.

The fourth round: "This is the crooked man, that stole the crooked apple that grew" etc.

If any player could not say the rhyme properly or left out any part of it, he had to pay a forfeit.

(5) *The house that Jack built* This was played in the same way as "The Crooked Crabtree", the first round being, "This is the house that Jack built" and so on.

(6) *Forfeits* Some one, who was to give out the forfeits, was blindfolded, and another person asked, "What is this one to do?" but didn't mention any name. They were all given various tasks to do, some girl to go out in the dark with some boy. This gave young people a chance of courting which seemed to be a feature of some wakes.

(7) *Quench the light*   It was an attempt by one to quench a small piece of candle lighting on the floor, while another person held the brush handle or spoon handle, by which the quenching was to be done, between his legs. Bets were made on this by the onlookers.

Other tricks at wakes   Horse play and practical jokes were a common feature of the town wakes. As remarked already, the "purty boys" or "Clare boys", as they are often called, looked forward to the wakes as a means of amusing themselves. Henry Keyes, my informant, has witnessed the following.

As the night went on, fellows would be watching to see who would drop off to sleep first. Those who'd be awake would then play some trick on the sleeping person. Anyone that did not want to partake in the joke would be told to leave the room and then those remaining would be all enjoined to secrecy and told what would happen if they let out the name of the person who was to do the trick. If the person was particularly proud of his moustache, one of the lads would cut it off only on one side and leave him with half a moustache. At that time the men were very proud of their moustaches and used to wear them fairly long and waxed at each end. The unfortunate sleeper would never discover his loss till the next morning. These practical jokes have also been known to cut a man's eyebrows or blacken his face with soot.

Sometimes they would cast lots to see who would go and rob and orchard. The lot fell to four fellows and they had to go, two to rob the apples and two to keep "nix". They came back with a sack of apples, which they all enjoyed.

Another thing done during a wake in the town was to go out and rob a hen-roost and potatoes from some garden and bring them back and cook them. This was done about seventy years ago.

Another practical joke done at a wake was to bring in sneezing powder or "electric" snuff and hand it around to the people and set them all sneezing.

Other types of tricks were played. For example, Henry Keyes told me he saw the following trick performed:

Corking the bottle   A man asked those assembled at a wake could anyone perform the trick of corking a bottle without putting his hands near it. He said he could do it himself and bets were made on it. One member of the audience said he could do it. His hands were accordingly tied behind his back. An empty stout bottle was procured and filled with water and the cork gently placed in the neck of the bottle, but not driven home. It was the task of the man, with his hands tied behind his back, to drive home the cork. He got someone else to balance the bottle on the edge of a table and then he approached the bottle and began to blow at it. The bottle was so finely balanced that after a few blows of the man's breath it toppled over, head downwards. It fell on the cork and the weight of the bottle with the water in it drove the cork right in, as tightly as if it had been driven in with a mallet. It took a corkscrew to get it out again.

Fighting at a wake "I was at a wake one night at a house in the Boker. An auld tramp came into the wake about one o'clock in the mornin' and he tired and hungry. He came into the kitchen where we were and the place was crowded. The table was full with fellows sittin' all around it. Someone took pity on the tramp and took down a big lump of meat out of the cupboard and bread and butter and gave it to the tramp. All the fellows sittin' around the table were laughin' and jokin' and they were hidin' the tramp and he atin' the meat, from any of the people of the house that would look into the kitchen. Some fellow started givin' out and sayin' the others were making little of the tramp. A terrible row got up and I seen them meself and they boxing outside in the street. Sometimes rows like that would start at a wake.

"I never seen any drunkenness at a wake."

The corpse jumps up "I heard me father saying one time that there was a wake up around White rock and a tramp came in. He had an auld scarf on him and they used the tramp's scarf to tie down the corpse. The legs of the corpse were all bent up and had to be tied down. After the supper the tramp said, "It's time for me to be goin' " and without any warnin' he took the scarf suddenly from around the corpse. It was tied with a slip-knot. The corpse sat up and let a groan out of it and in no time the wake room was cleared of people.

[All the above information about town wakes was given by Henry Keyes, unless where otherwise stated. J.D.]

WAKES IN SHELMALIER[94]

The following games were played around the Blackwater district; on the East Coast, just north of Wexford harbour.

Cock fighting Only two at a time could play this game. Each player had his feet tied at the ankles and his hands tied at the wrists. The knees were pulled up towards the chin and each player sat thus on the ground. The hands were brought down outside the upper parts of the legs above the knees and then brought in under the knees and thrust out then between the legs below the

---

94 The work of the same collector as "Wexford Town wakes". IFC 1399: 260–7.

knees. When the hands were got in that position they were tied at the wrist. This was done to each person, and then a sharp-pointed stick was put in the hands of each player. This was to be the spur used in the cock fight. Each player then approached the other, dragging himself along on his haunches, as the legs of each were tied at the ankles. Each tried to knock over the other, by pushing at him with his feet. If one was knocked over, he was at the mercy of the other, because with his feet and hands tied he would not be able to lever himself up again. When one got the other on his side, the player who was still upright would have the other at his mercy and would prod him with the stick or spur. Then one of the onlookers would sit upright again the player who was knocked down, and they'd be at it again. Before long the whole room would be cockfighting. Philip Tobin my informant for this and the following games, told me that he heard the old people say "that an auld lady that lived in the parish of Blackwater was better than any of the men at this game of cock-fighting", though as a rule women did not take part in any of the wake games.

Holding the candle to the eye   One eye was blindfolded by placing a hand over it. A lighted candle was held up in front of the other, and the person had to hold out his hand, which some member of the company hit with a strap. The person being struck had to tell who struck him; if not, he was struck again and again until he did tell. If he could tell who struck him, that person named would have to take the place of the first person, who was being beaten. So the game went on.

Douse the tailor   Two players played this. The two sat on a form crosslegged, like a tailor. Then either by tossing a coin or by agreement with each other, one tried to knock the other off the form. Each was allowed only one blow at the other. The player who had to sit for the blow covered his face with his hands thus: he crossed both arms, and placed the left-hand palm outwards against the right side of his face and placed the right-hand palm outwards against the left side of his face and thus tried to guard his head as well as he could. The other player then gave him a "douse" [common expression for blow: J.D.] in the side of the head and tried to knock him off the form. If the first player failed to knock his opponent off the form with one blow, then it was the other man's turn, to try to knock him off with one blow.

This was a particularly rough game, as a man with a hard hand could make your head sing for the night with one blow. It was also very difficult to retain one's balance sitting crosslegged on a form and trying to knock another off. Very often the force of your own blow would unbalance you, if the opponent was able to dodge the blow.

Pulling the mare out of the bog   Any number of people could play this game. One man was chosen to be the mare and he lay down on the ground full length. A bit of old rope was got to pull the mare out of the bog but apparently it served no purpose except that of a stage property. Another man was then chosen as the master or owner of the mare and he directed the game. The "owner" of the mare then ordered all those taking part in the game to take off their coats. He gave them a certain length of time to do this but not much. Then, when the allotted time was up, he went around beating with a leather strap those who had not got their coats off in time. Then he ordered them to take off their waistcoats, giving them a short time to do it, and beating those who did not do it in time. And so it went on, he ordered them to take off garment after garment, shirt, boots and socks, so that eventually they would have nothing on but their trousers.

Then they had to put on their garments one by one, getting a certain time to do so as before. The game waxed fast and furious at this stage, because all the clothes would be scattered about the barn, in which the games were usually played, and fellows would have great difficulty in finding them, so that very few, if any, would escape the strap in the putting on of the clothes.

Where are you, Jack?   [For some of the games Philip Tobin had no particular name. For convenience I give this game the name of the opening sentence: J.D.] Two people played this game. They were both blindfolded and had to go on their knees on the ground. A short piece of rope was then placed between them. The rope was about four feet long, or longer, perhaps, depending on the size of the room in which the game was played. The rope was placed on the ground and each player took a hold on the end of the rope, but leaving it to lie on the ground. Each player had in his hand a piece of old rag, weighted it at the end with sand or perhaps just knotted into a hard ball. The first man said, "Where are you, Jack?"

The other man replied, "I'm here in the dark." Then the first man replied to this by saying, "If you die before I die, do you take that!" and he made a blow at his opponent with the knotted rag. If he missed his opponent, then the latter would have his chance of making a blow, at the other.

Young miller, auld miller   In this game each player was given a name before the game started and the essence of the game was to remember the name each was given and to be able to give it out at a moment's notice, when called by the leader of the game.

All the players stood or sat about in a circle. One man was placed on his knees in the centre with his head bent down. The leader of the game stood over the kneeling man and began to thump him on the back while he called out as quickly as he could the names he had given to each player: "Young Miller, Auld Miller, Great Grey Miller, Rob the Hopper, Grase the Hopper, Auld Skip (or Slip?), Auld Slippery Heel, what's that man's name?" Then he would point to one of the men taking part in the game and ask another participant what was the name of the man pointed out. It would be one of the seven mentioned, "Rob the Hopper", perhaps. If the person couldn't tell the name of the one pointed out, he had to kneel in the centre, under the leader, and get thumped on the back. The leader kept thumping away on the kneeling man, while he shouted out the names.

More sacks on the new mill   All my informant knew about this game was that it was very rough and that fellows fell on top of one another on the floor until there was a whole heap of them.

My man Jack / The Priest of the Parish   This game was played in the district but my informant knew little about it, except the opening sentences: "The Priest of the Parish has lost his considering cap. Some say this and some say that and some say 'My man Jack have it'." [These two sentences are fairly well known among the elderly people in the Kilmore District, but I could not find anyone who could tell me how the game was played. J.D.]

The house that Jack built   Philip Tobin told me that the wake games died out in his district between fifty and sixty years ago. They were played only as long as the wakes were held in the barns. As soon as the wakes began to be held in the houses, the games stopped.

He also informed me that no women attended wakes at night in his district, except the neighbouring women who would be at the wake house preparing the supper and generally helping the people of the house. There was one instance of a woman taking part in the game of cock-fighting, but he heard of that from older people.

Fellows at that time used to look forward to wakes. They'd go to get tay, as it was hard to get at that time, and also for the feed at supper-time. The Rosary was said at ten o'clock at night and supper was at eleven o'clock. "There'd be supper with mate and all kinds of things, and tay again in the mornin' about four o'clock."

A Rathnure funeral custom [95]

When the corpse was going out, that is, when the coffined corpse was being brought from the house to the hearse for burial, "there was always a person with two blessed candles walking out backwards to the hearse, in front of the coffin," says Mrs Condon.

"Isn't it a strange thing, that no matter how windy the day was, the candles wouldn't go out!" She emphasises this: "No matter how hard the wind blew, it wouldn't blow out the candles!"

"Some woman that would be helping would bring out the corpse with the candles. It was always a woman that brought out the corpse."

Bodysnatching in the old days[96]

Auld Jim F. that bought the cow in Taghmon, that I was tellin' you about before, he riz a body for a farmer [Paudeen] he was workin' wud one time. They used to sell them to the doctors. The farmer called him out of bed one night at twelve o'clock.

"Are you asleep, Jim?" says he.

"I'm not," says Jim.

"Get up. I want you to do a little job for me. Do you know that young lady was buried today?" says the farmer.

"I do well," says Jim.

"Well," says he, "we have to rise that one's body tonight."

"Be man," says Jim, "I won't rise any body out of the grave. She'll haunt me all the days of me life."

"Go on, and don't be a bloody coward," says he, "I'll give you five bob for the night," says he, "and I'll give you a good drink of whiskey along with it."

So, be man, Jim agreed anyhow.

"Well, now," says he to Jim, "go out in the stable and put the tackle on the grey mare and put the dray car on her. Get two crowbars, now," he says, "and put them in the car. She's buried in a box tomb and we'll want the crowbars to lift the top stone off it."

At that time, Jim says, you'd get five years in jail for body-snatchin' without the option of a fine.

"On we goes to the graveyard," says Jim, "with our two crowbars and our dray car and we brought the mare and car into the churchyard, the way she wouldn't be detected on the road and tied her in a corner of the churchyard.

"We got our two crowbars and we goes to the tomb and lifted off the top cover of it. Begob, we lifted up the cover about a foot high and if we lifted it

95 Recorded by James G. Delaney, in 1954. IFC 1796: 405.   96 A story collected by James Delaney from Walter Furlong, a farmer aged 84, of Corrigeen, Grange, in 1954. IFC 1344: 355–61.

high enough to pull out the coffin, we'd have to lift the lid of it off altogether and we wouldn't be able to put it back again. So I tould him to get a bit of a stick to prop it up a certain height; as we didn't want to have the grave look disturbed, be havin' the cover off.

"He wouldn't depend on a stick and he got the bar on one side to give himself room to get out the coffin. He had it up about the right height to get out the coffin and I got in and got a foot at each side of the coffin, to lift it up. I was a fine strong man that time and it was no trouble to me. At the same time we heard the churchyard gate opened. It was about four o'clock in the mornin' this time.

" 'Be the livin' man!' he says, 'here's the police!' He let go the bar and took to his heels. Begor, when he let down the bar, the top of the tomb flopped into its place again and there I was sittin' on the coffin, and didn't know but the police was in the churchyard and the other man gone.

So I blessed myself. 'God be good to your soul, me poor crather, the divil break Paudeen's neck. I'll soon be dead along with you.' "

So he was just the same as a man before the firin' squad. No one would ever come to rise off the tomb again. But instead of the police, wasn't it another crowd come on the same mission.

Jim was listenin' and heard them say, "Someone was here already, there's a crowbar. If we're quick and get away, we'll cod them fellows."

"So, be man, when they heard us, they run, whoever they were." He could hear them say, 'Maybe they have her gone, and if we're caught we'll be just as guilty as if we had her. So we better make no delay'."

"Be the tarnal man," says [Jim], "I've a chance of me life still. The minute they open the top of the tomb I'll get out."

So they riz up the top of the tomb, three or four of them, right quick.

"Be man," says I [Jim] to myself, 'I'll give them a quare fright, before they have this coffin out.' So I took off me coat and wound it around me head and they riz up the top of the tomb with such a bang, that it slipped off altogether. The minute it slipped off, I jumped up with the coat around me head and let a most unearthly yell out of me. Well, they took to their heels. They fled helter-skelter in all directions. They thought it was the corpse after gettin' out. They never dreamt of a human being being locked up in the tomb, and they disappeared in a few minutes.

"Be the livin' man, I got me legs around the coffin. I lifted her out clane work out of the grave. I was a very strong fellow at the time.

"I went over to the corner of the churchyard and brought down me little grey mare and car. So, be man, I lifted the coffin into it nice and grand and it was no aisy job at all. I put the mare out on the road and got into the car and sat down on the coffin. There never a racehorse went as hard as that mare went home and I layin' a good switch on her. So, be man, I could hear the poor girl jumpin' inside in the coffin with the speed I was goin' at, but sure God help her, she didn't feel it. So, be man, it wasn't long till I got into the man's yard and he was asleep in the bed at the time."

"Get up, Paudeen," says I. "You cowardly rogue, you, and hand me out a five pound note. I have the corpse here in the yard for you."

"In the name of God, Jim," he says, "how did you get it out?"

"That's no affair of yours," says I, "how I got it out."

"I thought, Jim," he says, "we agreed to five shillin's."

"Five shillin's be damned," says I, "I'll go to the barrack this minute and have you transported, if you don't hand me out the money."

"Well, Jim", he says, "it was you stole her and not me."

"Well," says I, "who employed me and whose mare and car had I and whose crowbar? 'Twas you employed me and you run away like a cowardly hangman and left me there to die, and I could be dead afore now only God Almighty saved me."

So I went down across the yard and got into the car again, and sat up on the coffin.

"Hello, Jim," he says, "where are you goin' now?"

"Be the livin' man," says I, "I'm going' to the barrack with this coffin, and you'll be in the body of the jail before nine o'clock tomorrow mornin'," says I.

"Oh, come back, Jim," he says, "and I'll give you the five-pound note."

"You can do that as you like," said I. So, be the livin' man, he brought me into the house and gave me a five-pound note and begor, we carried the girl in and put her in a little scullery, until it was time to get her away. So begor, I went out and unyoked the mare and put her in the stable and I rowled up my little five pound note and put it in my vest pocket. "Begor, Paud," says I, "it wasn't a bad night's work at all!"

I said a few prayers for her soul's salvation and went into me bed and I slept like a thrush till mornin'.

That was the first body and last that Jim ever snatched. This old fellow Jim died about forty years ago aged eighty. He told this story to Walter Furlong himself.

Mrs Alexander

The editors have indulged themselves in giving three short versions of this lady's supposed return from the crypt. Deirdre Nuttall is descended from Mrs Alexander, and Diarmaid Ó Muirithe grew up in the house in Priory Street, New Ross, in which Mrs Alexander, it is related, gave her husband such a fright.

Version 1 [97]   Mrs Alexander was living in the country and she died about fifty years ago but before she died she had to make her will. Her will was to have her jewels on her hands when she died because she had about one hundred pounds worth of jewels.

A man who heard of her will went to where she was buried and he cut off one of her fingers with a knife and when he had the jewels off her finger she arose and the man ran out of the graveyard because he was afraid.

The woman walked out to her house and when she knocked at the door the servant girl who had opened the door dropped dead. Then Mrs Alexander went into the parlour where her people were and they were astonished to see her, but when she told them the story about her finger and the man, they were delighted and they promised a reward to the man who had cut off her finger but he would not give himself up.

She was not really dead but she was in a trance. She did not die for five years after.

Version 2 [98]   There was a woman named Alexandra, who lived some place near Bournmore. She was sick in bed and she went off in a trance. The doctors believed that she was dead. She was buried in a coffin like an ordinary dead person. She was a very sick person and she was buried with valuable rings on her fingers. A boy who was in need of money went into the churchyard, and went down into the tomb. He was cutting the rings off her fingers when the knife stuck in her fingers, and immediately blood came pouring out. She woke up and opened her eyes. The boy ran home, and reported the matter to the police. The police arrived immediately and found the woman standing in the tomb. She spoke to them, and she walked home. Her parents could not believe it. The doctors found out that she was only in a trance. She gave the boy a great amount of money. The woman lived for many years after that.

97 Written by Kathleen Ronan of Mountgarret, New Ross, a pupil of the Mercy Convent, New Ross in 1938 (Sister Philomena, teacher). IFCS 898: 9–11.   98 Written in 1937 by Thomas Furness of Brogue Lane, New Ross, a pupil of Michael Street School (Seán O Donnchadha, teacher). Young Furness heard the story from his father, John. IFCS 897: 11.

Version 3 [99]   Joyce Banks was her name, my grandmother's grandmother. [She was not an Alexander, although the families were connected and no doubt that is how the confusion arose and how the legends came into existence.]

Around 1800 Ross was stricken by a plague and people died of it like flies. She was a young woman. She wasn't long married when she got ill. She died quickly in the evening and they buried her at once in the family vault in St Mary's churchyard, and they didn't brick it up that night. The sexton opened the coffin because it was said that she was buried with a valuable ring. He cut her finger to get it; the blood came and he fled. She got up and went home to her house in Priory Street.

Her husband was shut up in his study, alone with his grief. When the 'dead' woman knocked, she used a special knock that she and her husband would use so that they'd know who it was. The servants were afraid and asked their master what he should do. He said it was nonsense, but eventually he heard the knocking and answered the door. It was her.

She went on to have about seven children. The sexton fled to Australia.

Some people think this story isn't true, but during the plague they wouldn't have kept records. How true the story was I don't know, but certainly my grandmother believed it, and she was particularly fond of her grandmother. The Beatty family tell exactly the same story.

A wake game played by New Ross children [1]

This is a rhyme game beginning with 1 and going on up to 12. It is very difficult and puzzling. If the players make a mistake in the rhyme they must give a forfeit, and a forfeit means paying a penalty.

Here's this!
What's this?
       Two ducks and a fat hen!

Here's this!
What's this?
Three plump partridges, two ducks and a fat hen!

99 Account given by Mrs Joyce Alexander, aged 87, of Macmurrough Farm, New Ross to her granddaughter, Deirdre Nuttall, in 1998. The lady in the story is Mrs Alexander's grandmother's grandmother.   1 Collected by Mary B. Dunphy of The Irishtown, from Anne O'Neill, aged 70, who was raised in the Bullawn. IFC 577: 313–16.

Here's this!
What's this?
Four air earls, three plump partridges, two ducks and a fat hen!

Here's this!
What's this?
Five white squirrels, four air earls; three plump partridges; two ducks and a fat hen.

Here's this!
What's this?
Six pair of parl darled earls; five white squirrels, four air earls; three plump partridges; two ducks and a fat hen.

Here's this!
What's this?
Seven grey mares all shod and shorn; six pair of parl darled earls; five white squirrels, four air earls; three plump partridges; two ducks and a fat hen.

Here's this!
What's this?
Eight crooked crows in a crabtree creaking, crooked was the tree and the crows all creaking; seven grey mares all shod and shorn; six pair of parl darled earls; five white squirrels, four air earls; three plump partridges; two ducks and a fat hen.

Here's this!
What's this?
Nine oul' ministers in the pulpit preaching, preachin' to 'em; eight crooked crows in a crabtree creaking, crooked was the tree and the crows all creaking; seven grey mares all shod and shorn; six pair of parl darled earls; five white squirrels, four air earls; three plump partridges; two ducks and a fat hen.

Here's this!
What's this?
Ten oul' women and their pipes in blazes, blazin' to 'em; nine oul' ministers in the pulpit preaching-preachin' to 'em; eight crooked crows in a crabtree creaking, crooked was the tree and the crows all creaking; seven grey mares all shod and shorn; six pair of parl darled earls; five white squirrels, four air earls; three plump partridges; two ducks and a fat hen.

Here's this!
What's this?
Eleven new blue pigeons picking pepper off of eleven new blue 'plither' 'plather' plates; ten oul' women and their pipes in blazes, blazin' to 'em; nine oul' ministers in the pulpit preaching, preachin' to 'em; eight crooked crows in a crabtree creaking, crooked was the tree and the crows all creaking; seven grey mares all shod and shorn; six pair of parl darled earls; five white squirrels, four air earls; three plump partridges; 2 ducks and a fat hen.

Here's this!
What's this?
Twelve white geese in the green fields grazing, green was the grass where the geese were grazing; eleven new blue pigeons picking pepper off of eleven new blue 'plither' 'plather' plates; ten oul' women and their pipes in blazes, blazin' to 'em; nine oul' ministers in the pulpit preaching, preachin' to 'em; eight crooked crows in a crabtree creaking, crooked was the tree and the crows all creaking; seven grey mares all shod and shorn; six pair of parl darled earls; five white squirrels, four air earls; three plump partridges; two ducks and a fat hen.

These games are never played at wakes or anywhere else now. The child of to-day is altogether a different psychological study to the child of thirty or forty or fifty years ago!

A story about a wake [2]

Long ago it was the custom to wake people in the barns and to get clay pipes and snuff to hand around to the people who came to the wake. This was done "for the soul of the dead person". It was also this custom to give away the dead person's clothes "for his soul". The latter custom is still carried out here.

One night, as the people were waking a dead man, he rose up out of the coffin and walked about. All the people at the wake were smoking pipes and taking snuff and talking, and they all jumped up screaming and ran out of the barn, falling over chairs and whatever was there.

It was discovered when the panic was over that the "corpse" wasn't dead

2 Told by Statia Doyle, a pupil at Aclare School, Campile, in 1938 (M.E. Campbell, teacher). Her informant was Josie Caulfield of Ballykeerogue, who grew up in Camblin. IFCS 873: 194–5.

at all. He was only in a trance. Still ever afterwards, although the man lived for years, everyone looked at him as if he wasn't right, and they all said that if he wasn't the devil he was under the power of the devil.

Rathimney graveyard[3]

There are ruins of an old church in the graveyard in Rathimney. The foundation of one wall is still to be seen; there is a sycamore tree growing over it. Pieces of an old headstone belonging to the family of Berneys are thrown on a grave. There were three sisters died when each one of them came to the age of nineteen, on the same date of the same month. The oldest headstone in the graveyard is dated from 1741; it is belonging to the Gaffney family. Opposite the graveyard there was a bullaun [waste ground in a field] long ago and there was a road through it; that was the way the coffins used to be brought. Unbaptised children were buried in the bullaun. A ditch was built around it and the road was blocked up. It is now a part of our yard. Some years later there was a woman going to the fowl market in Ballyhack very early one morning and she saw men lifting a coffin over the ditch that crossed the old road. There is a graveyard in Drealistown called the Poul; there are ruins of an old church in it. Where the church was is now surrounded by laurel. It is said that when King James was going to Duncannon to take the boat to France he went into Mass in the Poul. When a person is dying who is to be buried in the Poul, a light rises in the graveyard and goes to his house. A man died in America whose people were buried in the Poul, and it is said that the light went to the house in which the man was dying in America.

3 Told by Thomas Foley, a pupil in St Leonard's School, Ballycullane in 1938. His teacher was Mary B. Dunphy. Thomas's informant was his father. IFCS 871: 182–3.

Index

Doyle, Una, schoolgirl, Great Graigue,
Fethard 97
Doyle, Willie, informant, Glynn 38
Duggan, Billy, lifeboatman 151
Duggan, Dicky, lifeboatman 151
Duggan, Jack, lifeboatman 151
Duncannon 5, passim
Dungulph, Fethard 97
Dunkit 129
Dunmain, Ballycullane 22
Dunphy, Mary B., teacher, St Leonard's,
Tintern parish 18, passim
Dwyer, Michael, '98 man, 47

East Bank, Kilmore 141
Eblis 55
Egan, Mary, Boley, schoolgirl, Ballycullane
155
Egan, Vincent, schoolboy, Boley,
Ballycullane 20
Ennis, John, Carne boat-builder 138
Enniscorthy 10, passim
Entete, Forth and Bargy siesta 110
Eye fiddle 81

Fagan, John, schoolboy, Castlebridge school
170
Farrell, Mrs, teacher, Traceystown 96
Faythe, The, Wexford 80, passim
Ferrycarrig 90
Fethard-on-Sea 62, passim
Fitzgerald, Edward, informant,
Ballinaboola, New Ross, informant 7,
passim
Fitzgerald, Lady, Johnstown Castle 134
Fitzgerald, Lord Edward 47
Fitzgerald, Nicholas, informant,
Foulksmills 78
Fitzgerald, Patrick, schoolboy, Piltown,
New Ross 116
Fitzharris, Margaret, lace worker, New Ross
117
Foley, Henry, Terrerath 72
Foley, Laurence, schoolboy, Monglass,
Caime 25
Foley, Thomas, Rathimney, Gusserane,
schoolboy 81
Foley, Thomas, schoolboy, St Leonard's,
Ballycullane 204
Forrestal, Martin, informant, Knockea,

Campile 62
Forristal, Kathleen, schoolgirl, Knockea,
Campile 99, passim
Forth Barony of 82, passim
Fortune, Martin, schoolboy, Kilmannon,
Cleariestown 118
Fortune, Molly, schoolgirl, Ballinaslaney,
Oylegate 164
Foulksmills 28, passim
Franey, Tom, schoolboy, Marshallstown 93
Frizzel 7
Furlong of '98 48
Furlong Wat, Corrigeen 10
Furlong, James, schoolboy, Abbey Street,
Wexford 34
Furlong, Mary, informant, Abbey Street,
Wexford 34
Furlong, Mrs, informant, 3 Wolfe Tone
Villas, Wexford 95
Furlong, Mrs, informant, Coolroe,
Ballycullane 149
Furlong, Walter, informant, Grange,
Rathnure 10, passim
Furness, John, informant, Brogue Lane,
New Ross 200
Furness, Thomas, schoolboy, Brogue Lane,
New Ross 200

Gaffney, Honor, informant, Aclare 72,
passim
Gaffney, Kitty, schoolgirl, Aclare school 167
Garryduff, Campile, 18
Glynn 38, passim
Goff of Horetown 11
Gorey 18, passim
Gough, Edward, informant, Kilmore Quay
38
Gould, M., teacher, St Brigid's school,
Wexford 162, passim
Grace of Bannow, lobster pot maker 143
Grace, Mrs, Corrigeen 10
Grady, Martin, informant, Carrick-on-
Bannow 68
Grand Signor, The 49
Grange, Kilmore 17, passim
Great Graigue, Fethard 97
Greece 53 Turks 53
Greene, Richard, sea captain 94
Greenland 57
Gunnips, faction fighters 29
Gusserane 5, passim